THE
ADVENTURES
OF
MIKE BLAIR

◆

A Dime Detective™ Book

THE ADVENTURES OF MIKE BLAIR

Hank Searls

Series Consultant: ROBERT WEINBERG

THE MYSTERIOUS PRESS

New York • London • Tokyo

The stories contained in this volume were originally published in the following magazines:
"Shiv for Your Supper," *F.B.I. Detective Stories*, June 1949
"Kickback for a Killer," *All-Story Detective*, August 1949
"A Dish of Homicide," *Dime Detective*, November 1949
"Lethal Legacy for the Lady," *Dime Detective*, March 1950
"Let's All Die Together," *Dime Detective*, June 1950
"Keep Your Money Side Up," *Dime Detective*, August 1950
"For Auld Lang Crime," *Dime Detective*, December 1950

DIME DETECTIVE and MIKE BLAIR are exclusive trademarks of Blazing Publications, Inc.

 The Mysterious Press, 129 West 56th Street, New York, N.Y. 10019

This Mysterous Press edition is published by arrangement with Blazing Publications, Inc., The Argosy Company, in cooperation with Scott Meredith Literary Agency, Inc., representing Hank Searls

Printed in the United States of America

First Printing: July 1988

10 9 8 7 6 5 4 3 2 1

Book design by Nick Mazzella

Library of Congress Cataloging-in-Publication Data

Searls, Hank, 1922–
   The adventures of Mike Blair: a Dime detective book / Hank Searls.
    p.   cm.
   Contents: Shiv for your supper—Kickback for a killer—A dish of homicide—Lethal legacy for the lady—Let's all die together—Keep your money side up—For auld lang crime.
   1. Blair, Mike (Fictitious character)—Fiction.
2. Detective and mystery stories, American.   I. Title.
PS3569.E18A67 1988
813'.54—dc19   87-33251
                                                               CIP

ISBN 0-89296-918-0 (pbk.) (U.S.A.) ISBN 0-89296-919-9 (pbk.) (Canada)

Contents

THE PULPS: Yesterday's Classroom
  by Hank Searls   vii
SHIV FOR YOUR SUPPER   1
KICKBACK FOR A KILLER   19
A DISH OF HOMICIDE   37
LETHAL LEGACY FOR THE LADY   66
LET'S ALL DIE TOGETHER   96
KEEP YOUR MONEY SIDE UP   139
FOR AULD LANG CRIME   173
AFTERWORD by Robert Weinberg   212

THE PULPS:
Yesterday's Classroom
by Hank Searls

◆

You had to write fast, at a penny a word. You had to learn fast, too, for the learning was everything, and by the late 1940's, the pulps were disappearing.

A grim business, to face the blank page knowing that even if you churned out a full-length five thousand word short story that day the best you could expect was fifty bucks in three months, if it sold.

For even then, there were better ways to earn a living. It was said that you could earn three dollars an hour as a plumber, about as much as I was then making in the cockpit as a Navy aviator. Unless you were Erle Stanley Gardner or Rex Stout you simply couldn't whip out the pages fast enough to hack a living from the pulps.

So what motivated us—John D. MacDonald, Louis

L'Amour, myself? Why did we pound out the formula detective stories of the 1940's?

Few of us were full-time writers then. I was still a Navy photo pilot, mapping Labrador and Newfoundland, trying to support a family and a suitable Buick convertible, longing to be free to write full-time.

The money wasn't our real motivation. Those of us who began our writing careers in the pulps—*Black Mask, Dime Detective, All-Story Detective, F.B.I. Detective*—had better goals than coining pennies, a word at a time.

We were chasing fluency more than affluency. We were thinking of future one hundred thousand word novels. We were natural storytellers already, or we wouldn't have been writing. The bottleneck was between the brain and the typewriter. If you wrote one thousand, two thousand, three thousand words a day, allegedly words began to flow from your fingers unconsciously, and then you could concentrate on your thoughts, characters, dialogue, scenes.

Those of us who intended to become serious writers, and thought we had the mustard, looked on the pulp detective and mystery magazines warily. We regarded them with gratitude, of course, because they bought our words, but we were suspicious of the dangers they posed.

Couldn't you lose your style, spewing out stories at meteoric speeds? Wouldn't the famous "formula" demanded by pulp editors twist your approach? How many situations can you dream up for a private eye, a beautiful girl, and a killer without scrambling your brains? My hero Mike Blair, I note through the mists of memory, gets beat up in almost every story I wrote.

And what about "creative juices"? How do you overcome the psychic blow when you see that an editor has changed your title *Suitable for Framing* to *Kickback for a Killer?*

Even in the late 1940's, when the pulp magazines sold for a quarter, newspapers for a nickel, and milk shakes for fifteen cents, a penny a word seemed niggardly, considering the risk to your creativity.

Suppose you went stale before you broke into the

slick magazines? Weren't you selling your talent too cheaply?

Well, we did it anyway, because the alternatives to pulp magazines were scant. It was thought that to write radio drama you had to be in Hollywood or New York. The same went for TV, which was in such infancy that the Writers Guild had hardly established decent prices for a script if you *could* sell one.

Journalism was hard to get into, and itself a notorious wrecker of style.

Slick magazine fiction was better, but elusive. Besides, most fiction in *The Saturday Evening Post*, *Redbook*, and *Cosmopolitan* had to be as formula-bound as the pulps and prim as a primer. It was highly speculative, not much fun to write, and only worth a nickel a word itself.

We intended to remain with the sure thing. At least, once you established yourself with the pulps, they seldom rejected your stories.

And so we wrote and wrote. Where else could you learn and earn? Creative writing classes—there seem now to be dozens on every city college campus—were rare.

We seldom researched. I'm appalled, when I look back at the pulp detective stories I wrote in the late 1940's, at the factual errors: in one of my Mike Blair series, a highway patrolman breaks off a hot pursuit at a state border because he apparently thinks it's illegal to chase a fugitive across the line.

(Years later, when the pulps were dead and I was creating TV cop series and writing police novels like *The New Breed* and *Never Kill a Cop*, I became an L.A. County deputy and got it right.)

Today I shudder at cliches in the *earlier* pulp stories I wrote, when my starving-author attic was the copilot seat of a Navy World War II photo plane over the Labrador coastline, and the oxygen mask made my beard itch, and the unpressurized cockpit at 20,000 feet made lukewarm coffee boil over my manuscript pages.

I'm nevertheless grateful to the pulps.

For it worked. The thousands and thousands of words, at a penny a word, became easier. The fluency came, and each tale came out better than the last. The final appearance of my friend Mike Blair, *For Auld Lang Crime*, shows signs of originality, and isn't bad at all.

Where young writers today will sell their first fiction I don't know.

But I truly wish them luck.

Shiv for
Your Supper

◆

*Busted, and with drinks
on the cuff, private-cop
Mike Blair was angled into
playing watchdog to a
gambler's playful wife.*

The little bar off Union Square
was crowded during the lunch hour, but when the big
butter and egg men and their secretaries had finished
drinking their lunches, Duke, who kept bar, and myself,
a temporarily unemployed private detective, were left
alone in the cigarette smoke.

I wondered how many more drinks Duke's cuff would
hold. He didn't seem worried, and I told myself that my
company was worth more than mere liquor to Duke.

"Ever play the football pools?" he asked, handing
me a yellow card of selections over the bar.

"Used to, until I noticed Johnny Picco riding around
in a car while I was wearing out my shoes," I said. "Does
he still run those things?"

"Yeah," Duke said. "It's a good pool, though. Johnny
always pays off."

"He can afford to," I said, swishing my ice around
and hoping Duke would notice my empty glass. "Tony

1

Driscoll's his lawyer, and I do undercover work for Tony's clients. The last time we got Johnny out of trouble we soaked him a grand. Never a murmur out of Johnny. A hell of a nice guy, for a gambler."

The door swung open in a blaze of light and a slim, short man walked in. He waited until his eyes were accustomed to the dimly lit lounge and came over.

"Speak of the devil," said Duke softly, and then, "Hello, Mr. Picco. Collecting for yourself today?"

"No, Duke," said Johnny Picco. "How're they goin'?"

"Twenty-three bucks, Mr. Picco. Not bad so far."

"Keep it all today, Duke. Last week was a good one." Johnny sounded as if something were on his mind.

"Thanks, Mr. Picco. Thanks a lot."

"Better you than Uncle Sam," Johnny said, and turned to me.

"And how's it with you, Mike?"

"I'm not starvin', Johnny," I lied. "And I take it you're not either."

"No," said Johnny slowly, "not starvin', Mike."

He sat down on the stool next to mine and signalled for two drinks. Duke brought them and moved tactfully down to the other end of the bar.

"Tony Driscoll said I could find you here. That's why I came down."

"What can I do for you, Johnny?" I asked.

Johnny studied his drink for a while. Then he looked up and smiled grimly.

"It's my wife, Mike. I'm worried."

I had seen Johnny's wife, a beautiful blonde. I figured if I had a wife like that I'd never have another worry in the world. On second thought, I guessed I might sweat just a little when she was out of sight.

"I think she's playin' around," continued Johnny.

I felt sorry for him, but business is business.

"You want her tailed?"

"Yeah."

"I can do it for you, but you want to be sure you're goin' to use the information in the divorce, because it'll cost you dough."

"If you find out anything, I'll use it all right." Johnny's voice sounded strangely flat. I glanced at him and saw suddenly how he'd sewed up gambling in San Francisco. Behind the quiet, soft-spoken gambler was another harder Johnny with a glint in his gray eyes, a guy who looked as if he'd stop at nothing.

"Okay," I said, reaching for my notebook. "You can give me all the dope. What makes you think she's running around?"

"Just stuff I hear around town."

"When is she supposed to be playin' tricks?"

"How would I know? You know what my hours are?"

"No."

"Nine in the morning until three, four the next morning. Anybody tells you I've got a soft racket is nuts. Have to be in my office all day long—new outfit from L.A. trying to move in. Can't trust any of my boys."

If I had a wife like yours, buddy, I thought, *I'd hang around the old homestead, or hire a watchdog.*

"Where do you live now?" I asked.

"Nob Hill Plaza."

"What number?"

"The penthouse."

"Any way I can get in without anybody knowing it?"

"You can have my key, if you want. The houseboy will let me in."

"The houseboy would know if I used it, too, wouldn't he?"

"Yeah, I guess so." Johnny thought a while. "If you can get up on the roof of the Regency Club, next door, you can climb the fire escape right up to my roof garden."

I jotted it down.

"Anybody in particular she's supposed to be goin' with?"

Johnny glanced up with the cold look in his eyes.

"Yeah. Roger Parks, a small-time actor down at the Market Theatre. He used to play the horses, and I introduced him to Ann at a cocktail party. They tell me he's been taking her to some of these gin mills down near Palo Alto."

"Okay, Johnny. I guess that's all I need. I'll keep Tony informed, and you can contact him."

Johnny's fingers drummed on the bar. Finally he said:

"I don't want a divorce, Mike. If you find anything, I'll use it to run this guy out of town. If that doesn't work, I'll make him wish to hell it had."

Yeah, I thought, *and when the next actor comes to town, I'll be tailing your wife again.*

"That's up to you. I'll start tonight." I almost asked for an advance, and stopped as I saw Johnny reach for his wallet. He carelessly yanked a hundred dollar bill from a large family of the same and tossed it on the bar.

"Just to get you started right, Mike."

I waved nonchalantly as if I really didn't need it, but somehow it stuck to my hand and I put it away.

Johnny left and I had another drink, more or less to break the hundred. Then I drove up to Nob Hill and parked opposite Johnny's apartment house. It was a tall building, eighteen stories, and on top I could see the penthouse, about the size of a small country estate. I was glad I'd quit playing football pools.

I walked over and looked at the Regency Club next door. It was a men's club. I strolled up to the front door, and a doorman who must have voted for Washington stopped me. I flashed my badge and told him I was the fire inspector who had come to look at the roof. He passed me on to the elevator boy, a youth of about eighty summers, who took me as high as he could go and pointed to some stairs.

I came out on the roof of the club and found the fire escape, as Johnny had said. It looked like a cinch. I went back down to my car.

I smoked a pack of cigarettes and played the radio until the battery screamed in pain. Then I found the Owner's Manual in the glove compartment and tried to memorize page eight. After a while the rookie on the beat went by for the fourth time and stopped for a light.

Tactfully he asked me what I was doing. I told him I was waiting to kidnap the mayor's daughter. He must have been a police school graduate, because he grinned and left.

Then a young punk in a zoot suit strolled up and leaned against a light pole, a cigarette dangling from his lips. I tried to estimate where his shoulders ended and his padding began, and finally got tired of that.

I was looking at a worn-out map of Texas when I noticed activity across the street. First a convertible drove up to the door of the Nob Hill Plaza and a chauffeur got out and disappeared inside. Then something blonde in a mink coat swished down the steps and climbed behind the wheel. The car floated away from the curb with the blonde vision driving, and was a block away before my ears stopped ringing and I realized I'd been staring at Johnny Picco's wife.

My old buggy didn't want to start, and I almost lost her in the Powell Street traffic. She stopped at the Hotel Clifton and a blond giant with a spoiled face stepped into the car. I looked at my watch and jotted down the time in my notebook. The cavalcade started up again and headed for Palo Alto.

The car swooped down the Bay Shore Highway and finally turned off at one of the little neon-lighted joints off the road. Ann Picco and Pretty Boy got out and walked in, holding hands like a couple at a high school dance. I waited ten minutes and followed them in.

The place was lousy with college kids and cheap chrome fixtures. The girls in sweaters were still buzzing like angry queen bees over Mrs. Picco's mink coat. It was easy to see how Johnny had heard of his wife's meanderings. She stood out like a diamond in a pawnshop window, even though she and Sir Galahad went into a dark booth in the rear of the dive.

I walked over to the jukebox and invested a nickel while I cased the place. The booth next to them was empty. I slipped into the booth with my back to the partition and signalled for the waitress. She bounced over and took my order and I settled back to listen.

* * *

There was considerable talking in the next booth, but I couldn't distinguish the words. I finished one drink, and then another, and decided that this was the kind of a job I liked.

In a little while I heard them moving around behind me and then they appeared on the tiny dance floor, Ann without her mink coat. I gulped and looked down at my drink. Without the coat she was even more beautiful than I remembered. I toyed with the idea of a worn-out private dick moving in and then remembered the look in Johnny Picco's eyes. I was safer working for him than against him.

They danced two or three times, like a couple of professionals, and when they stopped some of the college kids clapped a little.

They came back to their table, both a little flushed, but the billing and the cooing had stopped. Their voices had gone up a couple of octaves and I could catch a word now and then. It was an argument, a drunken, juvenile sort of a fight.

"Ann," I heard Parks say, in a low, passionate whisper, "let's go back. Now!"

"Why, Roger, what for? We just got here." Her voice was cool and a little amused.

"Let's go, Ann."

"I don't see why you want to go. I'm having fun."

Their voices dropped again and then I heard Parks call for the waitress. He paid the check and stood up.

"Come on, Ann. We're leaving."

I let them get a head start and paid my check. I caught up with them on the Bayshore Highway and followed them to Parks's hotel. They stopped outside for five minutes while I pretended to be getting luggage out of my trunk compartment. I could see that the fight was still going on, and finally the car moved away again, with Roger Parks still aboard.

I told the anxious bellhop standing at the curb that I'd changed my mind and hopped back into my car. I lost them going up California Street, so I drove directly to the Nob Hill Plaza.

They were there already, and another conference seemed to be going on. Three times the door on his side of the car opened and third time it stayed open.

"Tell him to shove off, baby," I groaned. "Don't let him go up there."

She let him go up.

I jumped out and crossed the street, heading for the Regency Club. The old guy was still on duty. I told him I wanted to check the wiring on the roof while the lights in the club were on. He believed me and I went to the roof and swung up the fire escape. It was a long way to the penthouse, and by the time I reached the top enough whiskey had flowed through my pores to float the *Queen Mary*. I poked my head over the rail.

I could see, through a maze of expensive porch furniture and potted trees, that a light in the penthouse was on. I flattened myself against the side of the penthouse and drew my head back far enough to see through one of the French windows.

Roger Parks was loafing on a couch. Ann was standing by a built-in bar mixing a drink. She was talking, but I couldn't hear a word. Finally she walked within range of the actor. He reached up and switched off the light, and as he did he grabbed her arm. I almost went in to break it up, and then I remembered what I was there for. Quietly I tried the French door and it opened a little.

Then Ann's voice floated out, cool and clear.

"Get out, Roger."

I couldn't hear Parks's reply, but I could hear a little scuffling going on. I cheered for Ann silently and decided to move in if things really got tough for her.

I heard her cross the room and then a door opened and closed.

"Okay, sister," I whispered. "Nice try, but I guess you just don't have the stuff." I wanted a cigarette, or a drink, or both, and thought of what I'd have to tell Johnny, and shivered.

* * *

I waited five minutes without hearing a sound from inside. Once it seemed as if a door opened at the other end of the penthouse. Suddenly I heard a groan from the living room. It meant one thing. I shouldered through the door, groping for a light switch and stumbled over something soft and heavy. I knew what it was before I found the light.

He was lying in front of the couch, and a dark stain was spreading beneath him. A wicked-looking knife lay beside him—the kind we prized in the Pacific. I felt his pulse and looked at his eyes and knew he'd made one pass too many.

I took a quick look through the apartment. The front door was open, and I was surprised, because I'd thought I heard it close. She wasn't there. I found the houseboy asleep in the servant's room, and decided not to wake him until I'd thought things over. I went back to the living room.

I called Tony Driscoll first. No one answered. I thought of leaving the body and going out the way I came but decided that Mrs. Picco was going to need a witness, and I was it. I called the cops, on the assumption that they'd be interested.

"Get up to the penthouse on the Nob Hill Plaza," I said, feeling dramatic as hell. "There's been a murder."

Next I tried to get hold of Johnny Picco. Nobody answered at his office. I looked at my watch. It was only 3:20 in the morning. I sat down and lit a cigarette and waited for the gendarmes.

I was just finishing the cigarette when Johnny Picco walked in. He saw the body on the floor and his jaw tightened, but otherwise he never changed expression.

"What happened?"

I stood up and walked over to the French doors and gazed at the lights in the bay.

"She killed him, Johnny."

"Why?"

"He was getting rough. She's okay, Johnny."

Johnny sighed like a man who's just put down a heavy suitcase.

"But she killed him? Why?"

"She was a little drunk, maybe, but technically it was self-defense."

Johnny began to pace the floor. Suddenly he stopped.

"Let's get the body out of here. I can take care of it."

I swung around.

"You're crazy, Johnny. Tony Driscoll can get her off. I phoned the police."

Johnny's eyes glinted.

"I thought you were working for me."

"I am and I'll testify for your wife. But I'm not throwin' my license away to keep your wife's name out of the papers!"

"Where is she?"

I jerked my thumb toward the front door.

"Took a powder," I said.

Johnny seemd to think for a moment. Suddenly he stooped and picked up the knife.

"Hey, what're you doin'?" I asked him. "You'll have your prints all over that thing."

Johnny whipped out a handkerchief and began wiping the handle and the blade.

"My prints won't be on it, Mike. And Ann's won't either."

"What's the point?" I asked as he tossed it back on the floor, and then a big cop stood in the door, with Symanski, of Homicide, standing behind him.

"Who phoned the station?" asked the cop.

"I did," Johnny said, and I felt a cold shiver go up my spine. I turned to him.

"What is this?" I asked, but I already knew what it was. I could almost smell the odor of a frame-up drifting across the room.

"I called you," said Johnny to the cops. "I came home and found this guy standin' over the body." He pointed to the corpse on the floor. Symanski peered in and then walked swiftly over and knelt by the body. He looked up.

"He's dead, all right. Who is it?"

"A guy named Parks—Roger Parks," Johnny said. "He was playin' around with my wife. I hired this guy Blair to run him out of town. Looks like he took it in his head to kill him."

Symanski whipped out his notebook.

"Let's see. You're Picco, aren't you? Numbers game?"

"Bookmaker. And football pools," said Johnny.

Symanski turned to me.

"What have you got to say, Blair? Is business so tough with you private eyes that you got to make like torpedoes?"

"This, Symanski, is a cheap frame-up. That's all I got to say. For further information, contact my lawyer, Tony Driscoll. In the meantime, you better start looking for a beautiful blonde named Ann Picco."

"We'll handle the case by ourselves, thanks. You're both under arrest. Is this the knife?" He took out the handkerchief and picked it up. Then he laid it tenderly on the table. He went to the phone and dialed.

"Joe? Send out the wagon and tell Doc to get up here. It's murder, all right. Looks like Mike Blair, the private dick, did it, and maybe Johnny Picco is an accessory before the fact. Yeah, send out the press. Why not?"

I looked at Johnny. He was gazing at me, and his gray eyes didn't waver a bit.

"You sure you don't want to hang me right here?" I asked bitterly. "You paid your hundred bucks, you might as well get in on the necktie party."

I wondered if I were kidding or not. I had a lot of faith in Tony Driscoll, but it already looked like a tough case to beat, and getting tougher all the time. Suddenly I decided that if I were going to live I'd better do something, and fast.

"Symanski," I said, "let me talk to you outside." I nodded toward the terrace.

"Okay," he said cheerfully. "Watch Picco, Murph."

We walked through the French door and over to the rail.

"Johnny's wife did this, Symanski. I saw it. She and this guy Parks had a fight, she left to get the knife, evidently came back, stabbed him, and went out the front door. I was out here on the terrace."

Symanski laughed.

"Sure. And Johnny Picco is trying to protect his wife, who was running around with somebody else. You'd better think up a better one than that."

My heart sank. The story was weak, all right.

"Incidently," asked Symanski, "how'd you get into the house?"

A nasty idea crept into my head and I knew it was now or never. I tensed.

"I climbed up the fire escape," I said innocently.

"Where?"

"Right in front of you."

Symanski leaned over the rail and peered into the darkness. I braced myself and let him have it with a looping overhand to the back of his head. There was a crack that was my knuckle breaking and then a clang like Big Ben striking 1 o'clock, as Symanski's forehead hit the top rung of the fire escape. He sank backwards, limp as a flour sack. I stretched him out so that he looked comfortable, took his gun, and climbed over the rail.

I went down a lot quicker than I'd come up, ran across the roof of the Regency Club, and sprinted down the stairs to the elevator. I leaned on the button. Several years passed. Finally the pointer above the door began to move like the hour hand on a clock, and then the door opened.

The doorman was running the elevator now. He asked me if the wiring on the roof was okay. I told him we might have to tear the whole club down.

As I passed out of the club I saw the Bush Street Precinct wagon drive up to the door of the Nob Hill and about a thousand cops jumped out. I waited until the first wave had passed and then walked quickly across the street to my car. I pulled out from the curb and was halfway to the waterfront before I let off the emergency brake.

My knuckle began to throb and I knew it was broken and wondered if my neck would hurt as badly when they caught up with me.

I stopped at one of the little saloons down on the Embarcadero that stay open all night, and bought a straight shot.

I left the saloon and noticed a flophouse across the street. I drove six blocks away, parked my car, and walked back. The old geezer at the desk glanced at me suspiciously, saw that I had a necktie on, and raised the price of a bed in the dormitory to fifty cents. I tossed four bits on the desk and he jerked his thumb toward the stairs.

"Two floors up—any bed with nobody in it—no smoking up there—you got to be out of the bed by ten or it's another fifty cents."

"Can I snore?" I asked, and climbed the stairs.

I found an empty bunk next to some wino who'd been drinking ethyl gasoline, from the smell, and flopped down on it without even taking off my clothes. The last thing I remember was taking out my wallet and slipping it under my pillow.

I woke up with somebody shaking me and grabbed for my wallet. It was an old hag with a face like King Kong, and it seemed she wanted to make the bed. I sat up. The biggest collection of bums I had ever seen were climbing out of their bunks, each with his own private hangover. I got out quick, but not before two of them tried to touch me for a dime for a cup of coffee.

I walked out of the flophouse into a blaze of sunlight. Cautiously I looked around. There were no cops in sight so I headed for a lunchroom up the street. I bought a paper and sat at the counter, ordered a cup of joe, and looked at the front page.

There I was, big as life. My first thought was that the picture didn't do me justice, and then I looked at the mirror behind the counter and decided that whenever it had been taken, I'd been a lot more handsome. The growth of beard and the red eyes and the bags under them made a good enough disguise to get me by, and I gave up the idea of buying a shave.

I stepped over to the pay phone in the back of the joint and dialed Tony Driscoll's apartment.

He answered himself, and seemed wide awake, so I knew something was up.

"Tony," I said, cupping the mouthpiece, "did you hear what happened?"

"Hear what happened? This place has been crawling with the boys in blue all night."

"I'm at North Beach," I lied, just in case the phone was tapped. "What's the latest?"

"Can't tell you much now. Picco's sticking to his story. They can't find his wife. What actually happened?"

"She killed Parks. Picco says I did it for pay. Looks as if she might plead self-defense if they find her. How about me?"

"Frankly, you'd better stay under cover. They have a terrific case against you, with Picco sticking his neck out as he has. Phone me if they pick you up. Otherwise call me tonight around eight. Do you have enough cash to get by?"

"Yeah. Your friend Picco was kind enough to give me an advance. That'll look good, too, if it comes out in court."

I hung up and left for the saloon across the street. It was just opening up and the barkeep was sprinkling sawdust on the floor. I sat at the dark end of the bar and ordered a straight shot with a beer chaser. I passed the morning there very pleasantly, thinking of thirteen steps and a noose, and gas chambers, and a seat for one at San Quentin.

About noon the place started to fill up with longshoremen and sailors, and I pulled my hat farther down over my eyes. Two big stevedores next to me began discussing a football pool. I tried not to listen because I was a little tired of the subject.

When they went they left the selection card on the bar. It was green. I reached over and picked it up and a bell rang in my head. The last selection card I'd seen had been yellow.

I motioned to the barkeep.

"Who puts out this pool?"

He looked at me suspiciously and evidently decided that no plainclothesman would look as seedy as I did.

"Johnny Picco, the bookie, handled 'em until today. This mornin' before I open up some new guy comes around, says Picco is out of business. He says he's goin' to pay twenty percent to agents, so I take the cards. Whatta I care where the twenty percent comes from?"

It was evidently the Los Angeles outfit Johnny had mentioned. How the hell they'd moved in in such a hurry I couldn't figure. The morning paper probably hadn't hit the street until around five, and unless these guys had their cards already printed and waiting they couldn't have distributed them that quickly.

On the other hand, they wouldn't have had them printed if they hadn't known Johnny was going to be out of the way. Unless they had a fortune teller in the outfit, they'd never have known he was going to be in jail.

I thought for a while and then moved to the phone. I turned to the classified section of the phone book and looked up print shops.

A half an hour later I was still calling print shops, and almost at the end of the list. My finger was raw from dialing and I was ready to quit. I dialed the number of the HURRY-HURRY PRINTING SHOP, Calling Cards, Advertising, and a cheerful voice answered.

"Hurry-Hurry Print Shop, Calling Cards, Ad—"

"Yeah, I know. What was the idea of changing the odds on the Stanford-UCLA game? You guys nuts? That could cost me plenty of dough."

I waited for the voice to ask me what the hell I was talking about.

"We didn't change the odds, Mr. Spade. I have the

odds you gave me to print right here. Stanford and seven points."

"That so? Okay, guess I made a mistake. Say, when did I give you that order?"

"Let's see. Day before yesterday, Mr. Spade. Anything else we can do for you?"

"No."

I hung up. It looked as if Mr. Spade, whoever he was, was clairvoyant. Or else he'd planned two days in advance that Johnny wasn't going to be around.

The light suddenly dawned. I motioned to the bartender again.

"Say," I said, "is this guy goin' to collect for the pool tonight?"

"Yeah. Why?"

"I got a little bar over in Berkeley. Maybe I might be able to do business with him."

"Well, he'll be in tonight," he repeated. "Stick around."

I sat there all afternoon and well on into the evening. A grizzled old cop came in twice and looked the place over, and both times I almost climbed into my drink. About 11 o'clock the doors swung open and a young fellow in a well padded yellow sport jacket walked in and jerked his head at the barkeep. There was something familiar about him, but I was a little foggy and couldn't remember. The bartender went down and talked to him and I could feel them looking at me. Then the barkeep walked back and said:

"That guy is here now, if yuh wanna see him."

I strolled to the front of the bar.

"Torgus is my name," I said, sticking out my hand and trying to place the guy. "Pete Torgus. I own the Casa Rio Cocktail Lounge across the Bay. Thought we might do business."

The kid ignored my hand. "Yeah? Maybe we can. Come out to my car and I'll talk to you."

The bartender handed him a stack of selection cards and a lot of cash and we left. The kid got into a flashy convertible and I climbed in beside him.

"My name's Spade," he said.

Suddenly I remembered where I'd seen it before, and it was all I needed. I slid Symanski's gun out of my pocket and poked it at him under my arm.

"All right, sonny. Start drivin'."

His eyes shot to my face and he blinked.

"Look," he said, "If this is a stick-up, you're wastin' your time. I just started makin' the rounds, and all I got is what the barkeep in there gave me."

"I said start drivin'."

He started the car and pulled out.

"Head toward Twin Peaks," I told him. "No Sonny Boy, this is no stick-up. I'm one of Johnny Picco's boys, and you're goin' to pay us a little visit. Unless you start talkin' now."

"I wasn't cuttin' in on Johnny," he said quickly. "I read where he was in the jug, and I figured I'd take over until he got out, that's all."

"Yeah, you read it this mornin', so you had cards printed two days ago. And when you read it this mornin' you were plenty surprised, weren't you?"

"Whattaya mean?"

"You were surprised because you thought you'd knocked Johnny off last night. Isn't that right, junior?"

"You're nuts."

"Okay, if that's the way you feel. Tiny wanted to work you over anyway. Just thought you might prefer to go to the cops and spring Johnny, instead of lettin' the boys play with you for a while. You're goin' to the cops anyway, you know."

"Who's Tiny?"

"Where you from? Never heard of Tiny Forbes? Brother, that guy can make a preacher swear he's been playin' the horses."

Sweat was glistening on the kid's brow.

"What do you want to know?"

"I don't want to know anything. It's the cops that want to know. I know already. I know you were casin' Johnny's apartment house yesterday, because I saw you, standin' there on the street, smokin' a cigarette. I know you got up on the roof of the Regency Club next door and climbed the fire escape up to Johnny's terrace.

"I know you waited outside, behind the door, for Johnny and his wife to come home. I know you stabbed the guy you thought was Johnny, only it wasn't Johnny, it was the guy his wife was playin' around with. You know how I know?" I jabbed him with the gun. "I know because I was on the terrace too. I saw you," I bluffed, wondering how we'd missed hearing each other on the terrace, but deciding that a private eye and a guy bent on murder could be pretty quiet when they had to. "Then I heard you leave the place by the front door, right after Mrs. Picco."

"If you saw me, how come you didn't do somethin' about it?"

"Why should I? I work for Picco. If you want to kill some guy that's playin' around with Picco's wife, what do I care? But when they put Johnny in the clink for it, that's different."

"They ain't tryin' to nail Picco with it. The papers say they're lookin' for some private dick he hired."

"They'll nail Johnny too, if they can. But they can't, because when Tiny gets through with you, you're gonna sing, and sing loud."

"Look," he said hoarsely, "Reed sent me up from L.A. He'll pay plenty if you let me go, and we won't try cuttin' in up here again. How's that?"

"No soap," I said. "Come on, give her the gas. What're you waitin' for?"

"Okay," he said in a hollow voice. "You guys won't have to work me over. I'll go to the cops. Where's the station?"

We drove to the Bush Street station and I hauled him in. I asked for Symanski and he came out of his office in his shirtsleeves.

While the kid was talking I stepped to the phone and called Tony Driscoll. He was down before Symanski had the confession on paper. Tony looked worried until I gave him the big smile. Symanski stepped into his office and came out with Johnny Picco. Johnny seemed tired but otherwise okay. He looked at me and then at the floor.

"Sorry, Mike," he said, "I—"

Sorry, he is, I thought. *Tries to pin a murder rap on me to save his wife, and he says he's sorry.*

"Forget it, Johnny," I said. "I know how it is."

"I guess that confession lets you out, Picco," said Symanski, "but I'm putting the vice squad to work on your football pools, so you'll probably be back to see us pretty soon."

Johnny laughed and shrugged. Then Tony Driscoll stepped outside and motioned to someone in his car. She got out. It was Ann Picco.

"Thanks, Johnny," she said simply.

"Okay, honey. Staying home after this?"

Her big blue eyes looked into Johnny's and I wished somebody would look at me that way.

"Yes, Johnny," she said.

I wondered.

Kickback
for a Killer

◆

Mike Blair's forced swimming lesson cost bookie Joe Botelli two grand—and the beautiful blonde her life.

I stood at the door to my apartment and fished for the key in my pocket. My feet ached and my throat burned and the only thing that kept me from collapsing was the knowledge that a friendly bottle of scotch was waiting inside. All day long I had pounded the pavement looking for a blonde. Not any blonde, but a blonde with a birthmark the size of a dime on her neck and seventeen thousand dollars in her purse. I opened the door and froze.

She lay on the daybed in my living room, her long golden hair lying about her head. At first I thought she was asleep, but then I saw the dark red stain on the rug and knew that if she were asleep it was for the last time.

The face was young and sweet, not the kind you'd expect to find on a girl who'd steal seventeen thousand from her boss. I knew before I checked that there would be on her neck a small, round birthmark about the size of a dime.

Whoever had done the job had stabbed her with my letter opener—it lay on the rug in the stain. And whoever had done it had had a nice, clean mind—he'd carefully covered the body with a bedspread from my linen closet.

I picked up the phone and dialed Homicide. While I was waiting I took a quick look around. A cigarette with a delicate tinge of pink around the end was snuffed out in my ashtray. On the cocktail table in front of the couch was a book of matches, and on the cover was printed: "Sombrero Club. Shows Nightly. No Cover." The matches I slipped into my pocket. After that I poured myself a shot of scotch and sank into a chair. The numbness that hits you at a time like that was wearing off and my hands were shaking. I lit a cigarette and tried to think....

McCallister, head of the Homicide detail, was a new man from the East, and I'd never met him. He was short and slight with gray hair, gray eyes, a gray suit—even his skin seemed gray. He had a sharp, hooked nose and a taut slit for a mouth. Even before he looked at me he knelt and inspected the body. Then he got up, cruised aimlessly around the room, noted the open window, looked down the fire escape, and wrote a few words in a small red notebook. Finally he turned to me.

"What's your name?"

"Blair. Mike Blair."

I handed him my card.

"Michael Blair, Private Investigator," he read slowly. "Licensed?"

"Yeah."

"Let's see."

I handed him my wallet. With a chill I remembered that her picture was in it somewhere. He looked at my credentials and nodded.

"Well, let's hear your story. Then we'll get to work and find out the truth, and between what you tell us and the truth we ought to be able to hang this on somebody."

He looked at me steadily, and it was a nasty experience. McCallister's eyes tore you apart, rejected what they saw, and then put you back together again. Already I didn't like him.

"I came home from work and found this girl here, dead. Then I phoned you. That's all there is to it."

There was a long silence.

"Go on," he said.

"That's all," I repeated, feeling like a school boy caught in a lie.

"I don't suppose you've touched anything?"

"Nothing but the scotch."

"Search him, Clark," he said, and a plainclothesman went through my pockets.

"Just a set of keys and a book of matches and a handkerchief. Also a .32 in a shoulder holster," he reported.

McCallister gazed at me curiously.

"Why did you kill her?"

I felt a chill go up my back.

"Come on, now. You're not going to start that, are you? You think I'd kill her in my own place and then call the police?"

"It's been done." His eyes were like twin pools of ice.

"Listen, you two-bit Sherlock, one more crack like that and I'll—"

His hand shot out and he grabbed my lapel. He shoved, hard for a little guy, and I sat down in a chair.

His voice cracked like a whip.

"You'll sit there and answer when I talk to you. Understand? All right. You deny killing her. We'll let that ride. Have you ever seen her before?"

"No." That was the truth.

"That's a lie too. We'll let you cool off for a while down at the station and then we'll have another little talk. Clark!"

The plainclothesman drew handcuffs out of his pocket and moved over.

"Wait a minute," I said. I thought fast, and took a deep breath. "Give me a chance to get my affairs in order. I'm not going to leave town."

"Affairs? What affairs?"

"I'm working on a job now. Let me tell my client I'm quitting."

That did it. McCallister's eyes grew thoughtful as he weighed the advantages of having me tailed. He shot a glance at Clark, who sauntered to the door.

"How do I know you won't skip?"

He thought it over, evidently stalling for time until Clark could arrange to have me shadowed.

"Are you bonded?" he asked.

"Of course."

"How much?"

"Twenty thousand."

I picked up my wallet and showed him my certificate.

"All right, Blair," he said finally. "I'm going to let you go. Don't leave town. And be down at the coroner's inquest tomorrow. Phone the station tonight and we'll let you know what time." He walked back to the window and looked out again, drumming his fingers on the sill.

I left before he could change his mind. In the lobby were two detectives and a cop. I ignored them and walked out the door. I got a cab and told the driver to head downtown. Then I swung around in the seat and watched one of the detectives, a big guy who walked as if he were still swinging a nightstick, get into the next cab.

"Stop at the first big office building," I told the driver. He weaved through the traffic and pulled up at the Medical Center. I paid him and walked in.

I'd tailed enough people to know that I didn't like it when my subject got onto a crowded elevator, so I waited in the lobby pretending to be looking for a name on the list of tenants, until one of the elevators was filled. I squeezed my way past the starter and into the elevator just as my shadow walked into the lobby. He spotted me as the door closed, and I tried not to grin as I watched his mouth move silently.

I rode to the first floor, waited for a down elevator and went out through the garage. I didn't see the big guy again.

*   *   *

The manager of the Sombrero Club was a swarthy, dapper little individual with a tiny moustache. I found him at a table in the back, working over his books. I gave him my card and sat down. He nodded when I showed him the picture in my wallet.

"Yeah, I know her. She works here. Her name is Eve Lindquist. My new singer Why?"

"She was working under her right name? That's funny. Well, she doesn't work here anymore."

His face was impassive.

"Why?"

"Murdered. This afternoon."

"No! Who did it?"

"I don't know. Any ideas?"

He signalled a waiter and we got two drinks. He drained his glass and shook his head.

"No ideas at all. She was popular. Only been here two weeks. Say! She worked for Joe Botelli, the bookie, before she came here."

"She told you that?"

"Yeah. Why not?"

Since she'd disappeared two weeks before with seventeen thousand of Joe Botelli's hard earned clams, it seemed strange that she was using him as a reference, but there was no use telling the little guy all I knew.

"I just wondered," I said absently. "Well, I guess you'll want to make arrangements to replace her. Don't let me keep you."

The manager walked sadly away to his office and I finished my drink. The more I thought the thing over, the more the job smelled like a frame-up on yours truly, engineered by my client, Joe Botelli. Girls who steal seventeen thousand dollars don't have to go to work the next day, and if they do go to work they don't take singing jobs under their own names in the same town they stole the money in.

I began to wonder if my old buddy Joe had actually lost the money. Somehow it didn't figure, either way. Why would he pay me seventy-five a day to look for a girl if he knew where she was? On the other hand, if he knew he was going to kill the girl, it might be a good idea to have someone looking all over town for her, so that when the cops started asking around they'd hear about it. My heart chilled.

By now, I was sure, McCallister knew that I'd just settled my rent for the first time in three months. He'd know I'd been paid for something, and if he found out I'd been looking for the girl for a week—I decided to go find Joe Botelli.

From the outside the place was a cigar stand, but the office within was busier than a police station on Halloween. There were about fifteen desks, all with two or three phones, and Joe's boys were writing bets as if their lives depended on it. A heavy guy was lolling near the door. He got up and moved over in front of me. I handed him my card.

"I'm working on a job for Botelli. Tell him I'm here."

He looked at the printing as if he'd never seen any before, and then, after about four minutes thought, moved himself to Joe's office. In a moment he was back, motioning me with a hand the size of a side of beef.

Joe Botelli sat behind a massive desk, under an oil painting. He'd always impressed me as the executive type and he dressed to fit the part. He was immaculate in a pinstripe suit and a neutral tie. He had a ruddy face and a pleasant smile. Only his eyes gave him away. His eyelids dropped lazily, but when he looked up you could see a glint of steel. I'd often thought I'd rather be working for him than against him.

He stood up behind his desk.

"Evening, Mike. Sit down. What can I do for you?"

I sat down and lit a cigarette. I took a deep drag. On the couch across the room lounged Joe's right-hand man, a slack-jawed gunman known as Fingers Shane. He was cleaning his fingernails and not showing any interest, but just as ready for action as a coiled spring. I never liked to turn my back to Fingers, so I sat half toward him.

I looked at Botelli.

"Joe, I found your girlfriend."

He looked up and smiled.

"I figured you would, Mike."

"Yeah," I said bitterly. "You figured I would, all right. Get this, Botelli. Starting an hour ago, I wasn't working for you anymore. Starting right now, I'm working for Mike Blair, himself. Get your hat. I'm taking you in."

Out of the corner of my eye I saw Fingers jerk his hand to his coat. I whipped out my .32 and stood up. Fingers let his hand drop.

"Toss it on the floor, Shane," I said.

He reached into his coat and pulled out a .38 automatic. With a hurt look he tossed it onto the rug.

I turned back to Botelli. He was gazing at me in amazement.

"You gone nuts, Mike?"

"You know what's wrong. Get your hat."

Joe dropped his eyelids.

"Now, take it easy, Mike. Tell me what's bothering you, and maybe we can straighten it out."

"Look, Botelli, I don't know how stupid you think I am. When a guy hires me for seventy-five a day to look for a girl who's run away with seventeen grand, I figure that's okay. When I find she's been murdered in my apartment, I begin to get suspicious. When I find out she's been working in plain sight in a nightclub, under her own name, and using the boss she was supposed to have robbed as a reference, I begin to smell a frame-up. What do you begin to smell?"

"Eve was murdered?"

"Yeah. Surprised?"

"Where?"

"You know where. In my apartment."

Joe shook his head.

"She stole the money. Like I told you, I came in one morning and she wasn't here. Seventeen grand gone—the whole week's take. I didn't murder her. Now who the hell did?" He rubbed his jaw.

Fingers Shane spoke from the couch, "Look, boss,

there were only three of us knew she had the dough, us and this private eye. We didn't do it. He must have."

Botelli looked at me speculatively and shrugged.

"Could be, Fingers. Maybe he got smart and tried to shake her down. Maybe she wouldn't come across with the money and he knocked her off. I think we'll just tell the cops the truth and let them work on it. Get your coat, Fingers."

Botelli got up and moved toward the door. I stepped to the side, covering him, and as I did I caught a glimpse of a massive shadow behind me. Suddenly there were stars and rockets and Roman candles flashing before my eyes, and then a deep, black silence.

I could feel the motion of a car under me and my head felt as if it were in a vise. Painfully I opened my eyes. I was in the backseat of a small sedan. We were passing through a city, and in the glare of the street lamps I could see the tremendous bulk of the driver. There was someone sitting beside me and I closed my eyes quickly and played dummy.

"Stop here and buy a paper, Sonny," the man beside me said.

"Okay, Fingers."

I felt the car stop and a voice said, "Five cents. Thank you." The car moved on.

I heard the paper rustle beside me. Then I heard Fingers' voice.

"Got all about the girl's murder in it, Sonny."

"Yeah? What's it say?"

"Singer murdered. Body found in apartment of private detective. The body of blonde nightclub singer Eve Lindquist was found this afternoon in the Bay Heights apartment of Michael Blair, a private detective. Police said that she had been stabbed with a letter opener. Police stated that an investigation revealed that Blair had made inquiries as to the whereabouts of the singer on several occasions during the last week. Robert Mc-Callister, head of the Homicide detail, stated that Blair had eluded police—"

Sonny's voice from the front seat was heavy with self-righteousness:

"Why'd he want to kill a nice girl like that? She always treated me fine. She usta bring me cake and stuff she made herself."

Fingers' deep voice was cruel in the darkness.

"Don't kid yourself, big boy. When she left she took seventeen grand with her. That's why the boss hired this guy—to find her."

"No kiddin', Fingers?"

"No kiddin'. The trouble was, when this guy did find her—she was workin' at the Sombrero Club. He gets her up to his apartment and tries to shake her down himself. When she doesn't come through with the dough, he kills her."

"That still ain't no reason to kill a nice girl like that—for just seventeen grand. I'm glad Joe's lettin' us handle him."

The car moved on for a mile or so while I tried to think of a way out of the mess. It didn't look as if I could expect a break from Fingers or Sonny, and even if I did get away from them, there were always the cops. The car slowed and stopped. I could smell saltwater and I heard a foghorn moan. I shivered and opened my eyes. A flashlight glared in my face.

"Well," said Fingers. "The sleepin' beauty is awake. Get out!"

I stepped out and found that we were in the warehouse district along the waterfront. It was foggy and damp and the cobblestones glistened in the yellow light of a lamp down the street. Fingers gave me a shove toward the nearest warehouse and I staggered. He tried a key and opened the door.

It was dark inside, and smelled like a sewer. He pushed me down a wooden ramp to the water level. There was a speedboat tied up to a pier inside, rising and falling gently with the swells. Sonny climbed in and started it up. Fingers socked me and I fell into the bilge. Sonny cast off and then we were out in the foggy bay, slicing through the waves.

I was plenty scared and decided it was time to enter a plea.

"Look, Fingers—" I began.

He caught me with the flat of his hand across my mouth and I could taste blood, salty on my tongue.

"Shut up!"

The engine droned on for twenty minutes and then Sonny lay to. The foghorn moaned again, far away, and the boat rocked idly.

"We gonna weight him down?" asked Sonny.

"No. Joe wants them to find the body. Suicide." He turned and looked at me with dull eyes. "Say your prayers, brother. This is it."

I felt Sonny's grip on my arms and tried to jerk away. I might as well have saved the energy. I saw Fingers draw his fist and swing with everything he had. Then my head exploded in a flash of light. . . .

Hell, I decided, was not too bad after all. You just relaxed in the darkness and let the current sweep you away. You drifted downward and downward forever, it seemed, and let fate do all the work. I thought of all the worrying people did about dying and laughed inwardly. Then hell turned black and freezing and my head burst and my ears ached and I tasted salt and I had to get air. . . .

I don't remember waking up but when I did I was on the surface, floating on my back. It seemed that I had been that way for a long time. My shoes were off and my coat was off and I was kicking idly and drinking in beautiful gulps of cold, clammy air. My head still ached and I was more tired than I had ever been, but slowly I decided that I was alive. It was a good feeling.

Far in the distance I heard the foghorn again. I turned my head toward the sound and continued to float, kicking a little, but taking it easy. I still didn't expect seriously to make it, but I didn't want to tangle with death again.

As I floated, I thought about a lot of things, mostly to keep my mind off the cold. I thought about getting out of the private eye racket and selling apples somewhere, or settling down and getting married. And I thought about a pretty blonde whom I'd never seen alive, and I wondered why she'd been murdered. There was an idea kicking around in the back of my head—something somebody had said—but I couldn't pin it down. It didn't really matter, I decided.

The foghorn had been coming closer for a long time, and then it had drifted away, but taking its place had been the faint slap of water, such as you might hear close to a pier. I forced myself not to look around and continued to kick. A streak of silver began to shine in the east. I didn't know how long I had been in the water, but dawn was breaking—it must have been hours.

Finally I turned. A thousand yards away, rising in the fog, was the gray shape of a pier. Next to it was the towering hulk of a freighter's stern.

The last thousand yards were murder. The tide was changing and sweeping me out, evidently, because when I looked next the pier was almost lost in the fog. I turned over on my belly and began to swim. I was holding my own, now, even gaining, but my breath was coming in rasping sobs and saltwater trickled down my throat. The roof of my mouth was dry and my eyes stung. My legs began to drag in the water.

In a rage I struck out and pulled at the water. When I looked again the pier was directly above me. I grabbed a pile and hung on. There was a ladder of crosspieces all the way up the pile. I rested for five minutes and dragged myself up. I made it and collapsed on the wharf. I lay there for an hour, shivering, but too tired to get up.

I could have stayed there all day and been perfectly happy, but there was something nagging at my tired brain. Then I remembered that every cop in town, including the waterfront detail, was looking for me, and the wharf was no place to spend the day. I got up stiffly and walked down the pier. The rough boards hurt my bare feet. I glanced up at the freighter and saw the gangway watch, a big, blond kid in a turtleneck sweater, looking at me in amazement. I staggered a little and he smiled and turned away.

I sloshed up to the warehouse at the end of the pier and found a cab stand. I phoned for a taxi and waited. I wanted a cigarette and a cup of coffee and a dry suit and a drink and maybe a couple of days sleep and a one-way ticket out of town—otherwise I was happy.

The cab pulled up and the driver looked at me sharply.

"Rain down here?" he asked.

"Got drunk and fell in the water," I said. I climbed into the cab. "Just drive around a while. I want to think."

He turned in the seat.

"First, let's see if you can pay for it. I got a wife and kids."

I reached into my hip pocket and found my wallet. I handed him a soggy five dollar bill and he inspected it doubtfully. Finally he shrugged and shoved the cab into gear. I sat back in the seat.

As he drove uptown I thought things over. The best thing for me to do would be to get out of town, hire a good lawyer, and hide out until things cooled off. The trouble was that half the Homicide squad was probably watching the trains, and the other half was probably out at the airport.

Outside of giving myself up, there didn't seem to be much I could do. I couldn't ride around in a cab all day. Twice I leaned forward to tell the driver to head for the police station, and both times I sat back again. The idea of seeing McCallister was not pleasant. I needed a smoke to help me to decide.

"Got a cigarette?" I asked the cabbie.

He handed me a package over the seat. Absently I reached into my pocket and dragged out a matchbook— soaking wet. I started to throw it out of the window and then stopped.

"How about a match?" I asked the driver. He handed me a lighter. I lit up and sank back into the seat. Something was cooking in my brain. I gazed at the soggy book of matches. The printing was almost gone, but I could still make out the words: *Sombrero Club*.

*   *   *

The sidewalk by the cigar stand was crawling with shoppers and people going to work. I told the driver to keep the change and crawled out, trying to look as if I always walked around in wet clothes and no shoes and hoping that the cop on the beat was somewhere else.

A few of the shoppers looked at me curiously and hurried on. I went to the door in the back of the cigar stand and knocked. It opened slowly and I saw Sonny's beefy red face peering down at me. His mouth opened and closed and then he grabbed at me convulsively. He dragged me in and closed the door. The desks inside were deserted.

"What the hell—" said Sonny.

"What's the matter, Sonny? Surprised to see me?"

His brow wrinkled in an angry frown.

"How'd you get back?" he asked hoarsely.

"My mother was a duck," I said bitterly. "Where's Botelli and that hood of his?"

"You'll see 'em, buddy. Don't worry."

He laid one of his hams on my shoulder and shoved me half across the room. He caught up and jammed me through the door to Botelli's office.

He frisked me rapidly and pushed me to the wall.

"Stand there and look at the wall. And keep your hands behind your neck."

I heard the floor groan as he walked to Botelli's desk. He dialed a number and there was a long wait.

"Hello, boss. This is Sonny. Look, boss. That guy's back. Blair. The private eye!"

There was a moment of silence.

"I know it, boss. Sorry. I don't know how he got back. Well, anyway, we got him again. He just walked in, big as life. You comin' down, or you want me to handle it alone?"

There was a pause.

"Okay, boss. I'll keep him here."

My arms were aching with the strain of holding them above my head.

"Look, Sonny," I said. "This is okay in a movie, but I

haven't got a gun. How about letting me put my arms down?"

Sonny thought it over.

"Okay," he said finally. "But don't try anythin'. I'm watchin' you."

I took down my hands and faced slowly around. Sonny was standing by Joe's desk, covering me with a heavy service automatic. I walked to the couch and sat down and lit one of the cabby's cigarettes. I sat back and took a deep drag. I looked at Sonny and shook my head.

"I feel sorry for you, Sonny."

He flushed angrily.

"You feel sorry for *me?* That's a laugh."

"You were kind of sweet on that girl, weren't you?"

Sonny's bulk towered above me and for a moment I thought maybe I'd gone too far.

"Yeah. I liked her." His voice shook. "And then a cheap shamus comes along and knocks her off for a lousy seventeen grand. Aah, I oughta kill you myself, now."

His finger whitened on the trigger and I held my breath.

"Yeah, Sonny," I said quietly. "You kill me and then you'll never know who murdered her."

"I know who murdered her. I read the papers. A guy like you, the gas chamber's too good for."

"You think I'd have come back here if I killed her? No, Sonny. I didn't kill her. But I know who did."

I could see the wheels going around in his head.

"Okay, wise guy. Who killed her?"

"Why should I tell you? You won't do anything about it. You guys are all yellow."

Sonny's face turned beet red and his hand shook.

"Who killed her?"

"Take it easy, Sonny. Sit down, and I'll tell you a little story. Listen close."

He didn't sit down, but he listened to me.

"To start with," I said, "did she tell you she was quitting work here?"

"No. Well, she always wanted to quit. She wanted to be a singer. What's that got to do with it?"

"Do you think she stole seventeen grand?"

"If Botelli says she stole seventeen grand, then she stole seventeen grand."

"Maybe Botelli just thinks she was the one that stole it. Maybe it wasn't her at all. Maybe it was somebody else."

"Yeah? Why'd she quit without telling anybody?"

"Maybe she did tell somebody. Maybe she told the guy that stole the dough. Maybe she even left a note for Botelli. Maybe she left it with the guy that stole the dough. Maybe he didn't deliver it."

I waited for a few minutes while Sonny's overworked brain digested the idea. Finally he looked up.

"Who you talkin' about?"

"Who knew the money was missing? You didn't know it, did you Sonny?"

"No. Just the boss and Fingers, I guess. And you."

"That's right. And who knew where she was working? Did you know, Sonny?"

"No."

"Do you know now?"

"Yeah. The Sombrero Club."

"And who told you that?" I asked softly.

He thought for a while.

"Fingers told me, in the car, on the way down to the boat."

"And where'd he find out,"

"It was in the paper," said Sonny triumphantly. "Yeah, we'd just bought a paper."

"No, Sonny, it wasn't in the paper. And I didn't tell Fingers which club she was singing in. No, he knew it all the time, and yet he let his boss hire a private eye for seventy-five a day to find out. What's that look like to you?"

Sonny thought for a while. Then he glanced at me with what was meant to be a shrewd eye.

"Yeah? If Fingers did it, how come she was found in your apartment?"

"Fingers is a careful guy, Sonny. He knew if I looked long enough I'd find her for Botelli and the story would come out. So he called her up, gave her my address, maybe told her he had a message to give her from Botelli. Then he got into the apartment by the fire escape and waited. He let her in. I think he offered her money to leave town—at least she was there long enough to smoke a cigarette. She turned down the proposition, so he killed her. He picked my apartment so that when the cops found out who she was, they'd think I killed her for the dough."

Sonny rubbed his chin. Then the door opened and Botelli and Fingers walked in. Botelli didn't look himself. He hadn't had time to shave and his suit hadn't had its daily pressing. He walked up to me and looked me in the eye.

"So you made it back, Blair. And you came back here asking for more. What's the story?"

"I came back to apologize, Joe. You didn't kill her. Now if you'll just apologize to me, to the tune of about five hundred bucks for every hour I spent in the bay, I'll tell you who knocked her off, and we'll all go down to the station."

Botelli lit a cigarette. He dragged at it once and then ground it out nervously.

"Yeah? Well, whatever you dreamed up, you came to the wrong place. I'm finishing last night's job. And this time you're not coming back again. Fingers!"

Fingers walked over quickly, his gun held flat in his hand. He drew back the gun and his eyes glinted wickedly. I felt a momentary disgust at my own foolishness in coming back. Sonny was too stupid to see, or too yellow to do anything about it. I waited for the crashing blow of the gun across my face.

"Wait a minute!" Sonny's voice blasted across the room. The big service automatic looked like a toy in his hand, and his face was grim. Botelli and Fingers stared at him blankly.

"What the hell is going on," began Fingers.

"Shut up!" Sonny's voice was full of doom. "Listen,

Fingers, I want you to answer one question. How'd you find out Eve Lindquist was workin' at the Sombrero Club?"

A shadow of alarm passed over Fingers' face, but his answer was smooth.

"What do you mean? It was in the paper."

"This guy says it wasn't."

"What difference does it make?" Fingers weighed the gun in his hand and measured the shooting distance from it to my face.

"It makes plenty of difference," said Sonny. "If you killed her I'll—"

The gun in Fingers' hand hardly wavered, but the explosion rocked the room. Sonny groaned and dropped. Fingers moved the gun toward me and I dropped below the line of fire. I put everything I had into a right cross. My fist crashed into Fingers' pulpy face and he dropped. I dove for his gun and looked up at Botelli. He was standing over me, shaking his head. He had me covered, but good, so I left Fingers' gun where it was. I stood up, brushing myself off.

"Okay, Mike," said Botelli. "What's the story? Looks like there was more to this than I thought."

"There was."

I squatted and went through Fingers' clothes. In his inside coat pocket was a brown envelope. I opened it. There were seventeen thousand dollar bills inside, fastened with a paper clip. Also there was a letter in a neat feminine hand. I handed the whole works to Botelli.

He put his gun on the desk and read the note from the girl he thought had run out on him.

"So she didn't skip after all. She says she got a job at the Sombrero Club and she's giving the week's take to Fingers and she'll be back to see me in a couple of weeks."

He shook his head and went to the phone.

"I'm calling the cops. As for what happened last night, I'm sorry, and I'll write you a check for two grand. Provided, of course—"

"Say no more. I'm considering it a swimming lesson."

He called the police and told them to bring an ambulance. Then he turned to me.

"So it was Fingers all the time. And he tried to pin it on you."

"Right." I told him the story of what had happened.

"And," I finished, "he figured that if I thought the cops wouldn't be able to trace the body I might deny ever having had anything to do with her. He was right. I was scared, and I denied knowing who she was. Then, of course, the cops identified her. He knew they would. They traced her down and found that I'd been looking for her for two weeks. Put me in a bad spot."

On the floor, Sonny groaned. Botelli went to the wall and pressed a button. A bar opened up and he poured a drink. He kneeled and put the glass to Sonny's lips. Sonny moaned and sipped at the drink. Botelli stood up.

"How about a drink, Mike?" Botelli asked.

"Thanks," I said. "Thanks. I think I will."

A Dish of Homicide

♦

Tagging after a two-timing starlet started out to be a gag for gumshoe Mike Blair.

CHAPTER ONE

Deadly Copperhead

I was sitting at my desk, wondering about the office rent, when the door opened and in walked the most beautiful assemblage of female parts that had ever shrugged into a mink coat. She had hair the color of burnished copper and dead white skin and her eyes were as green and as hard as emeralds.

Suavely, as in a movie, I stood up, knocking over my chair. She's come to the wrong office, I thought. The theatrical producer is three doors down.

"Good morning," I said. It was three p.m.

She laughed. "Relax, buster. Are you Mike Blair?"

"Unless you're from the finance company."

She eased into one of the finance company's chairs. "I've heard of you," she said. Her voice was low and husky. It was a voice that had been around. "You worked

37

for a friend of mine...a former friend...when she was getting a divorce. Sugar Lynn."

I remembered Sugar, and it hadn't been strictly what you'd call work, but I nodded. "Oh, yeah. Sugar. The little singer. She divorced her husband to marry Howard Morrison, the cowboy star. I wonder if she did?"

"No."

I shook my head. "Too bad. Are you in the show business, too?"

"Off and on. Right now, off. When I found that I needed some—well, confidential work done, I remembered that Sugar had come to you."

"I have always considered Sugar among my most satisfied clients."

She lit a long cigarette and looked at me lazily, taking a slow drag.

"I'll bet," she said finally. "Well, this is a different kind of work."

I went to my office safe. I opened it and took out the bottle of scotch that I must have been saving for the first beautiful redhead that came to visit me in a mink coat. I poured Beautiful a drink.

"Is your name confidential, too?" I asked, handing her the glass.

"Dawn Sherril."

"Very pretty. Miss or Mrs.?"

"Mrs., right now."

"Oh," I said. I sat down at my typewriter. "My secretary has the day off," I lied, "so if you'll just give me your husband's address and the address of the other woman, I'll start tailing them tomorrow. The price will be twenty-five dollars a day, and expenses, but you can tack that on the divorce—"

"I don't want him tailed."

I swung away from the typewriter.

"You want him shot? You want his girlfriend murdered? Name it. Special on murders this week."

She gazed at me coolly, lying back in the chair, her cigarette held carelessly.

"You know," she said slowly. "For a guy who's supposed to know how to keep his mouth shut, you sure do a lot of talking."

"I'm sorry. Go ahead."

She reached into a handbag that must have cost a hundred dollars and pulled out a newspaper clipping. She tossed it on the desk.

It was from the column of an Eastern newspaperman.

Dawn Sherril, the former New York night-club warbler, is singing the blues to a certain guy in the West, and may earn a lifetime contract.

"Well," I said, "what's wrong with that? Who's the lucky guy?"

She hesitated. "I don't think you have to know."

"Look, when I work on a case, I know everything my client knows, or no go."

She thought for a while. "Howard Morrison."

"Howard Morrison? The same guy Sugar—"

"That's right. Any objections?" she asked me.

I shook my head. "He must like married women," I said.

"Maybe he figures there are less complications."

"Maybe he's nuts, too. Every kid in the country pays a dime a Saturday to watch him shoot up the screen. One piece of bad publicity and he's all through."

"There won't be any bad publicity. That's what you're going to prevent."

"Go on. You interest me."

"My husband saw the clipping and he's flying out from New York."

"I see. And what do you want me to do? Shoot down the plane?"

Her eyes flashed green flame and I shut up.

"No, comedian. I want you to pass as the guy I'm going around with, while my husband's here. At my expense, of course. And I think I can afford the twenty-five a day, besides."

"Dawn, daughter, you just hired yourself a private

escort. Would it be too much to ask why you need to hire somebody?"

Her eyes dropped.

"My husband is a bum. He's done time for blackmail, and he has a lot on me. I worked with him once. I was just a kid, and in love." Her eyes melted into tears. It was very effective. Then I remembered acting was her racket and that she was probably just rehearsing. "I finally left him because he wouldn't go straight. But he'd never give me a divorce, probably because he was waiting for me to snag somebody with money so he could blackmail me."

I looked at the mink coat.

"And you finally snagged somebody, as you put it?"

She nodded.

"Nice going," I said. "But where do I come in?"

"I want you to convince him that you're the man the column mentioned, that you haven't any money, and that you don't care about my past. If he thinks there's nothing in it for him, if he thinks we'll get married sooner or later anyway, he may let me have a divorce for a couple of hundred. If he knew who I actually was going to marry, he'd be after him for thousands. Besides," she added, "I'm not too sure Howard would marry me if he knew I'd been tied up with a blackmailer."

I looked at her in admiration.

"I'll be damned. Who would have thought a girl as beautiful as you could have figured all that out? Of course, Mr. Sherril will find you've tricked him after you marry Morrison, and he'll be on you like a leech."

She smiled sweetly. "After I marry Morrison, Morrison will be too busy to care."

I looked her over and nodded. "I guess he will," I said thoughtfully. "I guess he will."

We stood on the ramp at the airport and Dawn shivered in the cold. The mink coat was back in my office, with a diamond ring the size of a pea, but she still looked like a millon dollars.

The huge airliner taxied up under the lights, swung

in a circle, and stopped. Its engines coughed and died. A few passengers got out and one headed our way. I began to feel uncomfortable.

You can tell them a mile away—the born crooks and the crumbs. You can spot them by their eyes. Their eyes are cold and blank, and their faces are deadpan. This one was big and had blond, wavy hair, and I could see that he was the kind of a guy a girl might turn crooked for, if she hadn't been around. He walked up and nodded coolly.

"Well, Dawn, we meet again. The California climate agreeing with you?"

Dawn shrugged.

"And who is this joker?" asked Sherril.

"Mike Blair, the man I'm going to marry."

Sherril looked me over critically. I was glad, for our purposes, that my overcoat was four years old and I was wearing a five o'clock shadow.

"This is the guy you want to marry?" Sherril asked sullenly. There was disappointment all over his face.

Dawn nodded. "And what's wrong with him?"

I began to feel like a used car.

Sherril shook his head. "Let's go get a drink. If Joe Blow can afford one."

I was disliking Mr. Sherril more every minute.

"The name is Blair," I said, "Mike Blair." I flagged a taxi and told the driver to take us to the Hi Hat Club....

The place was crowded, but the headwaiter stared at Dawn and then gave us a table next to the dance floor. We ordered a round of drinks. Then Sherril sat back and cased the place.

"What do you do for a living, Blair?" he asked finally, still looking around.

"I'm in the oil business," I said, just to get him excited.

His face lit up and he glanced at me with new interest.

"Is that so? That's a good racket."

"Things are slow right now. My boss has a nice

station, right on Route 40, but people aren't traveling much anymore."

His face fell and he looked at me suspiciously. I stared back blankly.

"And you want to marry my wife."

"Yes, Mr. Sherril, I do."

"How the hell do you expect to support her working in a gas station?"

"Dawn is willing to struggle along until I get started."

Sherril regarded her closely. "What's the angle? You don't want to marry this guy for his looks. What's he gonna do, inherit a million clams?"

Dawn went into her act. I had to admire the way she did it. Her eyes turned starry and her face softened.

"You wouldn't understand, Pete. I didn't understand about love before, either. When it hits you, things like money don't matter anymore. I love him, Pete, and I'm going to marry him."

It was pure ham, and she was playing to a tough house, but she got it across. Sherril looked thoughtful.

"I don't know about that. I don't know. There's the little matter of getting a divorce, for one thing. And there's something else...."

"Dawn told me she worked with you in a confidence game," I said. "And I don't care. I still want to marry her."

Sherril looked at me and shook his head sadly.

"That's your worry, Mac. As a wife, she makes a good singer. I don't suppose she told you that she gave the cops enough to send me up for three years?"

There was a long silence. Then the lights dimmed and the band began to play softly.

Sherril went on, his voice low across the table, "Just the same, I don't want a divorce."

"Why?" I asked.

"I think I'll just let her sweat it out. I spent three years in the jug on account of her...she can spend the rest of her life married to a jailbird."

*   *   *

A spotlight shone on the dance floor and I started suddenly as a slender figure floated out from the wings. She was dressed in a flimsy strapless gown that made you hold your breath for her, and she was singing in a low, haunting voice that sent shivers up and down your back.

It was Sugar Lynn, her soft raven hair shimmering in the glow of the spotlight. I hadn't been to the Hi Hat since the recession hit the detective business—it had been over a year—but she was just as provokingly beautiful as ever.

She glided over to our table, looked coldy at Dawn and myself, and moved away, putting everything she had into her quiet, throaty voice. I heard Sherril draw in his breath.

"Who's that?" he asked. Neither of us answered him.

Sugar got a big hand when her song was over, and disappeared into the wings. In a moment she was out, standing at our table. Dawn looked up at her. When their eyes met, the temperature in the room dropped ten degrees.

"Sugar," said Dawn. "It's so nice to see you. You know Mike, of course."

"Of course," Sugar said coldly. "I see him all the time. Every couple of years."

I looked at my fingers and tried to think of something brilliant to say. I decided to skip it.

"I just thought I'd tell you that Howard has a reservation here tonight, Dawn, dear." Sugar's voice was dripping honey. "In case you wanted to unload any of your surplus cargo."

Dawn's green eyes never wavered. "Thank you, Sugar," she said. "It won't be necessary. Don't you have to mingle with the other guests?"

For a moment Sugar's face was naked with hate, and then she smiled and drifted off.

"Who's Howard?" asked Sherril.

"A mutual acquaintance," said Dawn absently.

Sherril looked at her doubtfully and then turned back to me. "As I was saying, I don't want a divorce."

"How much don't you want a divorce?" asked Dawn.

Sherril swished his drink absently around in the glass. "Oh, I'd say about three thousand dollars worth."

"Mike hasn't got that kind of money." She gathered up her handbag and turned to me. "Let's go, darling. We're wasting our time with him."

I nodded and got up, saw that Sherril was hesitating.

"Wait a minute," said Sherril. "Isn't there somewhere we can go to talk this over?"

"Not to talk three thousand dollars over, there isn't," said Dawn.

"Well, maybe the price is a little high for a grease monkey. Maybe we can work out a deal."

"We'll go out to my place," said Dawn sweetly.

I paid the check and the three of us started for the door. As we walked across the dance floor, I saw a commotion by the hatcheck counter. Somebody had just come in, somebody important, and the headwaiter and hatcheck girl were breaking their necks to take care of him.

He looked up and I recognized a face I'd seen on the billboards of neighborhood movies all over the country. He saw Dawn and started toward us, nodding hellos along the way.

"Dawn," the cowboy said. "Where have you—"

"Hello, Howard," said Dawn coldly. "We're just leaving. Sugar is here. Have a good time."

As we stepped outside, I saw that Sherril's face now was wearing a very puzzled frown.

"Where have I seen that face before? What's that guy's racket?"

Dawn shook her head. "Just somebody I met at a party once."

CHAPTER TWO

Cooling Off—Fast

We took a cab out to the suburbs and stopped at a little house that looked like all the other little houses on the block. But it was modern and clean and new, and cost a lot of rent. We walked in and sat down.

"This is a nice setup you have here," said Sherril. "You got a job, Dawn?"

She nodded. "I have a job. Eighty a week; most of it goes into the rent."

"Aren't you two lovebirds saving anything for getting married? Seems like I would, if I were you."

"Mike's got a little saved. A few hundred. That's all."

Sherril thought it over. "All right," he said. "I need money. I'll agree to a divorce for five hundred dollars."

I looked at Dawn and she nodded slightly.

"Two hundred now and three hundred when the divorce is final?" I asked.

"Okay. Let's have a drink on it."

Dawn went to the kitchen and a moment later her voice floated out. "Mike," she called. "Help me with the ice."

I went in and closed the door behind me.

She reached up behind a shelf and pulled down a package of bills. She counted out two hundred and added another fifty.

"Give him the two hundred," she said. "And get rid of him. I want to get back to the Hi Hat before that woman cuts my throat with Howard."

I brought the money out and handed it to Sherril. He counted it carefully and put it away.

"Okay, brother," he said. "I guess you'll marry her when the divorce is over. Don't say I didn't warn you."

I gave him his drink and waited until he'd finished it. "Now get out," I said. "You'll get the other three hundred when the divorce is through."

"Don't rush me, Sonny," he said. "Don't forget, she's still my wife. Maybe I don't feel like leaving her here with you."

I grabbed him by the lapel and lifted him out of the chair. "You heard me. I said get out and, brother, I really meant that!"

"Okay," he said. He started for the door and I

relaxed. Suddenly he swung around and his fist lashed out at me. I started to duck. Then my head exploded in a symphony of light....

I struggled up from the depths of oblivion. A buzzer was ringing impatiently in my ear. For a long while I stared at the unfamiliar furniture, trying to remember where I was. When I remembered, I grabbed the couch and lifted myself painfully. Sherril was gone. The buzzer kept droning. Then it stopped and sounded angrily three times.

I lurched to my feet and headed for the front door. I could hear footsteps retreating down the walk toward the street. There was a taxi in front of the house and someone was climbing into the front seat.

"Hey," I yelled. "Were you ringin'?"

The figure turned and started up the walk. "Yeah. Your cab's here."

"What cab?"

"The cab you phoned for, pal. It's here."

I stuck my head back into the room. "Dawn," I yelled. "Dawn."

There was no answer.

"I don't know who called you, but there's nobody home now. Did you see a big blond guy come out of here?" I rubbed my jaw.

"No, Mac. No big blond guy. And the next time your wife calls two cab companies and takes the first cab that shows up, paddle her for me, will you?" He spat in disgust and started down the walk. He jammed his cab into gear and was gone in an angry burst of noise.

I discovered suddenly that I was thirsty. I weaved through the living room to the kitchen door, my head still spinning. I opened the door and felt my heart turn over.

Dawn was crumpled in front of the refrigerator. An ice tray was clutched in her hand, and a bright red pool was spreading over the colored linoleum. I staggered over and squatted beside her. I lifted her head and looked at her eyes. Then I felt her pulse.

She was dead.

*   *   *

My head began to throb in waves and I felt sick. I sprinted through the house and out the front door, reaching for the gun in my shoulder holster. On the tiny front porch I stopped short.

The holster was empty. I groaned aloud and walked back into the house. On the way in I looked at the address. I picked up the phone in the living room and dialed the police.

A gruff, sleepy voice anwered:

"Parkview Police."

"There's been a murder at 307 Melbourne. You better get out here."

The voice was suddenly wide awake. "Who is this?"

I started to tell him and then changed my mind. "I'll be here when you get out." I said. "Probably."

I hung up and walked back into the kitchen, looking for my gun. I looked all over the kitchen and couldn't find it. I decided Sherril had taken it with him. Then I saw the open kitchen window and the thought hit me that he might have thrown it out. I peered out and saw a tangled mass of shrubbery. There was no use even trying to find it at night.

And being found with a redhead who'd just been murdered was bad enough, but if she'd been murdered with my gun . . . it didn't seem that cops would exactly see the picture my way. At any rate, sticking around seemed to be a good start toward spending the rest of the night in jail, while Sherril blew town for parts unknown.

If I was going, it was time to go. I stood for a moment undecided. Then I heard the wail of a siren far away in the night. It made up my mind. A moment later I was walking down the darkened street. I turned toward the lights of a neighborhood shopping district and ten minutes later I was on a bus toward town.

I didn't go to my apartment. I registered under a phony name for a room in a cheap hotel and got on the phone. When you make your living tailing husbands and tracing down runaway wives, you develop contacts at the airports and the train stations. I phoned my contacts and gave them descriptions of Sherril. Then I flopped down on the bed and lit a cigarette.

There didn't, at the moment, seem to be much more that I could do. I'd obviously been used as a fall guy by Sherril. He must have planned to murder his wife all the time, and just waited until he could cash in on the marriage ties.

The motive? She'd sent him up for three years. That was motive, and I'd been handy to frame. Whether he'd succeed would depend on whether the cops found my gun and whether I found Sherril. Until one or the other happened, there was nothing to do but wait.

It had been a hard night. My head throbbed and my bones ached and I felt a stubble on my chin and my nerves were tied up in knots. I ground out my cigarette and closed my eyes.

I opened them with a start.

The mink coat and the diamond ring!

I sat up suddenly. The coat and the ring were in my office, where they wouldn't hurt Dawn's act. "Tonight I'm poor but proud," she'd said, peeling off the coat and jerking off the ring. If the cops traced the gun, that's where the cops would be, right in my office. And a cop who doesn't believe that a private eye would murder a client for a diamond ring and a mink coat is a pretty rare cop indeed....

I grabbed a taxi and headed for the financial district. On the way down I smoked three cigarettes. In front of the building, we stopped and I got out. I paid the driver and walked through the deserted lobby to the service elevator.

I rode myself up and walked down the dark hallway to my office. With relief I noticed that the light inside was out, and unlocked the door. I wouldn't have been surprised to find the whole homicide squad waiting for me. There was no one there. The mink coat was draped over a chair. I went to the safe and fumbled with the dial. I took out the ring and slipped it into my pocket and picked up the coat. Then I started for the door—and froze.

Far down the hall I heard the whine of the service elevator. It stopped and I heard voices. My heart sank miserably. I dodged back into the office and locked the door. I looked wildly around for a place to ditch the coat and ring. The office had never looked more barren. I thought of tossing them out the window and then decided that if they found them on the street, it would be worse.

Finally, I compromised by jamming the coat under the desk. I flipped on the desk light and spread papers around. I put an old report into my typewriter and began to pound the keys.

I heard the voices die down outside and the squeak of dry leather moving slowly up the hall. I continued to type. There was a whisper and then a knock.

"Who is it?" I asked, with what I hoped was the proper amount of surprise.

"Police," a voice answered.

I got up quickly and opened the door.

A tremendous plainclothesman with innocent blue eyes crammed himself into the office. A policeman in uniform followed. I'd never seen either of them before.

"Are you Michael Blair?" asked the giant.

"Yes, sir," I said. "What can I do for you?"

He swept the office with a glance. "Working late tonight, aren't you?"

"Yeah. Business is good."

He walked to my typewriter and read the report I'd been typing. I hoped it made sense. It seemed to satisfy him. He turned back to me.

"How long you been working here tonight?"

"I don't know. What time is it?"

"It's one a.m."

"I've been here all night."

"Maybe," said Blue-eyes. "We think different."

He began to walk around the office, lazily, but not missing anything. He moved back to the desk and I held my breath.

"Would it be too much to ask what you guys want?" I inquired, to divert his attention.

"Not at all," he said.

There was a long silence.

"What do you want?" I asked finally.

"There's been a little touch of murder going around. We seem to think you might know something about it."

"Sure," I said. "I probably murdered him. Who is it?"

"It's not a him. It's a her. And you probably did at that."

He kept moving closer to the desk, and I thought fast.

"You boys don't happen to have a search warrant, do you?"

He went on poking carelessly around in my waste-paper basket. Finally he looked up and smiled.

"As a matter of fact, we do. Want to see it?"

I shook my head. "I'm not hiding anything. Tell me what you want and I'll help you look for it."

"I don't know what we want. We're just looking. Mind?"

"No," I said. "Go right ahead." I sat down behind my desk and felt the mink coat under my feet.

He walked to the safe and kicked it. "Do you mind opening this up?"

I looked at my fingernails. "I'll open it if you'll tell me what you're trying to prove."

The baby-blue eyes grew suddenly hard.

"You'll open it anyway. Or we'll cart it down to the station and have it opened, the hard way. And then you won't have a safe anymore." He paused and smiled. "Not that you'll ever need one again, probably."

I didn't like the note of confidence in his voice, but I opened the safe. He looked through the papers inside.

"Nothing here on a Dawn Sherril, is there?"

"Who's that?"

"The girl you lent your gun to. She was carrying your name and address in her handbag. She shot herself through the heart and then opened the window and threw your gun out into the shrubbery."

"What gun?"

"The gun you have licensed in your name."

I took a deep breath. "Oh, yeah. I know. That gun. As a matter of fact, I just—"

"I know, buddy. You just sold it last week. Right?"

I nodded.

Blue-eyes laughed, without much mirth.

"I've been on the force seven years. Never found a murder gun yet that somebody hadn't just sold the week before. And they never seem to change the registration. Never even able to describe the man they say that they sold it to."

I sat down behind the desk again. The sweat was coming out on my forehead, and I wiped it with the back of my hand. I needed a drink, bad.

"I don't know what you're talking about."

Blue-eyes began to speak in a flat monotone, as if he were reciting.

"A girl was shot tonight. In her home. A girl named Dawn Sherril. She was shot with a gun we found in back in the shrubbery. The gun was registered to a private dick named Michael Blair. That's you. In her handbag was a name and address. The name was Michael Blair. That's you, remember—with this address.

"A neighborhood cabdriver volunteered the information that he was called to Mrs. Sherril's home to pick her up. The cab company operator remembers the call. She says it was a woman's voice. The cabdriver tells us that when he got to the address, it took ten minutes to get anybody to the door. The guy that came to the door needed a shave. You need a shave.

"The guy that came to the door had on a gray flannel suit. You have on a gray flannel suit. He had gray eyes. You have gray eyes. And the guy that came to the door said there was nobody home. But there was somebody home—Dawn Sherril. Only she didn't need a cab. She needed a hearse. Search him, Muller."

The cop moved over and began to frisk me, from the top down. When he got to my coat he opened it and grunted.

"You didn't sell the shoulder holster, did you?"

I shook my head. Things were looking bad, but there was no sense in admitting anything.

Muller emptied my pockets onto the desk and whistled.

"Look at that rock, boss."

The diamond shone like a living thing. The big detective picked it up carefully and looked inside.

"D.S. from H.M." he read. "Dawn Sherril from ... who's that cowboy joker she was supposed to be running around with? Howard Morrison."

He looked at me and smiled politely.

"You aren't too cagey, are you, Blair? I guess you got this at the hockshop?"

"Maybe."

He began to go through my desk drawers. "Let's see if you got anything else. Anybody who'd kill a dame for a diamond ring is pretty hard up."

He looked through the last drawer and started to turn away. Suddenly he wheeled and squatted, peering under the desk.

"Well, what do you know about this?" He pulled the coat out and held it at arm's length. "Yours, Blair?"

"Yeah," I said. "It's a disguise."

"Cute," said Blue-eyes. "Well, Muller, lip the cuffs on. We'll take him in and book him on suspicion of murder."

I figured the thing had finally gone far enough.

"Wait a minute," I said. "I'll tell you all I know about this case. I know Dawn Sherril. She wanted me to pass as the guy she was going to marry, because her husband was due to fly in this evening—and she wanted a divorce to marry this Morrison joker. But she didn't want Morrison to know she'd been a blackmailer. Also, she didn't want Sherril to know she was in the chips, so she left her ring and coat here. The act seemed to work okay.

"Sherril wanted five hundred for giving her a divorce—but when he got it he slugged me, took my gun, and shot his wife. When I woke up, she was dead. I called the police. When I found out my gun was gone, I got scared, I guess. Also I wanted to find Sherril, and I figured you guys would slow me up. So I shoved off. I've got my contacts at the airport and train station looking for him now."

Blue-eyes smiled sweetly.

"What an imagination! The one-man police force out to trap a murderer and make the cops look silly. Just like in the detective stories. It's a great tale, Blair, but it's no soap. I don't believe you. I think things are tough in your racket, I think you knew this dame had a ring and a mink coat, I think you murdered her, got scared, tossed your gun away, called the police for an alibi in case we found the gun, and left. That's what I think."

"Look," I said. "At least check on Sherril. He came in on flight 307 from New York this afternoon—a big blond guy, flashy dresser, red tie, green suit."

The detective picked up my phone. He dialed Municipal Airport.

"Give me the airlines dispatcher," he said. There was a long wait. "This is Peterson, of the homicide squad," he said finally. "Find out if you had a passenger named Sherril on your evening flight from New York." There was a pause. "Okay," he said. "Thank you."

He turned back to me.

"No such name on the passenger list," he said. "Surprised?"

My heart sank. "Like I said, this guy is a convicted extortionist," I told him. "Those people don't use their right names. He's probably on parole and not supposed to leave New York."

"Yes," said Blue-eyes tolerantly. "Yes, indeed. Put the cuffs on him, Muller."

A picture flashed across my mind—a picture of myself languishing in a cell while the newspapers and a D.A. hungry for convictions built up a case against me, and a guy named Sherril bought himself an airtight alibi to prove that he'd never been out of the State of New York. I didn't like the picture—I didn't like it at all.

Muller was little for a cop. Little, but stocky, built

like a barrel, with nothing to grab. I let him get close to me and then threw my arms about his neck and swung him around. He cursed and tried to jerk away. Blue-eyes whipped out a gun and lunged across the office. I hung on to the cop and backed toward the door.

When I felt the knob in the small of my back, I shoved the cop hard and he reeled toward the detective. I dodged through the door and slammed it. A shot roared from inside the office and a slug ricocheted down the hallway. I was three quarters of the way down the corridor when they untangled themselves and got to the door.

Another shot sang past my head and then I was in the elevator, slamming the gate. I pushed the button marked *garage* and cursed as the elevator whined slowly into motion. I heard Blue-eyes above me. A deafening report sounded in the shaft. A slug clanged on the roof on the elevator, and I ducked instinctively. I heard the sound of feet disappearing down the hallway as the two of them raced for the stairs.

It was the longest elevator ride I had ever taken. It seemed as if two hours passed before I finally came to the garage. I yanked open the gate and walked quickly through the empty spaces. Then I was out in the night. Across the street was a squad car, with the lights on and a bulky figure slouched over the wheel. I turned south, away from the car, and forced myself to saunter instead of run. At the first corner I turned west, and at the next I turned south again. A siren began to moan in the night and grew louder and louder, and then was past, a block away. It died away in the distance, and I flagged a cab....

CHAPTER THREE

Don't Tank Me

The cabby drove me uptown and let me off at a neighborhood bar. I went in and ordered a shot of bourbon and a bottle of beer. While I was waiting, I phoned the airport and the train station. Neither of my contacts had seen Sherril, but the man at the airport said that the place was crawling with cops, and wanted to know if they were looking for him too. I said no, they were looking for a private eye named Blair, and hung up.

I went back to the bar and downed the shot. It saved my life. My nerves began to unknot and my head began to clear. I ordered another shot and started to think.

The fact that Sherril hadn't showed at the airport and the train station didn't indicate that he was still in town. He might have taken a bus, or more likely, decided to hitchhike to another town and take a plane to New York from there. I wondered if there were any way to get his address in New York. Dawn might have known it. Dawn might have told some friend where her husband lived. The trouble was that I only knew one friend of Dawn's—Howard Morrison—and she'd hardly have told him her husband's address.

Of course, there was Sugar. She wasn't exactly a friend of Dawn's, but they'd apparently been chummy once. The possibility that she'd know where Sherril lived in New York was a pretty slim one, but you have to start somewhere. I finished my second shot and paid the barkeep.

The Hi Hat Club was crowded, even though it was near closing time. I asked the headwaiter for Sugar. He gave me a cold stare and told me that she was in her dressing room and it was off-limits. I slipped him a fin. He decided that it was on-limits to friends of Sugar. I went back and knocked.

There was a long wait. Then the door opened and Sugar stood there in what might have passed for a negligee. She had a smile on her lips. When she saw who it was, her face fell.

"What do you want?" she asked icily.

I slid past her like a magazine salesman. "Just wanted to talk to you, Sugar."

She shrugged and pointed to a chaise lounge. "Make it short. I'm tired."

"I've got news for you," I said. "Good news for you."

She sat at her dressing table and began making up her face. "Yeah? I can hardly wait. Have you decided to take me out to a movie next month?"

"Dawn's been murdered."

I watched her face in the mirror. She was dabbing lipstick on her lower lip. Her face never changed and her hand never wavered.

"Really? Lynched?"

"I'm serious. She was shot tonight, just after she left here."

Sugar swung around on her stool. "By whom?"

"According to the police, me. Actually, her husband."

"You mean you're denying it? I'd be proud." She turned back to her mirror.

I looked at the back of my hands. "I'm in a bad spot, Sugar. Her husband got away. Unless I can find him they'll hang it on me."

"You're breaking my heart. What do you want me to do?"

"I thought Dawn might have told you where he lived in New York, when you two were so chummy."

"We two were never chummy, as you put it. I've never seen her husband, and I don't know his address."

"You saw him tonight."

"What do you mean?"

"He was the big blond guy sitting at our table."

She shot me a startled glance in the mirror. "That was her husband?"

I nodded. She started to say something and then changed her mind. "I don't know his address. Sorry."

I walked over to her and looked down at her.

"What were you going to say?"

She dropped her eyes. "Nothing."

I took a deep breath. "Look, Sugar. I'm in a hole. If you know anything about this thing, for Pete's sake, tell me about it."

"I don't know anything about it. Now I'd appreciate it if you'd get out and leave me alone."

"Something tells me, sister, that you know more

than you're telling. I'm staying here until I find out what it is."

She looked up and her eyes were blazing. "I'll call the bouncer and he'll toss you out. Or else turn you over to the cops."

Something told me that she was waiting for a date and that she didn't want me around when he showed up. I decided to bluff it out.

"I don't think you'll call the bouncer. I'm staying."

She looked at me thoughtfully. "You're right, Mike. You're a stinker, but I'm not turning you in. Your boy Sherril is here now. Or he was ten minutes ago."

"What? He came back *here?*"

"He turned up a couple of hours ago. Tried to make a date with me. I turned him down and the last I saw of him he was sitting in the bar drowning his sorrows."

"Thanks, honey," I said. "Thanks a lot."

I was halfway to the door when it opened slowly. Howard Morrison stood there with a grin on his face. When he saw me, the grin faded. I brushed past him and out onto the dance floor. I walked swiftly across to the bar. The bar was a modern one, slick, chromium plated, dark in spite of the violet fluorescent lighting behind the mirrors. It was still crowded.

At one end sat Sherril, alone, staring into his drink. I walked over and stood behind him in the crowd.

"We meet again," I said.

He turned slowly. His eyes were bleary and a shadow of fear crossed them when he saw me.

"Well," he said. "Dawn's dream man. What are you doing here? I thought you'd be busy."

"Where? In jail?"

He looked at me blankly.

"Come on," I said. "You and I are going to take a little trip to the station house."

He rose unsteadily. "You really have a taste for punishment, haven't you?" He cocked his fist and sighted at my chin, striking out blindly. I moved my head. I slapped him three times, hard, and he fell back against the bar, rubbing his jaw. I saw the bartender moving down with a dangerous look in his eyes.

"It's okay, buddy," I told him. "My friend's just a little tanked, that's all."

"You boys fight somewhere else," said the barkeep. "This is a respectable house."

"You heard what the man said," I told Sherril. I took him by the arm and shoved him to the door. "Come with me. I'll take care of you." I steered him past the doorman and pushed him into a cab.

"Drive around," I said to the driver. Then I shut the glass partition and turned to Sherril.

"Okay, Sherril," I said. "I'm taking you down to the station. First, I want to talk to you."

He shook his head. "Nobody saw me slug you. You'll never prove a thing."

"I've been slugged before. But I never woke up and found my client murdered before. And I don't like the experience."

Some of the glaze left his eyes. "Murdered? What client? What are you, a lawyer? What are you talking about, anyway?"

"I'm a private detective. Your wife was my client. And after you slugged me you shot her—with my gun. Remember?"

"Dawn was shot?"

"Yeah. Surprised? You have my sympathy. It must be a terrific shock."

He was sober now, and I watched him carefully.

"Dawn shot," he repeated slowly. "Dawn shot." He shook his head. "And she still owed me three hundred dollars."

"You know," I said, "that's one of the things you're going to tell me. Why you murdered her before you got the whole five hundred, and why you came back to the Hi Hat Club—the one place the cops would be looking for you if they'd believed me."

"I didn't shoot her."

"You don't say."

"When I left Dawn's place, I came back and tried to

get a date with that singer. She wouldn't go out with me. I've been in the bar ever since."

Somehow, in spite of myself, I began to believe him. It was illogical to think that somebody else might have done the job—nobody else would have had the motive. Just the same, Sherril hadn't left town, and if he'd planned to murder Dawn, he'd have been better off to wait until she'd had her divorce.

The germ of an idea entered my head, and the rusty wheels in my brain began to turn. It seemed incredible, but. . . .

"All right. We'll say you left the place after you hit me. Did you see Dawn before you left?"

"No. She was in the kitchen."

Now for the sixty-four-dollar question. "Did you call a cab?"

"No. I just left quiet-like. I was sick of the whole set-up. I didn't want her yelling at me for hitting her boy-friend. And speaking of hitting her boyfriend, I've had about enough of this Sherlock Holmes stuff, and—"

I could sense from the set of his shoulders that I was about to be slugged again. This time he was sober, and it was no place for a brotherly tap. I needed time to think his story over, and I knew that if I lost him again, he'd leave town. I let him have it with everything I had. My fist crashed into his jaw. He groaned once and slumped to the floor of the cab. I glanced at the driver. He was busy weaving through the traffic. I slid the glass aside.

"Take us back to the Hi Hat Club."

CHAPTER FOUR

Strong, Silent Slayer

We drove up in front of the nightclub. The doorman stepped up to the cab. "My friend passed out," I said.

"Forgot his coat inside. I'd like to go back inside and get it."

I went through the revolving door, glanced at a broad back in the blue uniform of the Parkview Police, and turned right around and back out into the night. Sweat broke out on my brow and I took out a handkerchief.

"Say," I told the doorman. "I don't like to go through the dining room needing a shave. My buddy left his coat in one of the dressing rooms back stage. You got a back entrance?"

The doorman peered at me suspiciously and then jerked his thumb toward an alley.

This time I was more careful and luckier. I sneaked through the side door and found myself opposite Sugar's dressing room. I crept to the door and stooped to tie my shoe, with my ear a half inch from the crack.

It was quiet inside. I stood up and began to turn the doorknob slowly. I pushed the door open with my shoulder, a fraction of an inch at a time. Then I put my head to the crack.

The lights inside were lowered. On the couch were Sugar and Howard Morrison. They seemed to be getting along well together.

I opened the door and cleared my throat. "Sorry to break this up, but I'd like a few words with you, Morrison."

Morrison jumped up and stepped toward me.

"Who the hell are you? What are you doing here?" He had, I was glad to note, a genuine Texas drawl, even in real life. Sugar got up slowly, a dangerous look in her eyes.

"You know me, Morrison. I'm the guy you just got through trying to frame for murder."

"Blair," said Sugar. "If you aren't out of here in two minutes I'm calling the police."

"I'll call the police myself. First your cowboy and myself are going to have a little talk."

Morrison shrugged. "Let him have his fun, Sugar." He sat down on the couch.

"Morrison. I'm going to tell you what you did tonight. If I'm wrong, correct me. And when we get through our talk, I'm telling it to the cops."

He laughed. "Go on, you interest me. But don't take long. I'm busy."

"I know what you mean. All good clean fun, but no strings attached. Right?"

"I don't know what you're talking about."

"Yes you do. A wife in the background might hurt your box office appeal. Strong, silent type. A cowboy star. Never even kisses the heroine—or the kids up front start booing. Getting married wouldn't be good. But it would be better than a lot of bad publicity, just the same. If you get bad publicity, Momma won't let junior go to the Saturday matinee. Right?"

"Look, buddy, I haven't got all night to listen to you rave."

I stepped toward him.

"You'll listen to me rave just as long as I want you to. See? Getting married would be bad, but running around with a married woman would be worse, if there was a scandal. Just the same, the clean-cut cowboy star picked Dawn Sherril."

I paused and lit a cigarette.

"The trouble was, Dawn has been brought up wrong. When you decided you were through with her, she wouldn't go away. She'd been tied up in a blackmail racket before, so what's she do? She says: 'Marry me, or I'll spread your name over every paper in the country.' Right?"

Morrison got up suddenly. His face was blazing. "Shut up. I'm not sitting here listening to this stuff any longer."

I grabbed his coat and shoved. He sat down on the couch.

"You decided to get at the source of your trouble by killing Dawn. But you knew that if she was found murdered, you'd be involved. Unless, of course, there was somebody else on the scene with a motive for murdering her. You had to work a frame-up. How?"

I took a drag of the cigarette.

"You knew she was married. Her husband might be

a good guy to frame. But you didn't know where he was. So what did you do? You advertised for him."

Morrison relaxed and shook his head. "Sugar," he said. "This guy's nuts. Plain nuts."

"You advertised for him," I repeated, "the best way you could have. You sent in an item to a gossip columnist. The item didn't mention you—just Dawn. It worked. Her husband showed up. When you saw us tonight, you knew one of the men with Dawn was her husband. You hadn't figured on there being a third party.

"After we left here, you asked Sugar who the men with Dawn were. She didn't know Sherril, but she knew me. She told you I was a private detective, but that didn't mean anything. You decided to go to Dawn's house and wait until I left."

I turned to Sugar. "He did ask you who we were, didn't he, Sugar?"

She shot a startled glance at Morrison. She shook her head slightly.

"And he did leave for a while, after we left, didn't he?"

Sugar walked to her dressing table. She ran her fingers through her hair nervously. "I don't know. I don't know. Why don't you leave him alone?"

I turned back to Morrison.

"When you got to Dawn's house, you sneaked up to the window. You watched for a long while, waiting for me to go. You had a gun. I imagine you intended to make it look like a double suicide, and kill both Dawn and Sherril. But for some reason, things didn't work out right. You saw me bring Sherril a drink, and tell him to get out, and then you saw him slug me. He left after that. You stood there, thinking it over, and while you did, Dawn came out of the kitchen.

"She saw me lying there, went to the window, and looked out. She didn't call after Sherril—she didn't want him back. As far as my getting slugged, that was none of her business—that's one of the things a private eye gets paid for. She didn't want Sherril back, so she locked the door. That's important, Morrison. She locked the door, went to the phone and called a cab to take her back here.

"Dawn was afraid of leaving you with Sugar for too long, and I can see why. Then she went to put the ice tray away."

Morrison was fidgeting now, and there were beads of sweat on his upper lip.

"Meanwhile, you were watching. Suddenly it hit you. You were better off than if I'd left and Sherril had stayed. There I was, out like a light, and Dawn was out of the room. Maybe I had a gun—Sugar had said I was a private detective. You went in. You searched me. I had a gun. Perfect. I was suitable for framing. So you shot Dawn and left."

Morrison laughed nervously. "Very clever. It just doesn't hold water, that's all. The only reason I left here was to go see myself in a neighborhood theatre."

"What theatre?"

He hesitated. "I don't remember. What's the difference. Your whole story's ridiculous. Now that we've—"

"Ridiculous? I don't think so. Not at all. How'd the murderer get in? Dawn would have locked the door. She didn't want her husband to come back. The murderer got in because he had a key. Who had a key? You had a key, Morrison, because you were paying the rent." I hoped my guess was right. "Guys who pay the rent always have keys."

"You're nuts." Morrison lit a cigarette. His hand trembled. Sugar looked at him curiously.

"Maybe. But there's a cop out here, probably looking for me. I'm telling him what I just told you, and we'll see if he thinks I'm nuts."

I turned my back and walked to the door. I'd made plenty of mistakes during the day, but that was the biggest. Almost before I heard Sugar's scream, I realized what I'd forgotten: Morrison must have taken a gun of his own with him when he went to Dawn's. He still had it.

Sugar yelled: "Mike!" The gun roared behind me,

and a crashing blow on my left shoulder sent me rolling across the dressing room. I lay there a moment, stunned, trying to see through a red haze. Far in the distance I could hear Sugar's voice.

"You've killed him. You've killed him, and you killed Dawn!"

"Shut up! When the cops get here, you're telling them it was self-defense. Understand?"

"You killed him. You killed him."

The red fog in front of my eyes lifted and I saw Morrison take Sugar by the shoulders and shake her.

"Calm down! Get hold of yourself! He attacked me and I had to shoot him. Understand?"

I disagreed, but attacking him seemed like a good idea. My left arm was beginning to feel as if it had been cut off at the shoulder, but everything else seemed as if it would work. I set myself and waited until Morrison let go of Sugar. Then I lunged across the room, aiming for his knees.

It was a beautiful tackle for a guy my age. Morrison crashed to the floor. His gun dropped and slid under the couch. I hung on to both of his legs with my good arm.

"Sugar," I grunted. "Get the cops, and hurry."

Morrison was powerful and had two arms that worked. I heard the door open and heard Sugar's high-heeled shoes tapping down the passageway. Then a smashing blow on the side of my head brought back the red mist. Dimly I remember holding on to a pair of squirming legs, and being dragged across the floor as if I was a limp old rag doll, toward the couch.

Then it seemed as if the roof fell in on my left shoulder. Just before the darkness engulfed me I heard a click; the click of a revolver being cocked. . . .

I looked up at the detective with the blue eyes. I was on the couch and the dressing room was crowded. I tried to sit up, and Blue-eyes put a huge hand on my chest.

"Look," I said. "Find Morrison. He's the guy you're looking for."

He smiled.

"Morrison's in the city jail. He's charged with one murder, and if it hadn't been for a cop named Shaughnessy and a girl named Sugar, we'd be charging him with two."

"Where are they?"

"Right here," said a voice with a pleasant Irish brogue. A red, beefy face looked down at me, and next to it floated a face like an angel's, a face with a pair of smoky gray eyes.

I reached into my pocket. "I don't know how to thank you, Shaughnessy, but here's a cigar, anyway."

I turned my head and looked at Sugar Lynn.

Sugar, I decided, I would thank later.

Lethal Legacy
for the Lady

◆

From a cold deck the gunsel dealt the flaming frail a pair of wings—and shamus Blair...a murder rap.

CHAPTER ONE

Three's a Crowd

The girl with the ash-blonde hair could sing. She had a voice, a good one, low and haunting, and she sang as if she'd lost something a long, long time ago—something that meant a lot. She stood on the slightly raised platform in the rear of the shadowy cocktail lounge, leaning on the piano, and singing in this sad, empty voice.

She had a voice, and a figure, and level gray eyes, and a cool, impassive face. She had everything, and she was singing to me.

I ordered a drink.

The song ended on a plaintive note. A few of the people at the bar and the tables clapped. The blonde gave them a half-smile and started for my table, swiftly touching the tight knot on the back of her head. She slid into the seat opposite me and put out her hand. I took it.

"Mr. Blair?" she asked.

"Mike to you."

She gave me a fleeting smile. "I'm sorry that I couldn't come to your office, but I had the six o'clock show to do, and I wanted to see you right away."

"Quite all right," I said. "This is my cocktail hour, anyway. You sing beautifully, Miss Forrest."

She shook her head. "No. I don't have much of a voice. It's only that I try to sing as if I'd just lost my man in a crap game."

I laughed. "You sound like your father."

"Did you know Ace?"

"Everybody knew Ace. What are you drinking?"

"Scotch and water. And thanks."

"Thanks for what?"

"For not trying to tell me what a fine, upstanding citizen my father was."

I shrugged. "He was honest, as gamblers go."

"He was a heel."

He was a heel. Elegy. A guy gets knocked off by a person or persons unknown, and there is great mourning throughout the land. His daughter, who ought to know, says: *He was a heel*. Well, he was. I finished my drink and pulled up my chair.

"Miss Forrest, why did you phone me?"

"Cindy." Her cool gray eyes smiled at me.

"Okay, Cindy. Why did you call me?"

"It's about my father's last request."

"I'm a private investigator, not a lawyer."

"This is a job for a private investigator. I want you to find a girl."

I toyed with the ice in my glass. "That's not so easy. I've been trying to find a girl all my life, and look at me now."

She smiled absently. "The girl's name is Lenore Marlowe. She's a dancer. She danced at the Moonbeam Club three years ago. My father went with her for a long time, and then he got tired of her and she dropped out of sight."

"Three years ago? That's a big order. What's she look like?"

"She's beautiful. A redhead, the sultry kind."

Well, good.

"All right. I'll do my best. Is there anything else I ought to know?"

She studied me. "I want you to bring her back, wherever she is."

I thought it over. "That might be a little tougher. Would you like to tell me why you want her?"

She hesitated.

"My father was a funny guy—he had a strange sense of humor. He didn't leave a will. And he hated me. Ordinarily, the Moonbeam Club, the money, everything, would go to me, of course, since my mother's dead. But the last time I saw him, two years ago, he told me what he wanted done if he died."

I ordered two more drinks and sat back to listen.

"He knew I hated him for being a gambler—I know, it could have been worse, but all my life, all through school, people knew, and I...I felt that I had to live it down. As a result I developed almost a psychosis about gambling. I got over it, really; I even play the horses sometimes myself, now, but two years ago I was very rabid on the subject."

She sipped her drink.

"He knew it, of course. The last time I saw him he told me that he couldn't make up his mind what he wanted done with the Moonbeam Club if he died. I think he knew that he might be killed in some sort of a mess, just as he was. He said that since he couldn't make up his mind, he wanted the three people he thought were entitled to the club to cut cards for it."

I whistled. "That's about a half a million bucks worth of property. Who did he say was entitled to it?"

"Myself, and Vince Populo, the manager, and... Lenore Marlow."

"The redhead? What was she to him?"

"Not any more than the other floozies he ran around with. But he knew I hated her, and he knew that I didn't like to gamble, and that's the lovely way he thought of to make me suffer."

"Did he put it in writing?"

"No."

"Does anybody know it?"

She shook her head. "No. I'm telling Vince tonight, and when you find the girl we'll go through with the fiasco, and that'll be that."

I studied her curiously. She was either stupid or honest; honest beyond belief. And she didn't look stupid.

"Are you sure you want me to find her?"

She nodded.

"I know what you're thinking. I know that you think I'm weird. But that was another of his little tricks. He didn't care who got the club—but he thought I'd ignore his wishes, and then have it on my conscience the rest of my life. Well, I won't. We'll cut for the club, and whoever gets it, gets it. Period."

I shrugged.

"Okay, Cindy, if that's the way you want it. But I think you might be making a mistake...."

Ordinarily it's not hard to trace a dancer, or a singer, or an actress. You wire the agent and he tells you where the last booking was and you start from there. So I got a wire, collect, that the last booking listed for Lenore Marlowe was the Moonbeam Club in San Francisco, three years ago. And that was that.

None of the showgirls at the Moonbeam Club had been there for more than a year, but the headwaiter had been there for six and he thought he remembered that the redhead had lived at the Hotel Cardinal, only don't tell his wife he remembered.

At the Cardinal, they told me that their last mailing address was a little hotel on Bush Street. I hopped a cable car to the little hotel on Bush Street and found that it had been torn down two years ago. Dead end. From there on, it would have to be legwork. And I don't like legwork.

I tried every nightclub in town, with no luck. Then

I started on the dance halls—same result. I tried three burlesque houses. Still no soap, although the manager of one said he knew lots of redheads, and would I like to meet a little number that just came in from Kansas City.

The last burlesque house was the bottom of the barrel—a little dump in Chinatown that smelled of stale cigar smoke and popcorn and rotten peanut shells. It was noon when I walked in. There was an old joker sweeping out the seats. I dragged my weary feet down the aisle and asked him for the manager. He said he was the manager and he didn't want any. I asked him about a redhead named Lenore Marlowe and he looked at me suspiciously.

"Why?"

"She's inherited some money. Kind of."

He cackled. "Yeah, that's what they all say. How much does she owe you?"

"Do you know her or not?"

He smiled. "Sure. A stripper. Never forget a...a face." He chuckled toothlessly. He moved his hands expressively. "Stacked! Did a strip here—let's see—in forty-six. Left here for Mexico City. Owed me two weeks advanced salary. Hope you find her."

I started up the aisle.

"Hey, when you give her that money she inherited, tell her to remember old Louis." He exploded in a paroxysm of mirth.

Well, it was a lead, and it explained why the agent didn't have her address. I cabled Juan Perez in Mexico City and got an answer:

MARLOWE PLAYED ONE SUMMER RICAR-DO CLUB HERE. STANK. DRANK LIKE TANK. FIRED. LAST HEARD FROM PANA-MA CITY. LOVE AND KISSES. JUAN.

Lenore Marlowe was apparently hitting the skids, but good. I phoned the cocktail lounge for Cindy and they told me that she was at the Moonbeam Club. I drove to the city limits and on to the club.

It was quite a place. From the outside it was a palatial roadhouse; inside it was all sectional furniture and knee-deep carpeting. When I asked for Cindy Forrest, the headwaiter took me through a room full of blackjack tables and slot machines to a door marked *Manager.* He knocked twice, waited, and knocked again. The door opened partially and a pair of suspicious eyes peered out.

"Mr. Blair to see Miss Marlow," said the headwaiter. I walked in.

Behind a desk that you could drive a car into sat a short, merry little man with a dark complexion and glasses two inches thick, smoking a cigar. Behind him, leaning back on a chair, sat a good-looking blond kid with hard eyes, a gunman from his curly hair to his pointed shoes.

On a couch sat Cindy, her beautiful legs crossed, smoking a cigarette. Next to her a lanky, horse-faced character in a rumpled shirt, an individual I recognized as Slim Caper, the slickest blackjack dealer west of the Mississippi. The guy behind the desk stood up and stuck out his hand. I took it. It felt like a limp fish.

"So you're Mike Blair? Well, I've wanted to meet you. Populo is the name—Vince Populo. And that's Sweet-Boy Hines—he was Ace's chauffeur before Ace was killed—and Slim Caper. Since Miss Forrest hired you, I presume you're acquainted."

I nodded. "Slim I met in Reno once. It was expensive."

Slim chuckled. "That's right. I never forget a pair of hands. You lost eight hundred and thirty-eight dollars in half an hour. Right?"

"Yeah," I said wryly. "Never play against the house."

"Well," asked Populo. "What have you discovered about Miss Marlowe?"

*   *   *

Already I didn't like Populo. He was too damned eager; he seemed to forget that his chance at the club was purely charity. I looked at Cindy. She nodded.

"I've told Vince about my father's...whim. You can speak freely."

"Yes," said Populo. "We're all on the same team. We all want to find Miss Marlowe and get this thing over with."

I'll bet you want to find Miss Marlowe, I thought. *Like I want to find my landlady.* I shrugged. I said to Cindy:

"I think she's in Panama. That's why I came out here. If you want me to catch Pan American I can get a passport and fly down there tonight. It'll cost, though."

Cindy nodded. "You'd better go. We'll have to find her."

"Okay," I said. "That's all I wanted to know." I turned to leave. "I'm going back to town, Miss Forrest, if you'd like a ride."

She got up. "Thanks, I'll take you up on that. I'm all through here. Wait until I rebuild my face."

She gathered her belongings and went out a side door. A subtle change came over Populo. He motioned to the couch.

"Sit down, Blair," he said. "I've got a proposition."

I knew what the proposition was, but I sat down.

"You're a businessman, Blair, and I have a deal for you. I guess you know what it is."

I smiled sweetly. "You want to cut down your odds."

He inclined his head slightly. I went on, "In other words, Lenore Marlowe can't be found in Panama, whether she's there or not."

"That's right." The glasses glinted.

"And what's in it for me?"

"A thousand."

"Come on, now. The odds against your winning half a million are two to one. I cut them to even money and you want to give me one stinking grand. You can do better than that."

"Five grand, and that's tops."

I stood up. "Five grand, ten grand, five hundred grand. You know what you can do with your money?"

Populo held up his hand. "Wait a minute, sonny."

"You wait, brother. I'll find that girl if I have to swim up the Amazon to do it."

Populo nodded to Sweet-Boy. The kid stood up, fingering a bulge in his coat.

"Blair," said Populo. "If you don't play ball you aren't going to be around after the game."

I walked to the desk. I took the cigar out of Populo's mouth and ground it out on the lapel of his brown, expensive sport coat. There was a smell of burning camel's hair. His face turned purple and he beat at his chest.

"Blair," he sputtered. "Blair, I'll—"

"Tell Miss Forrest I've gone out to get some air. In here, it smells."

As I walked past Slim Caper, I saw his lean, humorous face twist into a wink.

Cindy found me standing on the spacious porch of the club, smoking a cigarette. I helped her into my car and we started for town.

"Honey," I said. "Watch Populo."

"I am. Why do you say that?" She looked surprised.

I told her about the proposition. Her face became thoughtful. Finally she turned and smiled.

"Thanks, Mike. Thanks a lot."

CHAPTER TWO

Ace of Spades

I stepped off the plane at Panama and into a steaming, tropical furnace. After San Francisco, the place was almost unbearable. I took a cab to the best hotel in town and shaved and showered. Then I went down to the bar and had a tall, cold rum collins. It almost cured the heat, so I had another. The barkeep was an enormous, choleric individual wearing the map of County Cork for a face.

"I don't suppose you speak English," I said.

"Only the simplest words, me boy. Only the simplest words."

"Do you know a redhead down here by the name of Marlowe? Lenore Marlowe?"

"Oh, me boy, there're more redheads down here than ye can shake a stick at. What would ye be wantin' with this particular one?"

"She might inherit some money, if I can find her."

He looked at me closely. Finally he seemed satisfied.

"Blue Moon Club. Floor show at nine p.m. She'll be there."

He walked away, polishing a glass. I looked at my watch. It was four p.m. I had five hours. Five hours meant five more rum collins to keep me occupied.

Five hours meant ten or twelve rum collins, once I got rolling. And if it hadn't been for the bartender reminding me of the time, I might have spent the night, and been a hell of a lot better off. But he showed me his watch, and called a cab, and I was off into the tropical night.

We roared through the narrow streets at seventy or eighty miles an hour and screamed to a stop in front of a cheap, neon-lighted nightclub. I pushed my way past the surly natives outside, and through the swinging door.

Half the U.S. Fleet was inside, trying to float itself, and a few *turistas* from the States, and about three Blue Moon girls for every male in the place. I sat at the bar and a short, swarthy barkeep wiped the liquor away from in front of me. I ordered a rum collins and asked for Lenore Marlowe.

He mixed the drink and came back.

"Señorita Marlowe? She ees dancing now. You go back there, you see her. One dollar, American, for the collins."

I tossed a dollar on the bar and started for the rear. Two Blue Moon girls converged on me, grabbing my arm and the other running her hand through my hair.

"You buy me a drink, no?" they said in unison.

"No," I agreed, shouldering them aside. I walked through a door and a guy in the uniform of the Panama police stopped me. "Two dollar cover charge," he said, holding out his hand. I sighed and dropped two bucks into his hand.

A waiter came up and said: "Eet is not allowed you bring your drink in here." I gulped down the collins and handed him the glass with a sigh. This was Panama.

He showed me a table and said, "One rum collins, hokay?" He darted off into the darkness and I looked up at the stage. A fat, dark individual in a yellow sport coat, sweat streaming from his face, was shouting into a microphone in Spanish. He paused, wiped his brow, and repeated the announcement in English, "And now, ladies and gentlemen, we are 'appy to bring you, from the exclusive Stork Club in the Estados Unidos...Miss Lenore Marlowe, in her classic interpretation: Flame of Love!"

He waddled off, clapping vigorously. There were whistles and catcalls from the audience. The lights dimmed to a hazy violet, and she drifted out from the wings.

She might have hit the skids, but she still had what it took. She danced gracefully, her body writhing to the muted strains of the brassy orchestra. Her hair was a golden flame shimmering in the spotlight, and her eyes were two green pools of promise.

Her body was slender and curved in all the right places, and she knew how to use it. She was definitely not a bump and grind artist; she had a style all her own, too good for the audience.

When the harsh spotlight hit her and she disappeared, the house came apart at the seams. The audience went wild. A drunken sailor started for the stage and had to be restrained by two of his mates. The redhead appeared for another second and then stepped back into the wings, and the orchestra took up the strains of a Spanish dance. A couple of the Blue Moon girls dragged their customers out onto the dance floor, and the show was over.

My waiter came back with a drink. I whipped out a pencil and wrote a note. "Bring this to Miss Marlowe," I said, slipping him a fin.

"Si, señor." He dodged off into the crowd. I sipped the drink and waited. In a few minutes she appeared from out of the smoke and slid into the chair opposite me.

She was as beautiful off the stage as on it, but close up you could read the disillusion in her eyes, and close up her mouth was not as soft. She looked at me appraisingly and flipped my note onto the table, waiting for my opening gambit.

"Drink?" I asked.

She nodded and called to the waiter in Spanish. Immediately he appeared with a double shot of whiskey. She tossed it off and looked into my eyes.

"So you're a friend of Ace Forrest," she said.

"I knew him. He's dead."

"Too bad," she said, lighting a cigarette. "Who do we have to thank for that?"

Ace, I decided, was definitely not the popularity kid.

"They don't know. That's beside the point. I was sent down here by his daughter to bring you back to the States."

"His daughter? Why?" Her eyes were hard, now; hard and suspicious.

I hated to tell her.

"Ace wanted his daughter, and you, and Vince Populo, to cut cards for the club after he died."

She sat up suddenly, her eyes alight.

"What?"

"That's right. Nothing in writing—just a last request to his daughter. And she's going through with it."

She sat back and laughed. "You mean," she asked incredulously. "That girl sent you all the way down here to get me so I could cut cards for her old man's club?"

I nodded.

"I don't believe it."

I got up. "Okay. I'll take back word that you're not interested."

"Wait," she said, raising her hand. "Tell me more."

I sat down. "There's nothing more to tell you. That was his last request, and Cindy Forrest is going through with it. You have one chance in three to win a half a million bucks worth of property. Take it or leave it."

She shook her head slowly.

"I'll be damned." She paused. "And she hated me, too. You know, Mr.—" she looked at the note—"Mr. Blair, I always knew that girl was a thoroughbred. She didn't like me, but she was a thoroughbred. You can tell, when you see as few of them as I do."

I agreed. She went on thoughtfully, "I guess that the thing for me to do is to refuse." She puffed her cigarette. She looked at me almost childishly. "That's what I ought to do, isn't it, Mr. Blair?"

I began to like her. "Mike's the name. And it's entirely up to you."

She thought for a long time. "It's funny. All my life I've dreamed of a chance for something like this. And now that it's come. . . ." Her eyes were far away. "Clothes, and nice places. No more stinking dives, and no more heels to be nice to." She smiled.

"Ace used to tell me that if I stuck with him I'd be wearing diamonds. It's just like him to put me in a spot like this. All my life, if I won, I'd have it on my mind." She paused. Decisively she ground out her cigarette.

"That place belongs to Cindy. Deal me out."

Well, I thought. *I'll be damned. You never know.* I smiled at her and took her hand.

"Nice going, kid. How about a bottle of champagne?"

She nodded, her eyes swimming. We had the champagne and ordered another bottle, and drank it, and ordered another. Then the fat, greasy M.C. stopped at the table, nodded coolly to me, and showed his watch to Lenore. She sighed and arose.

"I have to go on once more. Will you be here when I get through?"

I grinned happily. "Wild horses couldn't drag me

away." This promised, I told myself, to be quite a night. It turned out to be quite a night, all right. . . .

It was the same act, but this time she was dancing to me. I lifted a champagne glass to her and she smiled. She whirled and pirouetted sinuously, her veils flowing about her. Then came the breathless moment when she stood like a Grecian statue before the gaping mob.

Behind me I heard an ominous click in my ear and then a blast that shook the house. Before I whirled I saw the redhead's face twist into a grimace of disbelief as she pitched forward over the footlights, a red stain spreading over her chest.

I was up instinctively. In the dim light I saw a shape moving toward the door and the glint of an automatic. There was another blast and a tinkle of glass from the spotlight, and then darkness. For a moment there was a deep, awed silence, and, suddenly, bedlam. A hand clutched me and I dodged away, after the shape in the dark, while the crowd pressed forward.

A woman shrieked and then another, and a man cursed in Spanish. I heard a bottle break and the thud of a body. A knife ripped at my coat as I fought my way out. The lights went on again and I took a last look at the redhead, crumpled helplessly on the stage.

Then I was out in the humid night, listening to the clash of gears and the squeal of tires. I looked wildly about for a taxi. There was none in sight. Behind me I heard one crazy shout—*"El Gringo."* The foreigner—Me.

The shout was taken up and rose to a roar. I heard the crash of a door and the slap of feet on the cobblestones. This was no place for me.

I dodged up an alley and cut across a muddy yard. I ran up a side street and doubled back, trying to find the business section of town. In three minutes I was exhausted and lost. But the voice of the mob was fading in the distance. I sat on a curb and thought.

Whoever had shot the redhead had escaped. And half of Panama City was looking for me. I tried to think of the clues I'd left behind. My name in the hotel register, and the note on the table of the nightclub. And I'd asked the bartender at the hotel where I could find the redhead.

It was enough for the most ineffectual police in the world. I dug a schedule of air flights out of my pocket. I looked at my watch. My reservation was for tomorrow, but there was a flight tonight—twenty minutes. It meant leaving my suitcase at the hotel, but what the hell. A taxi squealed around the corner and I flagged it....

The girl at the ticket counter was dubious. She pursed pretty lips and said, "Señor Blair, your reservation is for tomorrow. Tonight's plane is filled up."

I tried to keep my voice steady. "It's very important."

"Of course, if somebody does not show, we will be most pleased to change your reservation."

So I waited until plane time, and tried to count the passengers, and smoked half a pack of cigarettes, and sweated every time I saw a uniform come into the terminal. The thing seemed to boil down to one Señor Lampert, a New Orleans passenger, who hadn't appeared yet. The girl paged him over the speaker and then paged him again. Finally she turned to me with a smile.

"It looks like Señor Lampert has had a bad farewell party. We will give him your reservation if he comes tomorrow."

I didn't wait to thank her. I was scrambling up the ladder into the DC-4. I sat by the window nearest the terminal. I started to sweat. I sweated while the plane taxied out to the runway, and kept sweating while the pilot checked his mags. Finally we were off down the runway in a surge of power. I sat back and tried to relax....

Customs at New Orleans was rugged. I waited in line while they inspected baggage, feeling like a murderer on a scaffold. At first they didn't believe that I didn't have any luggage. They checked my passport closely and finally brought me down to the immigration office. A little guy with a long nose looked me over and decided that I wasn't Hitler. In the end they signed my clearance.

As I turned to leave, the phone rang. The little guy picked it up.

"Fugitive from Panama justice," he repeated pompously. "Murder?" He took the phone from his ear and looked up at me. My heart stopped. "Gotta pencil, Mac?"

I handed him my pen and started for the door.

"What's the name?" asked the little guy into the phone.

I slammed the door and started down the corridor. I grabbed a cab and had the driver take me to the train station. I bought a ticket to Jacksonville.

It was a long, dirty ride, but I was still one step ahead of the Panama Police, and gaining all the time. I flew from Jacksonville to Dallas, where at one airline counter I bought a ticket to New York under my own name and at another counter a ticket to San Francisco, under a name I'd never heard before. I'd left a trail across the South that would take them weeks to untangle, I hoped.

San Francisco looked like heaven to me, but it was no time to go into raptures. I bought a shave and a shine at the airport and decided to look up my client. I picked up my car and drove to the little cocktail lounge. It was six-thirty, and Cindy was just finishing her stint. She smiled when she saw me and cut off her song at the chorus. She moved to the table and sat down.

"Did you find her, Mike?" she asked quietly.

"Yeah." I ordered drinks. "Yeah, I found her."

"Where is she?"

"She's dead."

The color left her face. *"Dead?"*

"Murdered."

Her voice was tight. "By whom?"

I smiled obliquely. "I don't know. According to the Panamanians, me."

She was startled. I told her the story. When she heard that the redhead had decided to give up her chance for the nightclub, her eyes filled with tears.

"Oh, that poor girl. Down there in the tropics,

dancing for peanuts, and she wouldn't take advantage
of—"

"Yeah," I said. "It's tough. Well, anyway, I'm wanted.
What would you like me to do now?"

She studied me for a while.

"You're in enough trouble. I can't ask you to go on
with this; to get involved anymore. Tell me how much I
owe you, and if there's anything I can do about the
other."

I laughed. "Sure. That's all we have to do. Tell the
cops you hired me to go down there and find the girl.
Then we'd both be in the soup."

"I'm sorry I got you into this, Mike. But as I said,
you're free to quit now."

I shoved my chair away from the table and looked at
her.

"Listen, sister, what kind of a guy do you think I
am? You think I like being used as a finger by a cheap,
tinhorn gamber? You think I'm going to take that lying
down? You think I'm going to be the fall guy? Hell, no!"
I paused. "You know who did this as well as I do."

She hesitated. "Vince Populo? I can't believe it."

"Vince Populo. Not Vince himself—hell, no. One of
his boys." I lit a cigarette. "No, sweetheart, I'm in this
now. You're stuck with me. Until the final whistle."

She sipped her drink miserably. "Whatever you say,
Mike."

I nodded. "And another thing—when we solve this
one, if we do, we'll know who killed Ace Forrest. If
anybody cares."

CHAPTER THREE

Playing Against the House

Whatever I was going to do, it had to be quick. Crimes
committed out of the country come under the FBI, and
those babies work fast. Also, they had my regular hotel

address at the passport bureau. It was taking a chance, but I had to have a gun, and I decided that it had to be done. I drove to my hotel.

There was nobody in the lobby that looked particularly Federal, so I went up to my room. Cautiously I opened the door. There was no one there. I went to the closet and got my gun, picked up some spare shaving gear, and left. On the way out, the desk clerk called me over.

"There's a man asked if you were in this morning, Mr. Blair. He's been waiting to see you ever since. He just stepped out of the lobby for a moment. Said he'd be right back."

It was that close. I went out the back way and got into my car. I started for the Moonbeam Club.

It was dark by the time I got there. I left the long line of cars dislodging passengers at the entrance and parked my car myself, outside the lot, just in case I needed it in hurry.

I walked to the door and went in. The headwaiter looked at me curiously and asked if I wanted a table. I said no, I wanted to see Populo. He told me to wait, Populo was busy. I fingered the gun under my coat and said that I was busy too.

He changed his mind and led me to the office. He knocked and turned to me: "See? Nobody there."

I knocked twice, waited, and knocked again. In a moment the door opened. I slipped the gun out of my coat and walked in.

Sweet-Boy Hines was at the door and Populo was sitting behind his desk, smoking a cigar. He stood up, surprise on his face.

"Well, Blair. Glad to see you. Why the artillery?"

"Okay, Populo. Skip the act. Who killed the Marlowe dame?"

Populo looked at me as if I was crazy. "Did somebody kill her? Sit down. Relax."

I stayed up, keeping one eye on Sweet-Boy and the other on Populo.

"You know damned well somebody killed her. Who was it?"

He was the picture of injured innocence. "How should I know?"

"Look," I said. I was about to misquote Cindy, and I hoped that she wouldn't mind if she heard. "Your chance at this property is contingent on Miss Forrest's not changing her mind. Well, she's changing her mind unless the guy who killed the redhead is turned over to the cops. You can take it from there."

I backed toward the door. "It's up to you, Populo." I groped for the knob and found it. "And you have until tomorrow." There was a movement behind me and I whirled. I caught a glimpse of a giant in a waiter's jacket. Then there was a blinding flash and deep, silent, darkness....

When I woke up, it was with a splitting, grinding headache. Sweet-Boy was towering over me, staring at me intently. I was on the couch in the office. Populo was working industriously at the big desk.

"He's come to, boss. What you want me to do?"

Populo didn't look up from his papers. "Work him over."

I started to get up and got the flat of a gun across my mouth. I tried again, and took a glancing blow to the temple. I lay still and took two jabs in the face. There was no future in that so I struggled to a sitting position. There was a crashing blow on my neck and the lights went out again....

The second time I came to Populo was standing over me. "You had enough, Blair?"

As a matter of fact, I had. "Yeah."

"Look, Blair. I got enough troubles. People trying to move in on us, guys welching on bets. I don't need any private eyes pestering me. Get out of town. If I see you around here again, I'll put you out of commission for good. Understand?"

I nodded painfully.

"Give him back his gun and take him out the side door, so he won't get blood on the rugs," said Populo....

When I got back to town I called Cindy, to tell her that we weren't going to get anything out of Populo, and to adivse her to take over the club and quit the foolishness. The bartender at the lounge said that she'd had an urgent phone call at seven and gone out, leaving word that she'd be back for the nine o'clock show. I went down to the lounge.

It was nine when I got there—and still no Cindy. The manager was irritated. By ten I was getting worried. I phoned her apartment—no answer. I called the Moonbeam Club—they claimed she wasn't there. The thing began to smell.

I went outside to the taxi stand. There was a driver asleep in his cab. I stuck my head in the window and woke him.

"You been here long?"

"All night," he muttered sleepily. "Off and on." He peered at my face. "Say, what did you run into?"

"Skip it. Did you see a blonde come out of there, around seven o'clock?"

"Lots of blondes come out of that place. You don't mean the singer?"

"Yeah."

"I thought there was something phony about that. She come out about seven and started down the street. A black sedan pulls up alongside her and a big guy gets out and helps her in. . . . Say, is there something wrong?"

"You're damn right there's something wrong." I started for my car.

"You want I should call the cops?" yelled the driver.

"No. I know where she went."

So I drove to the Moonbeam Club again, with fear for the blonde gnawing at my guts and anger seething inside me. I took out my automatic and cocked it. It was one thing to send a hood to Panama to kill off a dancer in a fifth-rate dive. Kidnapping the owner's daughter was something else. Populo must have been desperate.

I parked my car by the side entrance and tried the door. It was open. I sneaked down the passage to Populo's office. I gave the two knocks, waited, and knocked again. They hadn't changed their signals. The door opened and I shoved my way in, gun out and finger itching on the trigger.

Populo and Sweet-Boy were still there. Slim Caper was lounging on the couch. When Populo saw me, he cursed.

"You don't learn very easy, do you, Blair?"

"Where's Cindy?"

"What do you mean?"

"Where is she?"

"At the place where she sings, I guess. Why?"

Populo and his injured innocence were getting too much for me. I felt the blood rising in my face.

"Look, kidnapping is a federal offense. If you don't produce her in two minutes I'm calling the FBI."

Populo shrugged. "Go ahead. But I think you're nuts. She probably just went out for a sandwich."

"Yeah? With a big black sedan full of guys. All good clean fun."

A shadow of concern crossed Populo's face. "A black sedan? Say—"

"Yeah, Snow White?"

"It was a black sedan that ran her father and Sweet-Boy off the road last week. Do you think—"

"I think the black sedan belongs to you. And I think you've got Cindy, and that's what I'm telling the FBI." I walked to the phone. The FBI might pick me up, but they had better facilities for finding the blonde than I did.

I lifted the phone, covering the room with my gun. Suddenly Sweet-Boy cocked his ear.

"Boss," he said. "There's somebody out there in the bushes."

Populo shoved his chair back and leaped for the window. For a moment he stood silhouetted in the light from the parking lot, and then there was the crash of a forty-five outside and he spun to the floor. There was a thud as a slug buried itself in the pine-paneled wall on the other side of the room. I dropped the phone into its cradle and hit the deck.

"Get the lights," yelled Populo. Slim Caper was across the room in two giant strides, and the lights clicked out. In the glow from the window, I saw Sweet-Boy draw his gun. He fired twice, blindly, into the night. Then there was the sound of a high-powered engine and a clash of gears. Populo grunted and hoisted himself to his feet. He peered into the darkness.

"Turn on the lights," he said. "There's your black sedan, Blair. Go chase that for a while." He walked back and collapsed in his chair, mopping his brow. "Sometimes," he said softly, "I think I'll get out of this racket."

My brain was whirling. "Who the hell was that?" I asked stupidly.

"Don't we wish we knew. Somebody's trying to move in on us, Blair. Can't you get that straight? They killed Ace Forrest and they killed that redhead, and they've got Ace's daughter, and they just tried to kill me. Somebody who knows about Ace's last request—somebody who figures if there's nobody left to draw for the club, he can get it cheap."

He jerked his chair to his desk and looked up at me. "Listen. Who gets this place if Cindy is dead? Me?"

I shook my head. He continued, "Hell, no. I'm just the manager. You think I want her killed? Why, as long as she lives I've got a chance to win the place, no strings. And if I lose and she keeps it, I'll still be manager. You think I had her snatched? Use your head."

I thought it over. He made sense.

"I guess not. But who is it, then?"

"You're a hotshot private eye. You tell me."

I slipped my automatic back into the holster. "Maybe I will," I said. "Maybe I will...."

It was too late that night to do anything, so I drove back to town and got a room at a cheap hotel on Bush Street. I flopped on the bed and tried to collect my thoughts.

If Populo hadn't had the redhead killed and the blonde kidnapped, who the hell had? An outside outfit trying to move in, like he said, maybe. Of course, it was to Populo's advantage to have the redhead killed, and the blonde might have been kidnapped to confuse the issue. That still left the mystery of who had taken a shot at Populo. That might have been faked too, of course.

No, nobody stands in a window, making like William Tell's son, just to impress a private eye. Besides, they hadn't known I was coming back—they wouldn't have had time to plan the act. And Populo said that there was an outfit trying to move in.

I closed my eyes and tried to sleep. I tossed and turned and punched my pillow. No soap. I thought of the blonde, tied up somewhere, gagged. I thought of the blonde at the bottom of the bay. I thought of the blonde in a ditch, moaning for help. I tossed my feet over the side of the bed and lit a cigarette.

Whoever had killed the redhead had known that I was going down to Panama to find her. It wasn't a coincidence that she'd been killed the night I caught up with her. It wasn't by chance that the shot had been fired from behind my right shoulder. I'd been used, but good. I'd been used as a finger, and framed.

So whoever had killed her had known I was going down. Who knew I was going? The blonde—she was out. Populo—he had plenty to gain by her death, but somehow I was beginning to believe him. Sweet-Boy and Slim Caper—and they both worked for Populo.

I walked to the window and looked out at the gray dawn breaking over the fire escapes and rooftops. Then I had it.

Passport pictures. Whoever had followed me to Panama had got himself a passport. In order to get the passport he'd had to get a passport picture. All I had to do was check on the photographers who specialized in passport pictures, and if I saw anyone's picture I recognized, I was in.

I switched on the light and picked up the phone book. I turned to the classified section, under photographers, and groaned. There must have been sixty of them doing nothing but passport work. I tore out the sheet. Today, I told myself, was going to be quite a day.

Legwork. Anybody who thinks the private eye has it soft ought to try the legwork. You take a taxi because you can't park downtown, and you climb up stairs, and you talk to stupid people. Most of them are suspicious as hell, and hate anything that even smells like a cop. Then you climb down the dingy stairs and try again.

Some of the photographers kept files and some didn't bother. Some made extra prints and filed them and others kept only the negatives. I got dizzy looking at negatives and there was no way of telling whether I'd missed the man I was looking for. Some of the photographers refused to take time to show me their files because I didn't know the name of the man I was trying to find. None of them kept their photos filed by dates.

I worked all morning, took time out to lunch on an olive and a martini, and started again in the afternoon. By four I was way out in the sticks and I'd checked off every photographer on the yellow sheet. I stopped at the only bar in the neighborhood and had a shot and a glass of beer.

I was beat. I was groggy from lack of sleep. If it hadn't been for the blonde I'd have given up hours before. I thought of phoning the FBI and decided that it would only take me out of circulation. I had another drink.

In the back of my mind an idea was hatching. I had a third shot to help it along. Suddenly it blossomed. Whoever had followed me down to Panama had made reservations on the following plane. The airport would have the passenger manifest—if I checked with them I could get a list of names to start with. The photographers who filed their pictures at all filed them by name. I went to the pay phone in the back of the bar and called the airport. I told them I was a daily newspaper's social editor, and asked for their list of passengers to Panama for Wednesday. There was a pause on the other end of the line. Then I heard the rustle of paper. An efficient female voice started reading the names, "Mr. Crowe,

Mrs. Crowe, Mr. Carstairs, Mr. Lampert...." I poised my pencil. Mr. Lampert... Mr. Lampert.... It was the name that they'd paged at the Panama Terminal.

Mr. Lampert had gone down on the plane after me and made a reservation for the plane coming back that evening. Mr. Lampert had been planning on a short stay in Panama. I had a feeling that if I found Mr. Lampert's passport photo, I'd recognize it.

"Thanks," I said hurriedly and hung up. I got change at the bar and started phoning the photographers who'd been too busy to show me through their files, this time asking for the picture by name. The last one I called was irritated.

"Look, Mac," he said. "Like I told you this afternoon, I'm too busy I should have time to play games. What was the name?"

"Lampert."

I heard him going through his files. "Yeah, I got him. He was in here Tuesday, it says."

"What did he look like?"

"How the hell should I know? Thousands of people come in here every year. I should remember what he looked like?"

"Well, you got his pictures right there."

"Look, Mac. I got news. All my pictures look the same. Why do you think I'm a passport photographer?"

"I'll be right down."

I climbed three dim flights of stairs into the grimy studio. The photographer, a bitter little guy with a green visor over his eyes, walked out of his darkroom.

"Oh," he said. "It's you." He went to his desk and rummaged around. He handed me a picture, postage-stamp size. I moved under the skylight and examined it. My heart raced. As he'd said, it was a poor picture—it could have been almost anybody. But it wasn't.

It was Sweet-Boy Hines.

When I gave the guy a buck out of exuberance, he said, "Don't strain yourself, buddy." I raced down the stairs two at a time and out into the street. I took a cab to my car and drove to the Moonbeam Club. On the way, I did a lot of thinking.

Once again, it looked as if Populo was at the bottom of the killing. Sweet-Boy worked for Populo, and he would have been the logical man for Populo to send to Panama. Maybe the killing and the kidnapping weren't connected. But I knew that they were. And I was sure that Populo wouldn't throw away his chances for the Moonbeam Club by kidnapping Cindy. Well, who had sent Sweet-Boy down south?

I remembered the night before. Myself at the phone, and Sweet-Boy at the window. "Boss, there's somebody out there in the bushes." And Sweet-Boy, the bodyguard, had stepped politely aside while his boss rushed to the window. Also, Sweet-Boy had been driving Ace Forrest when he was killed.

It looked as if Populo was getting the double-cross, with whipped cream on top. Also it looked as if I was going to have to take a chance on an ally I didn't particularly trust. But it was my only chance....

I passed a sign that said: *MOONBEAM CLUB— Dine and Dance—3 Miles.* I pulled into a roadside restaurant and went to the phone. I called the club and asked for Populo. After a long wait he came on the line.

"Manager, Moonbeam Club."

"Populo? Blair."

"Yeah," he said cautiously. "What do you want?"

"Is Sweet-Boy there?"

"Maybe."

"Look. I think he's the guy that pulled the Panama job."

"Wait." I heard him tell Sweet-Boy to go to the bar and get him a drink. "Okay. Go on."

"He had a passport picture taken Tuesday. Did you see him Wednesday?"

Populo spoke thoughtfully. "I gave him Wednesday to Saturday off. He had to go to L.A. on personal business."

"Yeah. Personal business. He's working for whoever tried to knock you off last night, Populo, sure as hell."

He thought that one over. "You mean he called me

to the window last night so they could— Why that dirty—"

"Take it easy. If you want my help, you're going to have to cooperate."

There was a pause. "What's your proposition?"

"Frankly, I don't give a damn about you—I want to find Cindy Forrest. You claim you do too. Okay. What kind of a car does Sweet-Boy drive?"

"A blue convertible. Can't miss it. The top's down today."

"Call me here when he leaves for town." I gave him the number and hung up.

I had a cup of coffee and shot the breeze with the waitress to quiet my nerves. I smoked a cigarette and played the jukebox and wondered whether Populo was going to play ball. The phone rang and I beat the waitress to it.

"Blair?"

"Yeah."

"Okay. He just left." There was a click in my ear. I raced for my car.

The convertible loomed over the hill, making knots. I waited until it was past and then tried to keep it in sight. I caught up with it at a stop light and almost lost it again in the downtown traffic. Finally it pulled up in front of a brownstone house.

I drove around the block and parked on a side street. I walked past the brownstone house, casing the place. There was a tradesman's entrance and an alley leading into it. I stepped into the alley and waited. No one followed me. I looked up.

A fire escape dangled temptingly six feet over my head. I inspected the alley. There was a garbage can awaiting the collector. I lifted it and set it down underneath the fire escape. I hoisted myself up. Quietly I climbed to the first floor and looked in the window.

CHAPTER FOUR

Cold Deck

The room was apparently the dining room, dark and wood-panelled. In the room were three men, two sitting with their backs to the window, and Sweet-Boy standing, facing them. He seemed to be objecting to something. Finally the larger of the men stood up, stepped over to Sweet-Boy, and caught him across the mouth with the back of his hand.

Sweet-Boy looked as if his feelings were hurt. The other man peeled a few bills off a roll and tossed them on the table. Sweet-Boy picked them up quickly and stuffed them into his wallet. I took a good look at the faces, so I'd remember them if they broke for cover, and slipped the gun out of my holster. I smashed the window and poked the muzzle in.

"Nobody move." They froze like statues. I reached in with my left hand and unlatched the window. I raised it and followed my gun into the room.

They lined up and I frisked them carefully, tossing their guns on the table. "Now, turn around."

They turned around. It wasn't hard to spot the brains of the outfit. The other guy had the stupid expression of the average mobster, but the man who'd paid off Sweet-Boy had sharp blue eyes.

"Listen," he said. "You're not a cop. What's your racket?"

"My racket is my own business. Where's Cindy Forrest?"

Blue-eyes smiled. "That's our business."

I stepped up to him and clipped him across the mouth, easy. A trickle of blood ran down his chin.

"Whose business?"

He didn't answer.

"Where's Cindy Forrest?"

He shrugged. "Across the Bay."

That was all I wanted to know. If Blue-eyes said she was across the Bay, then she was on this side of the Bay. If she was on this side, she was probably in the house.

All right. Blue-eyes was smart. So he was smart. Was he tough? I decided to find out. I knocked him to the floor.

He wasn't tough.

"Take him up, Mac," he moaned.

"All of us," I said. "All of us."

Blue-eyes struggled to his feet. We filed out of the room. As we passed through the hallway, I spotted another hood dozing in the parlor. I halted the platoon and collected him. It was too simple. We resumed our march up the stairs. At the top Mac stopped outside a door and knocked. The door opened and a hard-eyed kid of maybe twenty stood in the doorway.

"Suppose you let us in," I suggested. He glanced at me and went for his gun. I jammed the automatic into his ribs and he stopped. "Toss it on the floor," I said pleasantly. "You're too young to die." He threw the gun on the floor.

Sitting on a straight-backed chair was Cindy, not tied up, very glad to see me.

We followed the boys down the stairs, and I herded them into Sweet-Boy's convertible, to the great delight of a gang of neighborhood kids. I crammed four of them in front; Cindy, the young punk and myself in the back.

Vince Populo took one look at the crowd I drove into his office, stared, and started pushing buttons. He didn't relax until his own boys started filling up the room. Then he sat back and smiled at Blue-eyes.

"Well," he said. "King Kelly. Who'd have dreamed you'd come way out here. Did New York get too hot for you?"

"Look, Vince," Blue-eyes began.

"Shut up!" Kelly shut up.

Populo turned to Sweet-Boy. "You," he said pleasantly. "You know what's going to happen to you."

"Listen, boss...." Sweet-Boy's voice trailed off as Populo's eyes glinted.

"Blair tells me you knocked off the redhead. Is that right?"

Sweet-Boy didn't answer.

"And it looks as if you drove Ace Forrest right into kingdom come."

Sweet-Boy shifted uneasily.

Cindy spoke up. "Vince, I think you'd better call the police. We don't want to get any more involved."

Vince smiled patiently. "Miss Forrest, do you want to see your boyfriend tried for murder? In a Panama court?"

"Of course not."

"Then be a good girl and step outside until we convince Sweet-Boy that it would be better to hang in Panama than to die by degrees in California."

We sat on the porch and had a cigarette. I told Cindy how I'd found her and how I'd worried. She pressed my hand. In a few minutes Populo was out.

"Okay," he said. "They're all aching to sing now." He turned to me. "Nice work, Blair. I've sent them down to the station with three of the boys... and their story will clear you." There was a long silence.

"All right, Vince. Let's go inside and cut for the house," Cindy said.

Vince looked out at the setting sun. "Well, Miss Forrest, it's like this. I don't think I want to. All this has changed my mind, you might say."

Cindy laughed. "Save it, Vince. On you a halo looks awful. Ace wanted it."

We walked into the gambling room. My throat was tight and my heart was pounding. I offered up a silent prayer to the laws of chance.

The word had passed around. Waiters, dealers, croupiers drifted over from their tables to watch. Populo picked up a deck of cards and shuffled them absently.

"One cut?" Cindy nodded. "You first."

Cindy reached out, her hand steady and took a card. I held my breath.

"Three of clubs," she said quietly. My heart dropped. I cursed under my breath.

Populo started to reach for a card. Slim Caper stood behind him, smiling vaguely. Populo's hand stopped in midair.

"Mind if Slim draws for me?"

A chill raced through me. "Hey, wait a minute," I started. "That guy's the slickest—" Behind me I felt a movement from one of Populo's boys, and a gun dug into my ribs. I shut up, seething.

Cindy eyed Populo coolly.

"All right," she said. "Let Slim draw."

Slim shrugged. His long, sensitive fingers reached for a card. He picked it up, looked at it, and showed it around.

It was the two of hearts.

I glanced at Populo. He met my eye. Behind the thick glasses a lid dropped slowly in a wink.

"Well," he said. "That's that." He turned to the crowd. "Break out the champagne. Everybody drinks tonight, to the new boss."

We sat on the porch with an ice-bucket of champagne by our table, the blonde and I, and watched the golden sun kiss the storm clouds good night. Her hand was warm in mine.

"Mike," she said finally. "That was a cold deck. Wasn't it?"

"That's right, Cindy," I said. "Never play against the house."

Let's All Die Together

◆

While the police dragnet tightened about him, private eye Mike Blair rode a wild hunch—to track down the racetrack blonde's real knifer.

CHAPTER ONE

Dead Ringer

Some days you can't make a nickel. For eight hours I'd shadowed the blonde with the beautiful gams. The beauty shop, the furrier, the jeweler, and finally the dim, familiar cocktail lounge off Union Square. Three drinks and a lot of willpower it had cost me to sit in the shadows and fight the impulse to stare across the room at the full red lips and the thoughtful gray eyes.

Then the long moment when she had left her table and walked to the dressing room, oozing all the things that make a man wish he'd been born a million years before. Finally the shock when the fat, ugly attendant in the white uniform had stepped out of the powder room and handed me the note, carefully, as if my hands were dirty.

I didn't need to read it.

> *Whoever you are, forget it. I'm going out the window into the alley. Don't think it hasn't been fun.*

I crumpled the note and beat it for the door. I sprinted half a block and banked around a corner into the alley next to the lounge. I drew up and stared.

The lowest window was twenty feet above the pavement.

I cursed and headed back for the main drag. Half a block away, in front of the bar, the blonde was lifting one of her beautiful legs into a cab.

It was the only cab in sight.

The blonde turned and waved. Her teeth flashed scornfully and then she was off in a whine of gears.

Slowly I walked back to the bar. I sat at the table next to the one the blonde had left. I ordered a shot of whiskey and a beer chaser and began to swear again, silently, so as not to offend the waitress. I poured down the shot and half the glass of beer and ordered a double bourbon.

Behind me I heard a light footstep and felt a cool hand slide down my cheek. A soft, liquid voice said,

"Hell, Mike. Why so hilarious?"

I turned. Red, coppery hair; cool, sea-green eyes. My heart turned over.

"Sherry," I said. "Where the hell have you been?"

She slid into the chair across the table.

"Around, Mike. Why? Have you been looking for me?" There was a hint of laughter in her voice. I looked away.

"No."

"I didn't think so. How did you happen to stop here today? Did you forget I worked here?"

I felt the familiar tightness in my chest. "No. I came here on a job."

She smiled. "Still breaking up unhappy homes? Or are you tracking down an errant wife?"

I took a long drink of beer.

"I was working on a job for Nick. Until a few minutes ago."

"Nick Parenti? I didn't know things were that bad. Are you collecting mutual slips, or just shining his shoes?"

"You're funny as hell, aren't you?"

Her eyes filled with tears.

"No, Mike. I don't want it to be this way. I'm sorry." She smiled faintly. "What are you doing for Nick?"

I said it as nastily as I could, wanting to hurt her.

"I was trailing a blonde for him. Does that satisfy you?"

She didn't react as I'd expected. She laughed, a real laugh, not forced.

"Things really *are* tough for private detectives. So you're doing his legwork now."

I relaxed a little.

"No. Nick thinks somebody's trying to bust him, get him out of business so he can move in. He figures somebody's fixing races and placing bets. He thinks the blonde is a plant—she won three thousand yesterday and eighteen thousand today. He thought she might lead me to the boss."

She lit a cigarette and inhaled slowly. She gave me a long, thoughtful look.

"Poor Nick," she said. "My heart bleeds for him."

I glanced at her quickly.

"All over?"

"All over." She looked down and ground out her cigarette tensely. "All over, Mike."

That's when I had the feeling that this had happened before. I felt the anger rising in me. I tried to stop the words before they came. It was no use.

"Yeah," I said. "All over. All over again. Just like when we were kids. Nick and Sherry had a fight. Nick doesn't give a damn, and Sherry can always have Mike until Nick is ready to kiss and make up."

My throat was tightening now, and I felt as if I needed air. I stood up. The words tumbled out bitterly.

"Not this time, sister. The three of us have come a long way from that damned alley south of Market Street. Nick's in the chips, you're on your way to the big time, and even old Mike is getting smart. Not this time, *Maggie*."

The name that she hated brought a quick flash into her eyes and then she laid her hand on my arm.

"No, Mike. This time Nick and I are through. If you meant what you said two years ago—"

"I meant it, all right. Two years ago. Good-bye." I picked up my hat and dropped a five dollar bill for the drinks.

"Wait," she said. Her eyes were cool again, almost blank. "The blonde you were following...was that the girl who left just before you came in?"

I nodded, surprised.

"She used to hang out here. Her name is Helena— Helena Parks. She lives at the Royal."

"It's too late. The hell with it." I walked out into the afternoon sunlight....

Nick sat behind a desk as big as my whole office, stocky, dark, immaculate, more like an investment broker than a bookie. He looked up and smiled. It was the same smile that had put him where he was; frank, friendly, honest, but there was a cold hardness in his eyes that I hadn't seen in years.

Nick was worried, I realized suddenly; and all at once we weren't in the office at all—we were backed against a grimy wall south of Market Street with the rest of the gang eight blocks away, and the boys from Mission Street closing in, and that same cold glitter in Nick's eyes was holding them off as much as the glitter of the knife in his hand....

I sat down.

"I lost her."

Nick spun his chair around in an angry, impatient

movement. For a while he gazed out the window at the fog rolling into the bay. Finally he said, "Did she spot you?"

"Yes."

I saw his shoulder muscles tense, and the blood creep up his neck. I waited for the explosion. It didn't come. Instead, "Mike, you never expected to see me in an office like this, did you?"

I was surprised.

"I guess not, Nick."

"You can see the whole town from up here. The hill where the big shots live, and the hole where we used to live. It's a good town, Mike. A fine town. I've got lots of friends here. There's not a man in this town that can say I didn't pay off on a bet. Not a man."

I'd never heard him talk like this, and it bothered me to see him in such a fix.

"That's right, Nick."

"I've got a hundred people working for me down there. All friends. Runners, collectors, barkeeps. I've made a lot of dough. I could quit tomorrow, and never do another lick of work. What would happen to them?"

I didn't answer.

"Some people think I'm a crook. Maybe so." He swung back and faced me. "But whoever's trying to break me is a crook, too, and he isn't going to do it. *He isn't going to do it!*"

"Hell, maybe it's just a streak of bad luck. Maybe nobody's trying to break you."

Nick tossed me a telegram. He said, "The blonde won eighteen thousand today on Hi Pocket—nine to one odds at the post."

I read the wire. It was from Florida.

HI POCKET A RINGER. PETE.

I put the telegram back on the desk.

"Maybe they're not trying to get you, particularly. Maybe if you checked with some other bookies you'd find they got nicked too."

"I checked. There wasn't a better in Reno, L. A., or New

York that put more than a hundred bucks on that horse. Just the blonde. And the day before, the jock on the favorite was bribed." He paused. "There's a lot of dough behind this, Mike. A lot of dough. And I don't know where it's coming from."

"Why don't you set a limit?"

"I don't operate that way."

"Why don't you start laying off money at the track?"

"I don't operate that way, either."

I remembered what Sherry had said about the blonde. I came to a decision.

"Are you absolutely sure that you were taken?"

"You're damned right I'm sure." He leaned back in his chair. "You can sense it, when you've been in this racket as long as I have. Last week it was a little guy in a brown hat. He took me for thirteen thousand. I knew there was something going on, but what could I do? I can't turn down bets. I'd go out of business."

"If you're sure the blonde is a crook, I'll find her and get your money back."

Nick glanced at me. "How are you going to find her?"

I stood up. "She lives at the Royal. If she still has the money, I'll get it for you."

Nick shook his head.

"Not you, Mike, it's too risky. It wouldn't be theft, it'd be grand larceny, and we can't prove a thing. Forget it. I hired you to find the guy that's putting up the dough. If she lives at the Royal, I'll send one of my boys up—"

I was through the door and on my way to the Royal Hotel before I remembered that I hadn't mentioned meeting Sherry....

The Royal is a big hotel, but a private eye gets to know people. I stopped at the bar for a drink and asked Uncle Johnny, the barkeep, for the room number of a beautiful blonde named Helena. He winked one of his tired old eyes and told me she lived in room two-twelve.

I slipped him a buck, rode a crowded elevator to the second floor, and knocked on the door. There was no answer. I went below and walked up to the desk. I elbowed my way through the crowd and smiled pleasantly at the harried clerk.

"Two-twelve," I said.

It worked. Absently, he handed me the key and turned away.

Helena, whatever her racket was, apparently did well. I switched on the light and stepped into the living room of a suite that must have cost two hundred a week—all thick rugs and modern, creamy furniture. Even a console television set. Methodically, I began to take the living room apart.

On my hands and knees I crept over the rug, patting it. Then I started on the furniture, working slowly, but not bothering to put anything back. Somehow, I felt that if I found the money Helena would never swear out a complaint. It gave me confidence. When I came to the television set, I felt suddenly that I was getting warm.

I shoved it away from the wall and tipped it over backwards. With a thud and tinkle of glass it fell on the rug. I stood it up again, and looked down. On the carpet was a shiny patent leather pocketbook. In the pocketbook were more hundred dollar bills than I had ever seen. A thrill of satisfaction went through me and I straightened up. As I did, I glanced through the open bedroom door.

The bedroom was a shambles. It looked as if a cyclone had hit it. But it had been no cyclone. The bedroom had been searched, and efficiently. The window was open, and the drapes were blowing in the damp night air. I went to the door and switched on the light. I stopped and listened. Through the open bathroom door I could hear the drip of water. A sense of calamity began to creep into my veins. Suddenly my hands were clammy.

Get out of here, I told myself. I walked through the bedroom to the bathroom door. I listened outside. I heard nothing but the melodious *plink, plink,* of water, but something held me. Then I knew. It was the drip of water into a bathtub—a full bathtub. My chest tightened. I stepped in.

The blonde lay in the tub, head back, long hair swaying on the surface of the reddened water. One arm hung over the side. A stiletto was buried below her chest, and the horror etched on her face was not a pretty sight. Suddenly I was sick, violently, and then that passed and I found myself in the living room, sweating and shivering.

How long I sat there I don't know—it might have been ten seconds or an hour. Dimly I realized that I still had the handbag. I started to drop it and then thought of fingerprints. The thought steadied me. Quietly I walked to the door.

Then I heard it—the jingle of a key ring outside the room. I stiffened and looked around wildly. I took two steps toward the bedroom and heard the snap of a key in the lock. The door opened and a tremendous individual, shaped like a ginger ale bottle and obviously the house detective, stood in the doorway, smiling politely.

"Everything okay in here—" he began. He stopped. He surveyed the wreck of the living room.

"Say, buddy, you been having a football game in here?" He closed the door behind him, delicately.

"My Lord, brother, this makes work for the chambermaids. What are you doing here? One of Helena's boyfriends? Fun is fun, but you could hire a hall. Where's Helena? What's that you've got there?"

I took a deep breath and felt my nerves snap into place.

"Helena's in the bedroom, asleep. She was a little drunk."

He reached over and took the handbag.

"Yeah," he said absently. "Somebody phoned up they heard a scream." He lifted a handful of bills out of the bag and let them fall back in. He looked up sharply. "You always carry a purse? You don't look like that kind of guy. Suppose you just come in the bedroom with me and we'll see that Helena's sleeping comfortable. Okay?"

I nodded, my brain whirling. He grabbed my arm and piloted me toward the bedroom. His grip told me that if I were getting out of this one it would be by brains and not brawn. I did a week's thinking in the three steps I took with him, and came up with an answer.

"Spike," I yelled into the bedroom. "Out the window!"

For his size, the house dick was greased lightning. He shoved me to one side and dove through the door. I stumbled against a chair, leaped for the light switch, fumbled for an eternity with the doorknob, and was out in the hall. I slammed the door behind me and raced for the stairs. I burst out on the mezzanine floor and looked around desperately.

Over the rail I could see that the main floor was still crowded. From the mezzanine, a wide, ornate stairway led to the lobby. In the hallway behind me I heard the thud of oversized feet. I sprinted for the stairs and took the first six steps in one jump.

Above me I heard the click of an automatic and a bellow. Below I saw a few white, startled faces turning up at me. Then I was in the lobby, bulling my way through the crowd. I crashed through the swinging door and into a waiting taxi.

"The Third Street Station," I said. I was surprised to hear that my voice was steady and calm—unfamiliar, but steady and calm. The cabby inched away from the curb and crawled out into the traffic, as if it were his cab.

"Come on," I snarled. "Get a move on. I gotta catch a train."

The driver glanced back with a hurt look and the taxi lurched forward. We rounded a corner on two wheels and caromed down an alley. Then we were out in the Market Street traffic and in the clear.

At the station I tipped the driver and hurried in. I walked to the coach window and bought a ticket to Seattle. For a moment I talked to the girl at the window about how nice Canada was going to be this year, trying to make sure that she'd remember my face. Then I went to the phone booths and looked for Sherry Maddigan in the book. It wasn't listed. I sauntered through the station and out the Third Street side.

This was country I knew—every alley, every back fence, every railroad siding. I was home.

Thrown to the Wolves

I walked nine blocks, past the staring deadbeats in front of the two-bit hotels, past a pasty blonde with a question in her eyes, past the nickel beer joints and the union halls. I turned off Third Street up an alley just a little worse than the rest and into a grimy tenement.

Even now I felt the familiar thrill. As a kid, when I'd walked up these stairs, I'd counted the steps. If I got an even number it would mean that Maggie was home—an odd number would mean that her drunken old lady would throw me out again.

Now she was Sherry, not Maggie, and she didn't live here anymore, and her old lady was just another beaten-down, whining alcoholic. I knocked on the door.

It took plenty of knocking and there was a lot of noise inside before it opened. I didn't recognize the old woman at first. Bloated, fat, sloppy in a filthy bathrobe, orange hair bedraggled, she was even worse than I remembered. But she recognized me and she was in one of her jovial moods. I steeled myself.

"Michael," she said, her bleary eyes starting. "Michael, my boy." She threw her arms around me and I dodged backwards as I caught a whiff of stale gin. "Come in out of the dark, boy, where I can see you. Come inside and sit down."

I smiled politely and followed her into the messy flat. She swept a pile of newspapers off a table in the middle of the room and cleared a chair for me. She stepped into a kitchen that smelled of grease and dirty dishes and dragged out a warm beer. Expertly she knocked off the cap on the edge of the table and seated herself opposite me, breathing hard.

"Now, then, Michael, drink your beer," she wheezed. She motioned expansively. "There's plenty more where that come from. I ain't much on frills here, but I do keep me in beer. Of course, now you and Nick Parenti and Maggie moved over to the other side of town, I don't guess you drink nothing but champagne, with your big-shot friends." She looked at me slyly.

I forced a smile and let the warm, sour beer trickle down my throat.

"Now, if *your* mother, the Lord rest her, was alive," she crossed herself, "I bet you'da seen she had more than beer in her old age." Her eyes turned bitter. "But not Maggie. Oh, no. The medicine I need, and I ought to see a doctor about my heart, and all I did for that girl. And what does she send me?" She glared at me scornfully. "Ten dollars a week." She took a long swallow from her bottle. "Ten dollars a week."

All you did for her, I said silently, *and it's ten dollars a week too much.* I shook my head sympathetically.

"Where does she live now, Mrs. Maddigan?" I asked suddenly.

She started to speak and then a shadow of caution crossed her face.

"Well, now, I dunno. Why? Don't you know?"

"Not anymore."

"Well, I dunno either. She never comes down here no more. Too good for this neighborhood, that one."

You can say that again, I thought savagely. I forced myself to smile.

"Where do you phone when you need money?"

She shrugged. "A lot of good that does me to phone her."

"But you do know her number."

She set her lips stubbornly and looked away.

"What's the number?"

She shook her head.

I pulled out my wallet. "Look. You say you need

medicine. Here's ten bucks. Get all the medicine you need."

Her eyes lit up and she reached for the money. "Now, that's mighty nice of you, Michael—"

I held on to the bill. "The number."

She sighed and got up. She moved behind a screen and I could hear her pulling out drawers. Finally she came back with a dirty slip of paper.

"Here it is. And tell her I ain't never got a cent this week, and I gotta make a payment on the radio."

I pushed back the chair and stood up. She looked relieved—eager, I guessed, to hurry down to the liquor store for her medicine.

"Thanks for the beer, Mrs. Maddigan. And the number."

The air on the street was heaven after the smell of the flat. I walked up to Phil's, the neighborhood beer hall, and ordered a shot and a bottle of beer. I went to the back of the bar and phoned Sherry, cupping my hand over the mouthpiece. The phone rang and rang and rang again. I looked at my watch. Three a.m. She ought to be back from the last show....

There was a sharp click in my ear and I heard her low, throaty voice.

"Hello?"

"Sherry? Mike. I'm in trouble. Can you meet me somewhere? Right away?"

"Where are you?"

"At Phil's."

"At *Phil's?*" There was a pause. "I'll be down right away...."

We sat at a booth in the back of the room and I told her the story. When she heard how the blonde had died she turned white.

"Poor Helena," she said. "She was so pretty, and she had so much to live for."

"What did she have to live for?"

"She was just a kid, and some fellow wanted her to wait until he could get a divorce...a wealthy man."

"Do you know him?"

"No. He never came to town. She used to leave the city to see him."

"Where'd she go?"

"She'd never say. She used to come down to the lounge at night, when I was singing. I think the poor kid was lonely. Sometimes she'd leave with a man; but usually she'd leave alone. You couldn't blame her for loving fun. She was all alone in the hotel."

"Well, she's not alone now. Half the homicide squad and every reporter in town is in that bathroom. In a couple of hours, when they get the fingerprints off that purse, they'll be looking for Michael Blair, the great private eye."

Sherry's hand slid across the table and over mine.

"You'd better turn yourself in, Mike. They can't hurt you. You didn't do it."

"Can't hurt me? My love, Sherry, I got in the suite by fraud. I tore the place apart looking for the dough. The house dick caught me red-handed walking off with what was left of the eighteen thousand dollars. I was working for Nick Parenti, who is the one guy that might want the blonde knocked off—and you say they can't hurt me. Hell, they get me, they won't even bother to ask me if I did it."

A shadow of fear crossed her eyes. "What'll we do, Mike."

"Here's what I want you to do. This and nothing else. I can't contact Nick—it's too dangerous. I want you to ask him who he sent over there to get the money and ask him what he figures to do about it. He won't let me take the rap for one of his hoods." I paused. "I hope."

"Are you sure it was one of Nick's men?"

I looked at her. "What the hell do you think?"

She nodded thoughtfully. "And where will you be all this time?"

"I'm renting a room in one of these palaces down here for two bits a night, and staying there until I hear from you or Nick."

She shook her head. "No, you're not."

"What do you mean?"

"You're coming home with me."

"You're crazy as hell."

"Yes, you are."

"No, I'm not. Hell, they'd hold you as accessory after the fact. You'd spend the rest of your life milking cows at the State Farm for Women."

She leaned forward. Her face was tense.

"Listen, Mike. You can't stay in this neighborhood. You know that as well as I do. This is the first place the cops look when they want a man. When we were kids, there wasn't a day that went by that they didn't search one of these flophouses. Remember?"

I remembered, but I wasn't admitting it.

She added, "And you're too well known downtown to hide out there."

I was too tired to argue.

"I could stay at the Royal," I offered, trying to smile. "They'd be glad to have me."

"Sure." She stood and threw her coat over her shoulders. "Pay the check and let's go."

Sherry's apartment was in the artists' colony on the hill. The place was an apology for the way she'd had to live as a child. It was small, neat, and everything fitted. It was like her; warm, glowing, restful. It was a place for a man to stretch out and relax. I did.

I sat on the couch in front of the bay window and looked down at the lights on the water while Sherry mixed a drink. Sherry and Nick, I reflected, both from the slums, both fighting their ways to a place in the hills, as if they had to be physically transported as far as possible from their early days.

Even I felt a security up here that I hadn't felt earlier in the evening.

Sherry was moving behind me, turning down the lights. She set a highball in front of me on the cocktail table.

"Like it?" she whispered.

I looked at the faint gray glimmer of dawn over the

bay. The whiskey caressed my nerves and they untied slowly, almost audibly.

"I like it," I muttered. . . .

The sun was high when I awakened. It was streaming into the bedroom through the French windows, and from a house down the hill came the strains of *Santa Lucia* on a victrola. From the street I heard the clopping of a horse's hoofs for the first time in years and a foreign voice wailing, "Rags, bottles, sacks."

I stretched luxuriously, and then remembered that probably half the town was looking for me. I sat up suddenly.

"Sherry?"

Her voice floated out from the kitchenette. "Coming, Mike."

She walked into the room, and I gulped. She had on a white bathrobe, the thick stuff they make towels out of—nothing luscious about it but the way she filled it out. The late morning sun put golden lights in her coppery hair. She was carrying a tray: fresh orange juice, eggs up, sausages, toast, and coffee. She leaned down and kissed me. I leered up at her.

"What, no morning paper?"

She looked away quickly, too quickly. A chill raced up my spine.

"The morning paper, Sherry. Let me see it."

She turned to me miserably. "Eat your breakfast, Mike."

"The paper."

She left and came back with it.

The police had worked fast, fast enough for the early morning edition. They'd identified the fingerprints on the patent leather bag, it said, as those of a private investigator. A guy by the name of Mike Blair. It seemed that there was a dragnet out for him from Vancouver to Tiajuana. The one nice thing that the paper had to say was that I had maybe gone to Canada. I blessed the girl in the ticket booth.

I looked up. "Well, I guess I get a lot of free publicity out of *that*."

"Eat your breakfast."

I ate it, slowly, every bite. Sherry had dressed and finished the dishes when I came out, sitting in front of the window smoking a cigarette.

"Anyway," I said. "They don't seem to know I was on a job for Nick."

"I'll see him this morning."

"You don't have to, you know. If they find out he's tied up with me—"

"Don't be silly. I'll be back before I go to work. Don't you dare go out."

"You think I'm nuts?"

She kissed me and gathered up her handbag. "Anything you need?"

"A razor. A razor, and you."

She smiled and left.

I smoked a pack of cigarettes, read a detective novel, and even sat through a soap opera on the radio. When I began to feel like the average American housewife, I sat and watched the afternoon fog roll in over the Golden Gate, wondering if they'd picked up Sherry. Three times I lifted the phone to call Nick's office, and then set it back on its cadle.

Finally I ground out my remaining cigarette and went to the phone for the last time. I dialed Nick's number. A key grated in the lock. I hung up and whirled around.

Sherry was tired. Her face was white and drawn, and her shoulders sagged. I took her in my arms and kissed her. I let her go and she dropped wearily to the couch, kicking off her shoes.

"What happened, honey?"

She shook her head and I could see that she was trying not to cry. I mixed her a drink.

"At first he wouldn't see me." Her voice was small and tight. She took a deep breath. "At first he wouldn't see me, and I waited outside his office for an hour." She lifted the glass and gulped the liquor.

"Then I thought maybe it was because we'd had a

fight, so I sent word that I wanted to see him about a mutual friend. He sent word back that that's what he'd thought, and that he didn't have anything to say. Once I tried to get in and that big redheaded gangster he keeps as a bodyguard threw me out. Nick was standing looking out the window and he didn't even turn around."

I felt the anger rising in me. My stomach was churning and my fists were clenched. I got up and put on my coat.

"No, Mike," she said. She grabbed my arm. "That won't do any good. Sit down."

She went on, "Finally the redheaded gorilla left for a minute and I went in. Nick was sitting at the desk with that cold look he gets. I told him I knew where you were and that you wanted to know what he was going to do about the murder.

"At first he didn't say a thing. Just looked at me with those frozen eyes. Then he said that he wasn't going to do a damn thing. He said, 'Mike got himself into this, let him get himself out.'"

She paused and her eyes filled with tears.

"And then he said"— her shoulders shook and she covered her face with her hands—"then he said, 'Murder doesn't go in my league, and I'm not covering for any damned fool that gets scared and kills, whether he's working for me or not.'"

I walked to the window. It was dark now, and the fog was so thick that I couldn't see the next house down the hill. In the bay a foghorn moaned wearily. I turned back to Sherry.

"So he's throwing me to the wolves? That's what it adds up to, isn't it?"

She nodded dumbly. I sat down beside her and took her hand.

"Money does funny things to people, Sherry. Funny things. I'm beginning to see how Nick made his dough. If that's the way you do it, count me out." I got up again, shrugged into my overcoat, and put on my hat. Sherry glanced up, fear in her eyes.

"Where are you going?"

"You know."

She walked to the door and faced me. "Don't be silly, Mike. They'll pick you up before you ever get there. Or else Nick will call the cops."

I shook my head. "It's a chance I have to take."

"It won't do any good. He's not going to admit anything. He'll just have you thrown out. Stay here, Mike. We'll get a lawyer, or we'll get out of town—go to Mexico or Canada—"

I put my hands around her waist, lifted her, turned around and deposited her away from the door, and kissed her. She clung to me, her lips on mine. I shook my head and gently removed her hands from my shoulders. Then I walked out into the fog.

CHAPTER THREE

Who Done It?

Nick lived in one of the swankiest apartment houses on the hill—in the penthouse, no less. I rode up in the elevator and stepped into a dark foyer. I rang the bell, waited, and rang again. I tried the door. It was locked. I looked around and saw an antique wooden bench with a high back. I sat down in the shadows and waited.

It was a long wait, and a hard bench. Twice I almost fell asleep. I started to light a cigarette and decided against it. Every time the elevator whined I tensed, and every time it stopped below I relaxed. Then it whined again, and I heard it creaking up the shaft. I slid further down into the shadows, and heard the elevator gate slide open.

A dark, stocky figure stepped out, and a much larger figure stood framed in the elevator door. The giant was Moose Rainey, Nick's redheaded bodyguard. The thought of his tremendous hams touching Sherry started the blood pounding in my ears.

"Night, boss," he said hoarsely. "See you in the mornin'."

Nick nodded and turned. Moose slammed the door and the elevator started down. Nick fumbled with his keys and I stood up, my right hand in my empty overcoat pocket.

"Open the door, Nick. Don't holler, and walk straight in. And keep your hands where I can see them." Nick turned, his face impassive. He shrugged and opened the door. I followed him in.

The apartment was dark. I switched on the light and looked around. The place was beautiful. Nick, like Sherry, had taste. The scheme was Old English, even to the oaken beams in the ceiling. I motioned to a leather chair in front of a tremendous fireplace, and Nick sat down. I sat opposite him, watching him warily.

"Keep your hands in sight and start talking," I said.

"What's there to talk about? Say, you better get the hell out of town. There are a lot of people looking for you."

"Let's talk about that, then. Who killed the blonde?"

"I wonder."

"Look, Parenti, there're only the two of us here. I know it was one of your boys, and you know it was one of your boys, so let's start from there. What are you going to do about it?"

Parenti moved his hand to his pocket and I stiffened. His hand stopped. "Mind if I have a cigarette?"

"Yes."

He smiled wearily and let his hand fall to his lap. Deliberately I removed my hand from my pocket and lit a cigarette. I blew a cloud of smoke his way.

"We're going to sit here all night until you decide to turn over whoever killed the blonde to the cops. If you don't decide by five a.m., the cops will be looking for me for a new murder, and this time they'll be right."

Parenti shrugged. He took off his hat and sailed it across the room. Then he leaned his dark head back and closed his eyes.

"Who did it?" I demanded.

He didn't move.

"Open your eyes."

The eyelids flickered and opened.

"Who did it?"

He sighed. "Look," he said, his voice flat and bored. "Who you trying to convince? I know you went up there for the money. Whether you were going to turn it over to me or keep it, I don't know. I don't care. The blonde was in the tub, you didn't see her; she saw you going through the place and sat tight. It almost worked, but finally you spotted her. Then you got scared and killed her, thinking I'd keep my mouth shut about your being there. Maybe I will, too. But you got caught. So it's your problem now."

"Who'd you send up for the money?"

"Nobody."

A light flashed in my brain. "Say, you wouldn't have decided to do that job yourself, would you? Just to scare these people out of town? And incidentally to get the money?"

Nick laughed. "Hell, yes. Every time somebody wins eighteen grand from me, I kill them. It makes people like to do business with me."

"She was knifed. With a stiletto."

His eyes glittered. "So what?"

"I seem to remember that you used to carry one."

He seemed to grow bigger. His eyes drilled into mine.

"Shut up," he said softly. "Shut up, or so help me, I'll get you if it takes the rest of my life."

"The rest of your life is going to be about five minutes long if you don't start talking."

His eyes wavered a moment and returned to mine. I heard a soft movement behind me, and then there was a blinding flash and I plunged into a deep, aching darkness. . . .

Far away I could hear someone speaking, and I felt a hand going through my overcoat pocket. A hoarse, familiar voice muttered, "So the doorman says some guy come up here and never come down, so I come up to see if everything was jake." The hand left my pocket. "He ain't got a gun, boss."

"Just bluffing. Okay. He's killed once; I couldn't take a chance. Lay him on the couch."

I felt a pair of tremendous hands throw me roughly onto a leather couch.

"What'll we do with him, boss?"

"Take him across the bridge, put him on the highway, and tell him to get out of town. Tell him if I see him again, I'll turn him in to the cops. You do it. I'm going to bed. And no rough stuff."

"No rough stuff?" Moose sounded as if his heart were breaking.

"No rough stuff." Nick's voice was soft. "He used to be a friend of mine...."

It was a long walk to the nearest all-night filling station from where the bodyguard dropped me. Every time I saw a pair of lights coming, I had to make like the South Pacific and dive for a ditch. But I had a lot of time for thinking as I trudged along, and I came up with an answer.

I phoned Sherry, long distance. In an hour she was out to get me. On the way back across the bridge I told her the story. She listened quietly.

"And now what?" she asked when I was through.

"Now I'm going to prove to the cops it was Nick. Or one of his men."

"How?"

"I don't exactly know. If I can find out who the blonde was tied up with—" Something clicked into place. Nick had mentioned another winner—a little man in a brown hat. "Say, did you ever see this dame with a little guy in a brown hat?"

Sherry thought for a while, weaving through the traffic on the bridge.

"No, I didn't. Why?"

"I just wondered...."

The next morning Sherry screamed like a wounded eagle when I told her I was going out again. And she grew more bitter when I told her that I wouldn't be back until I found what I wanted.

I took a cab downtown to Nick's office. Across the street was a shoeshine stand. Keeping my hat pulled over my face, I crossed the street and climbed into one of the chairs. I buried my nose in a newspaper, told the boy to shine my shoes, and watched the entrance to Nick's.

When the boy was through I tipped him a buck, told him I was waiting for someone, and said I'd stay where I was. He looked at me suspiciously, as if I were a cop, and then went on to the next pair of shoes.

At noon I sent the boy up the street for a sandwich and tipped him another dollar. I'd read the whole paper between glances across the street, and found that I was still front-page stuff. But at least they weren't running my picture, I reflected, and I was safe as long as my face was buried in the paper.

At three in the afternoon I was ready to quit. In and out of Nick's had gone housewives, flashy jokers in sport coats with "tout" written all over them, kids from the college extension up the street, young girls, old men, all kinds of people. But no little man in a brown hat. I took my feet off the footrests and stretched. Suddenly I stiffened.

In front of Nick's a little man hesitated momentarily, looked up at the building, and darted in. A little man in a brown hat. I waited tensely. If he was the man I was looking for he wouldn't be inside long.

He was the man I was looking for, and he wasn't inside long. He came down fast, with the gigantic red-headed bodyguard beside him. The little guy was almost collapsing under the weight of the hand resting on his shoulder. His face was white, and he seemed worried.

Moose had a set smile on his red face. Unless you were watching, you would never have seen the tiny shove that sent the little man on his way, and almost knocked him over.

I was out of the shoeshine parlor and crossing the street as the little guy scurried into the crowd. He was in a hell of a hurry, and it was hard to keep up with him.

Finally Brown Hat dodged into a second-rate hotel. I stopped outside and watched through the plate-glass front.

He walked through the tiled lobby past the traveling salesmen and two or three of the girls and into a little bar off the lobby. I waited a few moments and stepped into the bar through the street entrance.

The little man in the brown hat was at the end of the bar, sipping a glass of beer. I sat two stools away from him and ordered a shot and a glass of beer, and opened my paper. I drank the shot and glanced at the barkeep, a bitter-looking individual with a gray face, angrily polishing glasses.

"It's a crime about this blonde was murdered in her bathtub," I said, loud enough for the little guy to hear me. I watched him jump and gulp his beer. The bartender went on polishing glasses.

"You know," I continued. "The papers don't say it, but that eighteen grand the guy was trying to steal— down at the track I heard she just won it from a bookie. I heard she won it on a fixed race—some other outfit was trying to run this bookie out of town, and he had her knocked off by this guy Blair as a warning to lay off."

The bartender went on with his glasses. I sneaked a glance at the mirror behind the bar. The little guy had a strange expression on his face, as if he'd just seen a ghost. His hand trembled and suddenly he knocked over his glass. The barkeep looked at him in disgust and mopped up the mess.

"Another beer for the gentleman," I said. I turned to the little guy. "You know, if they could tie up this blonde with the outfit that was trying to move in, they'd have a real case against this bookie. Of course the cops don't know she won the money from him, or the papers would have got hold of it."

A look of fear and suspicion darkened the little

guy's face. Then he relaxed and a crafty gleam wandered into his eyes.

"You can't never tell," he muttered. He finished his beer and walked briskly out into the lobby, like a man who has just thought of a sure way to kill off his mother-in-law.

I paid the bill and strolled into the lobby. The little guy was standing by the phone booth, rubbing his chin. He looked cautiously around and darted in. I walked back of the phone, sat down in a leather chair, hiked it next to the booth, and opened my faithful newspaper. I heard a nickel drop in the slot.

"Long distance—Reno, River 2364, collect. Mr. Smith calling." There was a long wait. "Mac? The boss there?" Another wait. "Boss, this is Shorty in San Francisco. Parenti just kicked me out of his place. Yeah, I know, but I just got an idea that can't wait. Look, boss, how about spilling all about Helena to the D.A. down here? Tell him you were trying to break Parenti, and Helena was working for you, and let him figure out for himself who killed her?"

Silence. Then, "Yeah, you can prove it. Prove the horse was a ringer—so it was a ringer, what they goin' to do about it? Makin' book's illegal too. When they send Parenti up, we wait a month or two and then move in."

More silence, and then in an ingratiating voice, "Yeah, boss, sure I thought it up myself. Who else? Okay, boss, I'll be goin' back tonight on the sleeper."

I got up and moved to the cigarette counter. I turned and watched the little guy as he left. There was a jaunty bounce to his step now. A real genius. . . .

I stretched out on Sherry's couch and sipped a long, cold drink. Sherry moved around in the kitchenette. There was the smell of sizzling steak in the air. The whiskey relaxed me, and I felt like the smartest piece of talent in forty-eight states. This, I reflected, was the way to operate. Just like judo, let the other guy do the work.

"Of course," I called to Sherry. "This won't get me off the hook, even if it works, unless they put enough pressure on Nick to make him tell the truth. He can still claim he sent me up there to do the job, and then we'll both burn. But I think when it comes to saving his own hide, he'll talk, and he'll talk straight. Unless, of course, he did the job himself."

Sherry didn't answer. I shrugged and took another drink. "You know, sometimes I think I'd have made a good politician—"

"Dinner's ready," Sherry interrupted. Her voice was flat. I unglued myself from the couch. I walked over and lifted her face. Her eyes were wet.

"What's the matter?" I asked quietly.

She looked away. "I don't know."

"What is it?"

She shook her head. "I really don't know, Mike. I just hope you're sure of what you're doing."

I sat down and dived into my steak.

"Of course I'm sure. I can't be any *worse* off, that's for sure. This way, even if they get me, they'll get Nick too."

"That's what I mean. Are you sure Nick had anything to do with it?"

I paused, my fork halfway to my mouth.

"Who the hell do you think killed her?"

She didn't answer. I put my fork down carefully and looked into her eyes. Softly I said:

"Listen, Sherry, you don't think *I* killed her, by any chance?"

"*Mike!*" Her eyes were startled. "Don't say that. Don't ever say anything like that again."

"Okay. Now eat your steak."

She shook her head miserably and pushed her chair away from the table. "I'm not hungry." Suddenly she blurted, "And I *don't* think Nick did it!" She sobbed once and ran into the bedroom.

I felt the bottom drop out of my stomach. Not again, I whispered, not again. Not when she knows he's a heel, and a murderer.... I felt the old anger surging up and I shoved at the table. It turned over with a crash. I grabbed my hat and coat and walked out into the night, slamming the door as hard as I could....

I tramped to the top of the hill and stood staring into the fog, the familiar ache still inside me. What did he have over her, I asked myself, as I used to in the old days. A guy who would let his friend hang to protect a murderer—or was *he* the murderer?

I lit a cigarette. It calmed my nerves and I tried to think in a straight line. Sherry didn't believe that Nick had had the blonde killed. Well, maybe he hadn't intended it that way; maybe he'd sent someone up to get the money and whoever it was had murdered her on his own. Moose, for instance, would be stupid enough to do it. And maybe Nick had preferred to believe his own man to me.

That didn't make sense either—Nick had known me too long. The only other explanation was that Nick himself had murdered her. My mind was working now, coolly and logically. Suddenly I knew that whatever else Nick was, he wasn't a killer.

I flicked my cigarette down the hill. Something was wrong in this case...something smelled bad. Who else would it have been?

Then I had it. The thing burst on me like a light. I cursed and headed back down the hill. I was late, plenty late, but there was still a chance.

CHAPTER FOUR

As the Bird Flies

Sherry's car was in front of her garage, waiting to be put away for the night. The key was in the ignition. Everything I needed—except a gun. My gun was in my apartment—it might as well have been on Mars. I slid behind the wheel and stepped on the starter. The window above me opened and I heard her voice. "Mike?"

"I'll be back tomorrow," I yelled. "Maybe." I backed out onto the street.

I had a long drive before me, three hundred miles, first through the traffic over the bridge, then across the humid Sacramento Valley, then through the Sierras. By the time I got to the mountains it was dawn and I was shaking my head and rubbing my neck to keep awake.

I scooted over Donner Pass and there it was—the sleeper from San Francisco, racing through the snow sheds. It was going to be close, and still sixty miles to Reno. I roared through Truckee, hoping that the sheriff was still in bed, and then I was on good road again, good all the way to Reno. I lit a cigarette and tramped on the accelerator.

The worst was over, and the San Francisco train was still in the mountains behind me. I was making seventy now, and the speed woke me up. In twenty minutes I should be in Nevada, with no speed limit and no highway patrolmen to worry about. . . .

I glanced into the rearview mirror and chilled. Behind me was a black dot, and blinking in the morning sunlight was a red light. I thought of being stopped—no proof of ownership of the car, Sherry's name on the registration, unshaven, bleary-eyed. Hell, it wouldn't be a ticket—they'd hold me.

And if they held me I was a cooked goose; there wasn't a cop in the state that wasn't looking for me. I pushed the gas pedal to the floorboard. The speedometer trembled and climbed to eighty. And that was tops.

Behind me the blinking light grew closer. I began to look for the agricultural inspection station at the state line, and a new worry nagged me. If it was open this early in the morning they'd stop me, and I'd be a goner. The sweat started out on my forehead.

I roared over the Truckee River at eighty, around a curve, and into a straightaway. I watched the mirror and counted off the seconds until the patrol car appeared around the bend. I counted up to twenty-three and then the red light was with me again.

I rounded another turn, slid off the shoulder in a

cloud of dust, fought the wheel, and was back on the road. My heart pounded madly. This time the count was eighteen and the car filled up a quarter of my mirror. I listened and heard the faraway wail of a siren. The Truckee River flashed under me again, and ahead was a group of buildings that I recognized—the inspection station.

Out of the buildings walked a man in the uniform of the state agricultural department, carrying a sign. Behind me the siren was blasting into my ears. The patrol car began to pull to the left to pass me. I jerked the wheel and blocked him and flashed over the state line as the startled fruit inspector set up his sign:

STOP FOR AGRICULTURAL
INSPECTION

Behind, I could see the California patrolman slow reluctantly, and my heart slowed with him. I was in Nevada, man's country, where if a guy was racing the night train from San Francisco it was strictly between him and the train.

It was seven in the morning when I got into Reno. Already the place was beginning to heat up for the day. I found the station and parked the car. I walked in and discovered that the San Francisco train wasn't due for twenty minutes, so I sat at the coffee counter. The waitress was fooling with the coffee gear.

Absently I noted that even in her plain white uniform she was constructed from the rear as no waitress at a railroad breakfast counter had a right to be. She turned, and I drew in my breath. Her hair was jet black, smooth and shiny, and her eyes were a dark, startling blue. Her nose was small and straight, her lips had the slightest hint of a pout. When she smiled, I saw that her teeth were even and white. I took hold of myself and ordered a cup of coffee, black.

She brought it and leaned on the counter. "You look tired," she said suddenly. "Are you?"

"Does it show?"

"Yes," she said simply. "You should get some sleep."

"Okay. Right here?"

She laughed. "We have hotels. Even in Nevada."

"Name a good one."

"Three Gables."

"You must own it."

"I live in it."

Well, I thought. *That certainly was quick.*

"Don't get any ideas," she said, and her eyes never wavered. "I just thought you looked tired, and you seemed like a stranger, and I thought you might not know of a place to stay."

"Are you always that accommodating to strangers?"

"No. Only when they don't *look* like wolves. Sometimes I'm wrong."

I drew my finger across the counter. "Chalk one up for— What is your name, anyway?"

"Alma."

"I'm pleased to meet you, Alma. I'm Mike. Mike—" I stopped just in time. They have papers, I reflected, in Reno too. "Just call me Mike."

"Okay, Mike," she said cheerfully, and began to wipe off the counter. I looked at my watch. I had two minutes. Reluctantly I stood up. "Well, Alma, next time I need a cup of coffee...."

She smiled. It was a nice, honest smile. "Or a hotel?"

"Or a hotel." I walked away, feeling a hundred percent better. Coffee, I mused, did that for a man. Or maybe it had been Alma.

The passengers from San Francisco were struggling down the platform, laden with bags and sleep. I waited in the shadows until the crowd had passed. My heart sank. The little man in the brown hat was among those missing. I started to turn away—and then I saw him.

He was fighting a suitcase as big as himself and I almost felt sorry for him. Almost.

He passed me and headed for the taxi stand. I went out a side entrance and climbed into Sherry's car. I watched him talking to the taxi starter. The starter signalled and a cab drove up. Brown Hat got in and the driver pulled away from the curb.

I trailed the cab through town and out onto the highway. We drove for about eight miles and then the taxi pulled off into a driveway. I cruised on by and saw the little guy getting out in front of an expensive looking ranch-type dwelling.

A mile down the road, I parked the car off the highway, and started back on foot. My heart was hammering in my chest. The closer I got to the house, the harder it hammered. I wished again that I had a gun, even a BB gun, even a bean blower. I'd fooled Nick with the hand-in-the-pocket-routine.

But I knew now that Nick thought I'd killed the blonde; naturally he wouldn't take a chance. If I was right, though, these people knew I hadn't killed her, and they might not go along on a bluff.

I cut through an orchard and stopped in the shadows. Carefully I surveyed the place. There was a garage attached to the house, a back door, a front entrance. There didn't seem to be anyone around. I decided on the back door.

I hurried across the lawn and tried the kitchen door. It was locked. I was about to try the garage door when I looked up. The kitchen window was open, with no screen. I lifted myself and looked inside. There was nobody there. I glanced over my shoulder and hoisted myself in.

In the front of the house I could hear talking. On the sides of my feet I walked to the swinging door and stopped. I began to move the door, slowly and carefully. The refrigerator started with a click and I jumped. I forced myslef to relax and pushed the door another inch. I stuck one eye to the crack and looked through. The next room was a dining room and held a long table.

At the head of the table, finishing what appeared to have been a whole platter of bacon and eggs, was the fattest man I had ever seen, wearing the reddest face. Behind him stood an old woman, apparently the artist who had cooked the bacon and eggs. The fat man was beaming and rubbing his belly.

"Myrt," he said. "You are a boon to my old age. You cater to my every whim."

Myrt giggled nervously.

"Now get the hell out of here and fry me some more. You think I can get along on five lousy eggs?"

Myrt ran for the door. It was now or never. I tensed, put my hand in my pocket, and stepped into the dining room.

"Put your hands on the table, Fat Stuff," I said.

Fat Stuff looked at me blandly. "Do you mind telling me who you are?"

"Yeah. Put your hands on the table."

He put a pair of puffy hands on the table. I heard a footstep in the front room and stepped out of line with the door. The little guy came in, minus his brown hat, and bald as a light bulb. He saw me and a flash of recognition raced over his face. His mouth dropped open.

"Yeah, it's me, Shorty. The guy in the bar. The guy that gave you the Big Idea. Now put up your hands and don't move." I turned to Myrt. "And that means you, Myrt." Myrt raised her hands as if she were reaching for a high line drive.

"Sit down," I told the little guy. "Keep your hands on the table."

I turned to Fat Boy. "Who else you got around here?"

"Nobody. Son, if this is a holdup, you won't get a thing. You better go try the bank."

"It's no holdup. You and Shorty here are going for a ride with me. Down to the city. You're going to drive, and Shorty is going to be your copilot, and when you get there, we're going to the police station. You're going to sing."

The fat man laughed.

"You have a quaint way of putting things. What are we going to sing about?" he asked.

"About a blonde named Helena. And incidentally,

there's a guy around here named Mac, I think, and he's going too."

The fat man's smile eased for a moment and then returned. He turned to the little guy.

"You know, Shorty, if I didn't know you any better, I'd think you met this guy in San Francisco. I'd think you'd been talking too much."

Shorty opened his mouth and the fat man said, "Shut up." He glanced at me. "What makes you think that we're going to do any singing? Assuming that we know what you're talking about."

I ignored him.

"Call Mac," I said. He sat and smiled. "Call Mac," I repeated, moving my hand.

He called Mac.

Mac ambled in, a seedy-faced kid of about twenty, with flat, slate-gray eyes. Gunman was written all over him. He was chewing a toothpick. When he saw me he stopped, raised his hands automatically, and spit out the toothpick. He never changed his expression. Mac, evidently, had seen a lot of gangster pictures or had been held up before.

"You sit down too," I told him.

He sat down too.

"You," I said to the fat man. "What's your name?"

The fat man studied me curiously, still smiling broadly. He ignored the question.

"You know, Mac," he said finally, "I don't believe this guy has a gun."

My heart dropped. I growled, "You don't? All right, make a move and find out."

"I don't think he has a gun," the fat man repeated slowly. "Find out, Mac."

I moved the hand in my pocket, my heart pounding. I wished I'd frisked Mac, but it was too late now. Mac seemed to be giving the matter a lot of thought.

"You heard me, Mac," said the fat man, still smiling and studying me.

Mac came to a decision. Slowly and coolly he moved

his hand inside his coat. I started toward him, but it was no use. His hand came out with a forty-five automatic. Suddenly he chuckled, mirthlessly.

"What da ya know about that?" he said. "Say, boss, that's all right. How'd ya know?"

The fat man began to giggle and then to laugh. His tremendous belly shook and he gasped for air. He stopped and then started again. Finally the laughs subsided, and he struggled to speak.

"I didn't, Mac. I didn't...."

I sat at the table while they went through my wallet and talked about me.

"So you're Mike Blair," said the fat man. "The guy that killed the blonde."

"You know damn well I didn't kill her."

The fat man chuckled. "That's what the papers claim, Mike. As Will Rogers used to say, 'I only know what I read in the papers.'" This he thought was hilarious, and he started again. All at once he sobered.

"What kind of a tie-up you got with Shorty here?" he asked suddenly, nodding toward the little guy.

"We're brothers," I said nastily. "He sold me the whole story for a free beer."

Shorty turned an unhealthy green.

"That's a lie, boss. I only seen this guy once, in a bar. He done all the talkin'."

"Say, he didn't put that idea into your head about sticking Parenti with that murder rap."

The little guy looked sheepish.

"I thought it was a little too bright for you." The fat man's brow wrinkled. He put his chin on his hand and closed his eyes. Suddenly he opened his eyes, dull and a shade of dirty green, and grinned at me.

"You know, that was a good idea. You still mad at Parenti, son?"

I thought it over. "Maybe."

"Maybe we'll be able to use the idea after all. How would you like that?"

It looked like a way to stall. On second thought I knew that whatever he'd dreamed up, I was the fall guy.

He continued. "You're a smart guy. I can see that. How would you like to make two grand and get a nice vacation in Mexico?"

I thought fast. There was a catch to this, but I might as well go along with it. I shrugged. He went on.

"How would you like to write the D.A. a letter, tell him Parenti hired you to kill the blonde and get the dough? We'll give you the stationery, a stamp, two grand, and a ticket to Mexico City. How would you like that?"

I tried to play it smart, but my Irish blood was too much for me.

"How," I asked pleasantly, "would you like to go to hell?"

The fat man chuckled delightfully. "Okay, Mac," he said. "Convince him."

Mac shoved his chair out from behind the table and walked around it. Slowly he lit a cigar. It looked too old for him. He puffed twice and then his hand moved quickly. A searing pain shot into my eyelid as he ground the cigar into my face. I started to get up and a crashing blow on my neck sent me to the floor. Two kicks in the solar plexus did the rest. The room grew dim around me. In the distance I could hear the fat man chuckling.

"Mike," he reminded me. "This lad's young. He can do that all day."

To prove he was right Mac kicked me again. I stayed where I was.

"Get up," said Mac politely. "Sit down again. He's our guest, ain't he, boss? He shouldn't be lyin' there on the floor." He kicked me again and I struggled to my feet. I lurched for the chair and felt it whisked out from under me. As I fell he kicked me again. A flash of pain shot up me.

"Okay, Mac," said the fat man. "Let him up."

I struggled to my chair again. This time it stayed put.

"See, Mike?" said the fat man. "Mac thinks you should write that letter too."

I shook my head. The fat man shrugged.

"All right, Mac. Take him up the Mount Rose Grade and dump him. They'll find him in the spring."

Mac hoisted me from my chair, a thin smile on his blank face. He turned me around roughly and shoved me toward the kitchen. I looked at Myrt, the cook. She was smiling and nodding virtuously. *Crazy as a loon,* I knew suddenly.

I changed my mind about the letter. It can happen in a spot like that, no matter what kind of a hero you think you are. I turned, hunched my shoulders.

"I'll write it."

The fat man smiled paternally.

"That's a good lad. Myrt, some writing paper out of the desk. And don't pick up the paper in your hand. Bring the whole box."

Myrt disappeared into the front room and came back with a box of stationery. The fat man took a pen out of his pocket and handed it to me politely.

"Now," he said. "Take a piece of paper, not the top one, and write down what I tell you. Shorty," he said, "phone the station and tell them to reserve a compartment for four on the afternoon train to San Francisco."

Four, I thought, my mind whirling. Who was the fourth? Not the cook. Somebody else? No, it was going to be me, Mike Blair, in person. Well, at least they weren't going to kill me here—they were going to take me back to San Francisco. To turn me and my "confession" over to the cops? No, that was too risky.

But a confession found, for instance, on a conscience-stricken suicide; that was something else. I had a feeling that I wasn't going to see San Francisco. Unless I got awful smart awful quick. An idea was rattling around in my feverish brain, a long shot, but maybe....

"You ready?" asked the fat man. He wasn't smiling now and his pig eyes were lost in thought.

"Say: 'To Whom It May Concern.' Got that? 'Nick Parenti paid me twenty thousand dollars to kill Helena Parks in the Royal Hotel. He did this because she won eighteen thousand dollars—' You getting this?"

I nodded slowly. I was getting it, but it wasn't what

I was writing. I fought to keep my hand from trembling. The fat man continued.

"'Because she won eighteen thousand dollars on a fixed race. I want to get this off my chest before I kill myself.'"

I stared at him, trying to act as if I'd just been tricked by my best friend. I jumped up, my hands shaking, and tore the paper across the middle. I let the pieces drop to the table.

"Wait a minute," I stuttered. "What do you mean, before I kill myself? You said—"

His face was deadly serious now. Softly he said, "Blair, if you don't get another piece of paper and write down what I say, Mac will have you screaming for suicide in a half hour."

I looked at Mac. He was licking his lips eagerly. I sat down and took another piece of paper out of the box.

"Write what I said, sign your name, and hand it over."

I did. He picked up the paper in a handkerchief and read it. He nodded and looked up with a smile.

"You write a beautiful hand, Mike. A little shaky, maybe. A college man?" He folded the paper, still using the handkerchief, and slipped it into his pocket.

Quietly, slowly, I let my hand slide over the top half of the first note, the torn one, and slid if off the table. I crumpled it in my lap and pushed the ball of paper into my pocket....

CHAPTER FIVE

Hot-Squat Grand Slam

Outside the station it looked as if everyone in Reno was going to San Francisco on the afternoon train. The fat man walked on my left and Brown Hat on my right and Mac brought up the rear, hands in his pockets. The fat man made me carry his suitcase. "To make it look good," he said. It was a heavy suitcase, and I longed to hurl it into his bloated belly.

We went through the entrance and I shot a glance at the coffee counter. A slim, graceful form moved swiftly up and down the counter—Alma. My heart leaped. I put down the suitcase.

"Let me buy a pack of cigarettes," I asked the fat man.

He hesitated and then smiled. "Sure. Mac'll go with you, in case they think you're too young to buy them."

As I walked up to the counter, Mac close alongside and watching every move, Alma glanced up and saw me. She smiled and I shook my head slightly. She looked puzzled and moved toward our end of the coffee stand.

I picked up a pack of cigarettes. I crushed the ball of paper in my pocket and palmed it in my hand. I gave her a quarter and let the ball of paper fall on the counter. My heart sank as it rolled off behind the stand. I looked into her troubled face, my eyes begging her to understand.

Mac shoved me roughly and jerked his head toward the fat man. I gave her one last look. Maybe, I thought, the last beautiful girl I'd ever see....

The fat man crowded himself into the compartment and established himself on the seat facing forward. He lit a tremendous cigar and leaned back with a sigh. Mac and Shorty and myself jammed ourselves into the opposite seat. I felt like a lamb in the stockyard. It was a long ride, and nobody said much.

Brown Hat went to sleep as we started up the Nevada side of the Sierras, the fat man buried himself in a racing form, and Mac sat back and stared at me, chewing a toothpick. I lit a cigarette and began to think. I had about the chance of an ice cube in a furnace, I told myself. I began to wonder just what was holding them up.

I didn't wonder long. It was dark now, and the train was hurtling along the Truckee River. Suddenly it slowed and began the long climb up the Donner Grade. My stomach tightened. I could have cut the tension in the compartment with a knife. Brown Hat woke up with a start. The fat man put down his racing form and looked at me speculatively. The palms of my hands began to sweat.

"Stand up, Mike," he said softly. I got up slowly, my knees shaky under me. The fat man reached over and slipped a piece of paper into my coat pocket. "Cheer up, Mike. Think how happy this will make the cops—the whole case cut-and-dried. They'll find you in the Donner Grade tomorrow. Tomorrow night every cop in Frisco will sleep like a baby."

Somehow it didn't make me feel any better. The fat man nodded to Mac. Mac got up slowly, opened the door, and looked out. Then he stepped back and motioned me out with a jerk of his head.

Brown Hat stared, his expression a mixture of horror and fascination. I started to speak and couldn't. Mac shoved me and I found myself in the passageway.

"Move," he snarled. I moved.

He crowded me to the vestibule between the cars. A young fellow and a girl were standing there smoking. *Stay here*, I told them silently. *Stay here until we get to Sacramento*. The young fellow smiled at the girl and dropped his cigarette. He ground it out under his foot, opened the door, and they went back inside the car. I groaned inwardly.

Mac took another look through the vestibule windows, pulled his gun out of his pocket, and opened the side door. The night air was cold and the smoke from the engine was bitter in my nostrils. We were swaying over the top of the pass now, and I heard the lonely whistle of the engine as we passed the summit. The clacking of the rails increased in tempo. Mac looked out of the corner of his eye at the drop below.

"This is the end of the line, Blair. They're gonna think you jumped out of an airplane when they find you down there. Have a nice time goin' down—it's gonna be hell when you hit." Swiftly he stepped behind me. I stiffened.

At least, I thought, when they find me I might as

well have a bullet hole in me—nobody throws me off a train like a candy wrapper, without killing me first. I pivoted and swung and missed. Like a flash Mac twirled his gun in his hand. I saw it gleam dully in the vestibule light and then there was a crashing blow on the side of my head. I felt myself falling and grabbed at the only thing in sight—Mac.

Again the gun came down. This time it missed my head. Pain raced up my shoulder. But it cleared my brain. I swung him around and clutched at the gun. The train lurched; for a split second we poised on the brink of eternity; a desperate hand clawed at the collar of my overcoat.

I caught a glimpse of a fear-crazed face, jerked at the gun, heard a scream falling away in the darkness, and staggered backwards into the vestibule.

I sat on the floor and grabbed for my cigarettes. My fingers were shaking like leaves in a hurricane. It took me half a book of matches to light up. I was dizzy, sick, my head ached, I would have given my right arm for a drink, but I was alive. And finally, for the first time since I'd followed the blonde into the cocktail lounge, I had a gun. It gave me ideas. I flipped the cigarette out into the night, closed the door with a clang, and strolled back to the compartment.

I braced myself in the passageway and put the gun in my pocket. Then I opened the door and stepped in. Brown Hat looked up nervously and his face froze in a look of terror. The fat man was reading the racing form. He didn't bother to glance up.

"Nice work," he said. "He give you any trouble?"

"Not much," I answered pleasantly. "Thanks for asking."

Slowly, incredulously, the fat man raised his head. His lips moved. "Why that brainless son of a—"

I raised my hand.

"Speak kindly of the dead, Slim. Who knows? You too may fall off a train someday. Any day."

The fat man sat back and chuckled.

"You're a pretty bright kid, Blair. Pretty bright. But now what are you going to do? Try to keep us in here? Both of us?"

I moved my hand in my pocket. "Yeah. It won't be hard."

"You don't think you're going to get away with that little-gun-that-wasn't-there routine again, do you, son?"

I shrugged. "You can't blame me for trying."

"Shorty," said the fat man suddenly. "Get up and see if he's got Mac's gun."

Shorty shook his head, watching my hand.

I smiled at the fat man. "You do it, Chubby," I invited. "Come on. You're a gambling man, a bookie. If I don't have a gun I'll give you back the suicide note. Okay?"

The fat man didn't move. I took the note out of my pocket. "Eat it!" I said suddenly. The fat man turned white. I took a step toward him. "Eat it," I said again. With my left hand I jammed it into his face. He pursed his lips. I let him have it with the back of my hand. His mouth fell open and I crammed the paper in. Carefully I wiped my hand on his lapel.

"Chew it well, now. We don't want to get indigestion, do we?"

He chewed it for a long, long time, and then, so help me, he swallowed it.

"Now the big smile," I said. "Remember the smile?" He actually tried to smile. I sat down and lit a cigarette. I was feeling better every minute.

"Blair," said the fat man suddenly. "What are you trying to do? You won't get away with this. You're wanted in San Francisco—and now you've killed Mac. They'll hang you from the first lamppost they find."

"For killing Mac I should get a medal. I guess he just stepped out there with me for a quiet smoke?"

"That's our story."

"You'll be damned lucky if you tell any story. You know why?"

The fat man didn't answer.

"Because Nick Parenti is meeting this train in

Sacramento. Nick and his gorilla. They've driven all the way from San Francisco just to welcome you." I hoped I was right.

The fat man looked startled.

"Go ahead with your racing form," I said. "Not that you'll need it where you're going."

"What do you mean?"

"They got a gas chamber for murderers in this state."

The fat man shifted uneasily. "The blonde? I was playing poker at the Silver Lady all day the sixteenth. A hundred people can testify to that."

"What about him?" I jerked my thumb toward Shorty. "Was he there?"

The fat man's eyes gleamed. He said slowly, "I don't know where he was." The little guy moved his mouth. Nothing came out.

Once in Sacramento, I didn't have to wait long to find out that Alma had found the note and Nick's phone number. The train had no sooner stopped than I heard compartment doors opening down the car, and apologies, and more compartment doors, closer, and more apologies. Then our door opened and there were no more apologies.

Nick Parenti stepped in, his hand under his coat. The big redhead followed him, wearing his hand the same way. Nick looked at the fat man.

"Hiram Schultz," he said quietly. "As I live and breathe. Don't tell me it was you? I might have known."

The fat man grinned weakly and stuck out his hand. Nick looked at it, his own hand came out of his coat and a gun swung in a short arc. There was the crack of metal against bone and the fat man groaned and grabbed his wrist. Nick turned to me.

"Sorry, Mike," he said. He stuck out his hand. I took it.

"Forget it," I said. "I'm sorry too. I should have known it wasn't you. I guess you want to know the story."

Nick nodded. There was a knock and a low, lilting voice came through the panel. "Can I come in now?" The door opened and Sherry crowded in, tired and drawn, but as beautiful as ever. I grinned at her and she smiled back faintly.

"Well," I started, "I got to thinking about who killed the blonde. Sherry didn't think it was you, and it makes me wonder. In the first place, you acted as if you thought I killed her, falling for that bluff about the gun in my pocket. Unless you thought I'd already killed, you wouldn't have worried about my shooting you.

"But who the hell had killed her, then? I was pretty sure it wasn't *me*. Then I remembered something. I'd followed the blonde all day after she won the dough. She'd spent plenty; beauty treatment, furrier, jewelers. Presumably that dough was supposed to go back to what's his name here—Schultz. Evidently the blonde didn't see it that way.

"Apparently Schultz didn't trust her. Shorty here must have been tailing her too. Shorty sees her spending all this dough and calls Schultz. Schultz says okay, she double-crossed me, kill her and get the dough back. And use a stiletto—that was an afterthought—to maybe throw the scent your way in case the cops found out she'd won the money from you.

"So Shorty does it. He's scared, but he gets in the hotel suite and hides. Then he knifes her in the tub. Finally he starts looking for the dough—in the bedroom, where it wasn't. But then he hears me at the door. That *really* scares him. He goes down the fire escape.

"Well, I knew from a phone call he made that he was going to Reno, so I beat him up there."

Nick looked puzzled. "How'd you get word to me? Some dame called up from Reno, said she had a message that she didn't know anything about. Claimed the message said to call me and tell me to meet the train in Sacramento, Mike was in trouble. It sounded phony as hell, but I figured I'd better come."

I looked at the fat man. He was staring at me.

"That message was just part of an old, torn-up

suicide note I wrote once. Right, Schultz?" He shook his head dumbly. "And I guess I must have passed it to the waitress when I got the cigarettes at the station. Check?" Schultz looked as if he were going to break down and cry.

I turned to Sherry.

"I'll take you to Reno to get your car. I guess you'll have to drive back alone. These two bums aren't going to talk without a lot of working over by Red here, and I don't want to get to town before they clear me." A happy smile broke over Red's face, and he looked pleasantly at the fat man.

"I'll send you a check," said Nick. "Thanks, and good luck, Mike. These monkeys will talk if it takes us a week. Get up, gentlemen, the rest of the trip is by car."

I turned to Sherry. "Coming, honey?"

Sherry's eyes were downcast. Suddenly she raised her face. There were tears in her eyes. She laid her hand gently on my arm. I could see it coming again, and I waited for the anger to well up in me.

"I'm sorry, Mike. I'm going back with Nick."

She said it tenderly, as if she expected me to break down and cry. Strangely, I found that I didn't give a damn. For the first time in a week I felt free.

"Okay, honey," I said cheerfully. "I'll drive your car down when I come back." She looked surprised, and a little disappointed. I stepped into the passageway.

"Mike," she called after me. "Where can I write you?"

I thought of a pair of blue eyes and dark, shining hair.

"I don't know," I yelled back. "You might try the Three Gables Hotel."

Keep Your
Money Side Up

◆

When the rod-happy card-
sharps tried to heist a
Barbary Coast flame's
cold-deck winnings, sha-
mus Mike Blair rolled up
his sleeves—and started
playing for coffins.

CHAPTER ONE

Flame's Buddies

I was lying on a strange iron
bed in a strange bare room and my head throbbed.
Something told me I had been rolled, but outside of that
I was feeling no pain.

It had been quite a night.

A tune was racing through my head, and a flashing
smile, and flaming red hair and taunting lips....

A foghorn moaned, so I knew I was still in San
Francisco.

This, for some obscure alcoholic reason, made me
very happy. I tried to whistle. Nothing came out. I
touched my mouth. My lower lip felt like an inner tube.

Apparently somebody had made some changes in my lovely mug.

I sat up. The walls spun around me, and the mattress rocked. I swung my feet over the side of the bed. I needed a drink.

On a battered dresser stood a bottle—not the best brand of wood alcohol, but maybe the second best. I lifted it and peered at it. It was purely a dead soldier. There was a cigarette butt in the bottom.

I groaned.

"You up, Casanova?" The voice was cheerful, and it was female, and it came from the next room. I followed the sound and staggered into a tiny kitchen. There were two eggs frying on an electric plate and a jug of wicked-looking coffee. Tending the whole mess was the most beautiful cook I had ever seen.

She had red hair and taunting lips. She was wearing a flimsy housedress and she was flung together like the girl on a hardware calendar. She seemed vaguely familiar. I felt as if I ought to know her name.

"*Hello,*" I said as if I'd known her all my life.

"Hello, Casanova," she said. "Remember me?"

"How could I forget?" I lied gallantly.

"What's my name?"

"Name?" I stumbled. "What's in a name, anyway? You are as gorgeous as a spring day. I will call you Gorgeous."

"You, Casanova, are drunk. You will call me Flame, which is my name."

"Flame? Very, very pretty. A little corny but very, very pretty. It matches your hair."

"That's why I picked it."

"The hair?"

"The name. Have a cup of coffee."

I had a cup of coffee. It was just a little thicker than pea soup, but it cleared my misty brain.

"And now, Flame, do you mind telling me how I got here?"

"Not at all, Casanova. I brought you up because I

hate to see a good man sleeping in the gutter, which is where you planned to spend the night."

"The name isn't Casanova. It's Mike. Blair."

"Last night it was Casanova. Casanova Blair, king of the underworld, czar of the Barbary Coast, emperor of the waterfront."

I shook my throbbing head. "I must have been drunk."

"Yes," she said. "You were drunk. You were cooking with gas. You were so fractured that they almost threw you out of the Club Tornado, and when you're *that* fractured, brother, you're pulverized."

"Club Tornado...Club Tornado." The name struck a chord. "A dive down in North Beach, with palm leaves all over and goldfish swimming in a tank behind the bar?"

"That's it."

"And you're the singer. Right?"

"That's right."

"You were singing requests for me. Right?"

She nodded. "Until the request got too rugged. Some of the things you asked me to sing!"

A little man began hitting me on the head with a large sledgehammer. I had another cup of coffee.

"I seem," I remarked, "to remember something else."

"That's right, Mike."

I felt my lower lip. "Something about a fight."

"You were in a fight, all right. That's why I brought you here."

"Why did I start a fight? And how does the other guy look?"

"Other *guys,* Mike. And you didn't start it. They did."

"There was more than one?"

"Yes, there were three. And they had guns."

My heart dropped into my fluttering stomach. "Guns? I *must* have been drunk."

"You were drunk, all right, but it didn't slow you up any. You were out of this world."

I looked at her closely.

"Are you sure you aren't thinking of somebody else? Ordinarily I can't punch my way out of a paper bag."

"She laughed. "Well, you could last night. Of course, you talked as if you owned the town. That might have had something to do with it."

"I did?"

"You said you were the biggest wheel in San Francisco. Casanova Blair, pride of the crime belt. All you had to do, you said, was whistle, and you could fill the place as full of hoods as a prison yard at lunch hour. That slowed them up, and in the meantime you started pitching bottles."

"And they had *guns?*" I couldn't get over it.

"They had guns. They were shooting at you, too. That only seemed to make you madder."

"What was it? A stick-up?" If I'd broken up a heist at the Club Tornado, it ought to take care of the liquor situation for a while.

"No, Mike, they were after me."

"After *you?*" This was even better. "What for?"

She hesitated. "Maybe they thought I had some money. But you stepped in." She gazed at me seriously. "Drunk or sober, you were fine, Mike."

"Oh, well—" I began modestly, shrugging.

She stepped toward me. "Shut up," she said. "You're scared stiff at what you did, and I know it, and I love you for it." She put her hands lightly behind my neck, drew down my head, and kissed me, hard. Her lips were warm and soft, and there was a faint smell of good, clean soap in her hair. I felt my blood pressure rising.

She stepped away. "You wouldn't let me thank you last night."

"I *wouldn't?* Say, what was I drinking, anyway? This doesn't sound like me at all."

She shrugged. "I guess not. Well, how about some eggs?"

My stomach turned over. "Not right now, thanks," I muttered weakly. "You wouldn't have a drink around somewhere, would you?"

She took a bottle out of the kitchen cabinet and set it on the table. She sat down to her eggs. And I drank my breakfast. I refreshed my bloodshot eyes with another look. She was out of this world. I wondered why she was singing in a hole like the Club Tornado and living in a dive like this.

"You're new at the Club Tornado, aren't you?"

She nodded. "I'm new in San Francisco."

"What are you doing singing in a dump like that? A girl with your looks ought to be hitting the big time."

She shook her head sadly.

"No voice," she said. "As you'd know if you'd been sober. A song in my heart, but just no voice. Booking agents go crazy at first, but there always comes a time when I have to sing, and that finishes me. Of course, in a place like the Club Tornado, nobody hears me anyway, so it's all right."

The fluttering in my stomach was beginning to settle down. "You can sing to me anytime, honey. Anytime at all."

She smiled, and the dingy kitchen was brighter. I tried to gather up the ends of my own private lost weekend. I had been on some sort of job, a job for a client. Client, client. It wasn't as if I had a lot of them.

Suddenly it came to me—Mrs. Chalmers. Mrs. Chalmers was purely routine. She suspected Mr. Chalmers and his private secretary. So I had tailed Mr. Chalmers to the Club Tornado and found that the Missus was right about Mr. Chalmers but wrong about the secretary.

Actually, it was a waitress in the company cafeteria. Now all I had to do was break the good news to Mrs. Chalmers, tell her to be sure to mention me to her friends, and pick up fifty bucks. I shoved my chair away from the table.

"Well, honey, thanks for the lodging and the liquids. Are you singing tonight?"

She looked up quickly. "You aren't leaving?"

"It's breaking my heart, but I'm a working man. I thought I might drop down to the Club Tornado tonight, to see if your voice is as bad as you say."

"I don't think the Club Tornado will open tonight. You should have seen it when we left." A shadow crossed her eyes. "Don't leave, Mike."

It sounded attractive as hell, but fifty bucks is fifty bucks. I got up and walked behind her. I ran my hand through her hair. "I'll be back this evening. If you don't have to sing, we'll go out and spend some of the cabbage I'm picking up today. Stick with me, honey. You'll be wearing diamonds."

She turned and grabbed my wrists. Her hands were shaking. "Please, Mike. Don't go."

I wavered. "What is it? Is there something bothering you?"

She walked to the window. "No. Skip it. Go ahead. I'll be here when you come back."

Mrs. Chalmers took the news well; in fact she seemed overjoyed. I could almost see the alimony shining in her eyes. She wrote me a check for fifty clams and I went to my office to pick up my mail. There was nothing but bills, so I banged out a couple of reports.

For some reason, I couldn't concentrate. The redhead was on my mind. She was beautiful, and she was very much available, but that wasn't all. There was something about her that bothered me.

She was frightened. She was so frightened that she'd *begged* me to stay with her. What was she worried about? Then I remembered what she'd said about the fight. The men had carried guns, and they had been after her. She'd said that she didn't know why, unless they'd thought she had money; but that didn't ring true.

Why would they go into a bar full of men and try to hold up the singer? They wanted her for something else, and suddenly I felt that *she* knew why. I grabbed my hat and quickly hopped into a taxi.

I lunged up the dark, creaking stairs to her apartment, three steps at a time. I knocked. There was no answer. I tried the lock and walked in.

The place was a shambles. It looked as if Gargantua had been playing leapfrog with the furniture. It was scattered all over the living room. The drawers in the kitchen were pulled out and tossed on the floor. The mattress in the bedroom was slit, the pillows were torn, and there were feathers on the floor ankle-deep. Flame's clothes were tossed everywhere.

No one was home. Well, maybe she'd been looking for something in one of her drawers. Maybe she'd stepped out for a moment to buy a paper. Maybe she'd gone to work.

And maybe she'd been snatched.

For a moment I wondered if I wanted to go on with this. I wasn't a cop anymore, and Flame wasn't my client, and there was nothing I could do anyway, except waste time. I touched my lower lip and asked myself if I wanted more of the same. For all I knew, Flame was a cheap crook, a stool pigeon maybe, who'd been ferreted out by a hoodlum who owed her something.

Then I remembered the look in her eyes when she'd asked me to stay....

I decided to find her. The trouble was, there was no place to look.

Idly, I kicked at the clothes on the floor. I looked around in the kitchen and the bathroom. Not a clue, naturally. I decided to go to the Club Tornado. Maybe she *had* gone to work, after all.

"Hold it, buddy."

I jumped as if I'd been jabbed with an electric needle. I swung toward the door.

A natty young fellow, with clear gray eyes and thin lips, stood in the doorway. In his hand he cradled a stubby .32 automatic.

"Hold it," he said again. "Where is she?"

"Who?"

He stepped toward me. "Let's not play games. Where is she?"

I decided not to play games.

"Flame? I don't know. I just got here. Maybe she's at work."

"She's not at work, and you know it. Where's the money?"

"Now *there*, Mac, you got me. I don't know anything about any money."

"Where's Nino?"

"I don't know any Nino, either. I just met Flame last night. I don't know where she is, if she isn't at work. I don't know who messed up her apartment. If you're a friend of hers, you better get to looking for her, and cut out the detective story stuff."

He didn't seem to be listening. He gazed at my face thoughtfully. "What's your racket? I don't remember seeing you at Nino's."

"That's not unlikely—I never heard of him."

"What're you doing in Flame's apartment?" His voice was tight. It looked as if I was rapidly becoming one corner of an eternal triangle. I thought pretty fast.

"I'm a theatrical agent, caught her act last night and thought I might get her a booking at a better place."

"Where's she working?"

"At the Club Tornado."

He motioned me with the gun. "Come on. We're going. And she had better be there."

He slipped the gun into his coat pocket and left his hand in with it. He stood aside as I went out the door, and with his free hand gave me a very quick and expert frisking. He whistled for a taxi and we sat in the rear seat, very chummy, me with the .32 in my ribs.

I began to get irritated.

"Listen, buddy," I said. "I can get you for assault with a dangerous weapon. I—"

"Shut up," he said.

CHAPTER TWO

Meet Mr. Slay-Boy

We drew up in front of the Club Tornado, and my friend paid the driver. The place was just opening up. We walked in. The Club Tornado looked like its name.

The goldfish tanks behind the bar were shattered. The goldfish, apparently, had lost their happy home in the brawl last night. There was a tiny, ominous hole in the wall behind the piano, and the rest room attendant was sweeping up broken glass. The bartender, a long, loose-jointed character with buck teeth, was shining glasses. He was very disconsolate. He looked up and saw me and turned white.

"*Say*, you're the guy. Listen, Blair, the next time you wanta play hero, do it somewhere else."

"That's a fine way to talk to a guy that broke up a robbery in your cheap joint. I thought you jokers would roll out the velvet carpet for me."

"Yeah? Look at the place. We hire a bouncer for the strong-arm stuff. And we carry insurance for robbery. So next time you get the urge to be a Boy Scout, try the bar across the street."

My buddy with the gun raised his eyebrows. He slid onto a barstool and nodded to me, his hand still in his pocket.

"Go on," he said to the barkeep. "You interest me. What did what's-his-name—" he jerked his head at me. "What did Blair do last night?"

The bartender shrugged. "Some strong-arm boys busted in and started for the singer. A holdup, that's all. Everybody is taking it real easy except Casanova here. He's got to shoot off his mouth and start heaving bottles." The bartender swung his arm around. "Look at the place. And it almost got into the papers."

My buddy looked at me thoughtfully. He turned back to the bartender.

"You say they started for the singer first?"

"That's right."

"Where is she tonight?"

The barkeep shrugged. "Hasn't showed up. Maybe she figured we wouldn't open up after yesterday. Well, she can't sing anyway."

"Would it be all right," I asked my friend, "if I had a drink? Or don't you approve of drinking?"

He nodded and ordered himself a martini. I ordered a shot of bourbon and a glass of beer.

"Cheers," I said. "Would you please take your hand off that gun so I can enjoy my drink?"

He smiled tightly. "I guess you're not tied up with Nino, if you broke up that job last night. Why'd you stick your neck out for Flame?"

"Like I said, I'm a theatrical agent. I hate to see talent shoved around."

He shook his head. "You're not a theatrical agent. You're a cop."

Certain parties in the police department would have loved to have heard that one.

"*That's* a lie," I said.

"You're right," he said pensively. "You're not a cop. You're a private eye."

Only the boys who live near the underworld can spot a cop or a private eye. Once they do, there's no use trying to fool them.

"Yeah. I'm a private investigator. Why? You have anything you want investigated?"

He thought for a while.

"As a matter of fact, yes. I want you to find Flame."

"Why?"

"I have reasons. First, why were you in her apartment if you're not a theatrical agent?"

"I like her looks. I wanted to take her out tonight. But when I got there she was gone, so I decided to look around. I'm just one of those very curious guys."

His voice was low.

"You wanted to take her out? Well, just get that idea out of your head right now. It'll be healthier for you."

"Oh?" I sipped my beer. "You know, Buster, you're beginning to get on my nerves, waving a gun at me and talking like that. I don't appreciate it, and I don't scare, so why not quit?"

"Listen, Casanova, or whatever your name is—"

"Mike. Mike Blair. And you?"

"Kid Farrow. Blair, lay off Flame Condon. Unless

you want to end up under a stone." He sounded as if he meant it.

I shrugged. "That's up to her. You say you want to find her. Why?"

"You want to take on the job?"

"I don't work for free."

"If you find her, I'll pay you."

"Oh no. I don't operate that way. Twenty-five bucks a day, and expenses. And fifty dollars in advance."

He reached into his pocket and hauled out a roll. He peeled off fifty dollars and slapped them on the bar. His fingers were slim and sure, and he handled money like a gambler. I picked up the money and stuffed it into my wallet.

"Okay," I said. "Now you can brief me on everything you know. I assume that the same guys that tried to snatch her last night got her today?"

He nodded. "If she was snatched, they snatched her."

"Why?"

He looked at the bartender, shining glasses a short way up the bar. "Say," he called. "Are you missing any of this? You want us to move closer, so you won't strain an eardrum?"

The bartender looked up, drooling injured innocence. "Whatta ya mean? I'm not listenin' to ya."

"Come on," said Farrow. I followed him to a booth. He glared at the bartender and leaned over the table.

"I'm a gambler," he said. "I make my living knocking over the big boys. There's this place in Reno—Nino Costa's. Big-time operation, five roulette tables, eight crap tables, about a dozen blackjack games. Well, I took a blackjack game for twelve grand in one afternoon.

"I guess Nino let it get that high because he figured he'd roll me before I got out of town. Only, I shook the hood he put on me and left town that night, for New York."

"Yeah," I said. "Very clever. What's that got to do with Flame?"

"Flame was singing at Nino's. We were—"

I thought of the beautiful redhead falling for a jerk like this. "Go ahead," I said impatiently. "I guess you gave her the dough so if they rolled you, they wouldn't find it."

He nodded quickly. "That's right."

"That was thoughtful. Then what did you do?"

"As I say, I lit out for New York. I told Flame to hang on in Reno for two weeks, and then quit and come to San Francisco. She sent me her address when I was in New York."

"So Nino's boys found out where she was, and decided to pick up the dough before you did. Right?"

"I guess so."

It began to look as if the boys who had Flame were playing for keeps. I didn't like it.

"Suppose I give you back your fifty bucks and we call in the FBI? If she's kidnapped, they'll find her. By the time I track her down, she's liable to be dead."

"I don't want the FBI in on it."

"Why not? All you did was win some money. You have nothing to hide. Or have you?"

He spoke slowly, his lips tense.

"I don't want the FBI."

"Even if it means this guy Costa might knock her off?" I thought it over. "All right. I'll work on it for twenty-four hours. If I don't have any luck, I'm calling in the Feds. Take it or leave it."

"If you call the cops, I'll get you if it's the last thing I do."

I began to dislike Kid Farrow.

"What's the matter? You afraid you won't get your money back if we call the cops? What do you want? The girl or the money?"

He looked at me sullenly.

"That's what I thought," I said. "All right. As I say, I'll work on it until tomorrow. If it looks as if I'm spinning my wheels, I'm bringing in the cops." I finished my beer and started for the door.

I stepped out into the foggy night. I heard Farrow call my name and ignored him. I started down the street, looking for a taxi. I heard the door of the Club Tornado open and close.

"Blair? Hey, Blair!"

A man in a gray overcoat, collar turned up, stepped out of an alley ahead of me and sidled past. A short, fat man, with his hat pulled down. I heard Farrow's quick footsteps, following me.

Then there was a muffled shot in the gray void behind. I spun and dodged into a doorway. I heard the slap of running feet on the wet pavement and the clash of gears. A car pulled away from the curb, lights dim.

Cautiously I poked my head around the corner. I heard a groan. I broke into a run for the Club Tornado, my heart pounding. I stumbled over something soft and heavy and looked down. It was a man. I stooped and turned him over.

In the yellow glare of the street lamp I saw his face—Kid Farrow. A dark stain spread over the sidewalk, running off into the gutter. And in the gutter was a police .38. Whoever had shot him wasn't going to get caught with the gun....I felt for a pulse. There was none.

Well, I thought, it couldn't have happened to a nicer guy. And now there'd be no objection to the FBI. I stepped into the Club Tornado, determined to wash my hands of the whole thing.

The bartender was just hanging up the phone. When he saw me, he almost dropped his uppers.

Instead, he very calmly just raised his hands.

"What the hell?" I said. "Call the cops. There's a guy been murdered outside."

Slowly the barkeep lowered his hands, watching me keenly.

"Call the cops," I said again. "What's wrong with you?"

"I called 'em. I called 'em when I heard your shot."

"*My* shot? I didn't shoot him and you know it."

"No," said the bartender quickly. "I never said you did. I never said you did, Mr. Blair. You gonna stick around and wait for 'em?"

"Of course I'm going to stick around. Why not?"

The bartender looked away. "Sure. Why not?"

"Wait a minute," I said. "What are you going to tell them? I just have a feeling—"

The barkeep looked at me eagerly. "You got nothing to worry about. I'll tell 'em it was self-defense. I saw him run out there and call after you. And he had a gun on you when you came in—I saw that."

The guy was certainly getting ready to hang me!

"Listen," I said. "I didn't—" In the distance I heard the lonely howl of a siren. "I didn't—"

What was the use? He wouldn't believe me, and the cops wouldn't believe me.

Even my very own mother wouldn't believe me.

I stepped back into the night....

CHAPTER THREE

Laddy on the Lam

The trouble with a guy on the lam is that he always heads for the cheapest flophouse in town. And strange as it seems, that's where the cops go to look for him.

But not old Mike. I was too smart for that. I was going to take my fifty bucks and register at the best hotel on Nob Hill. Then I was going to wait until things cooled down, and light out for Reno to solve the Flame Condon kidnapping, and incidently clear my fair name of the charge of murder.

I thought of all this as I stumbled through the alleys in the fog. I thought it all out as I swung onto the Powell and Mason cable car. I thought of it as I entered the ornate lobby of the Nob Hill Hotel and slogged through a carpet so thick you could drown in it.

I told the room clerk that I'd like a quiet room. I was still thinking of how smart I was when I signed the register. And I was feeling absolutely brilliant by the time I dropped off to sleep.

I slept like a drugged alligator for about three hours. Then something deep in my subconscious awakened me. I had forgotten something. Whatever I had forgotten loomed bigger and bigger in my mind.

I lit a cigarette. I tried to remember what I'd done. I knew my fingerprints were on the glass at the Club Tornado, so all the cops had to do was check with the FBI and the Navy file would tell them who they were looking for. All right. The bartender had heard Farrow call me by name, anyway. Nobody had paid any attention to me when I registered in the hotel.

When I had registered at the hotel—

That was it! I tried to think of the name I had registered under. Joe Smith? Robert Brown? Casanova? John Doe?

No. I'd registered under my *own name!* Just plain Michael Blair.

What a hot criminal *I* was.

A guy like me couldn't shake a blind detective with a broken leg. A guy like me should see a psychiatrist.

I jumped out of bed and threw on my pants and shirt. I draped a tie around my neck and tossed on my coat. I started for the door.

I heard whispering outside. Then, "Okay, Blair, open up."

I whirled and looked for the fire escape. There were twelve stories of good gray fog outside my window, and the fire escape was three rooms down.

I walked across the room and opened the door. The room filled with San Francisco's finest... in and out of uniform. A big, dark-eyed detective named Morello, who had gone to school with me on the wrong side of Market Street, eyed me curiously.

"I thought I recognized the name. Well, Blair, it seems as if you're in the soup. Why did you do it?"

"I didn't."

"Naturally," said Morello. "Naturally. Well, come on."

"Listen," I said. "Listen Morello. That barkeep had the wrong idea. I know who killed that guy. He was a short, fat character, and he stepped out of an alley in front of me. He drove off in a car."

Morello scratched his nose. "Did you see the guy's face?"

"Not very well. It was foggy."

"What kind of a car?"

"Like I say, it was foggy."

"Come on...."

I sat in Morello's office. He lounged behind a battered desk, smoking a cigar. He offered me a cigarette. I took it.

"Well, Blair, it's been a long time."

I nodded. This was going to be the friendly treatment.

He smiled. "What are you doing for a living now? What's the latest dope?"

He knew what I was doing for a living, and he probably knew I knew. I sighed.

"After I got out of school, I went on the L.A. police. Now I'm a licensed private investigator. Divorce and insurance cases."

"Is that so? This guy Farrow, the deceased. Where did you meet him?"

"Before we start playing quiz games, am I under arrest?"

Morello shrugged and pushed out his lips. "Well, yes."

"What's the charge?"

"Suspicion of murder."

"You don't expect me to talk without a lawyer, do you?"

Morello flicked his cigar. "In a case like this, why not? It doesn't look too serious—maybe self-defense. Why fool with a lot of red tape? Tell us what happened, and maybe we can get you out on bail."

Same old stuff. Underplay the crime, convince the criminal that everything will be all right if he just cooperates, get his signature on a confession.

"Look, Morello, I was in this racket once myself. You can cut out *that* stuff."

He tried once again. "We went to school together. Give me a break. Make me look good."

"I appreciate your problems, Morello. I liked you in school, and I like you now. But I didn't kill the guy, and I want a lawyer."

He shrugged. "Which lawyer?"

"Tony Driscoll."

He pressed a button, and a little turnkey came in. "Lock him up, Pete. And call Tony Driscoll...."

I'd been on the wrong side of the bars once before, for breaking into the wrong room in a divorce case. That time, they'd tossed me in with a bunch of drunks. It had been kind of chummy, in a smelly sort of way.

But this time the taxpayers were providing me with a private cell, outside exposure, inside plumbing, and an inner-spring plank to sleep on. I climbed onto the bunk and lit a cigarette. I dropped off to sleep and dreamed of scaffolds, and gas chambers, and hot seats, and flaming red hair....

At some unearthly hour the next morning a bell jangled and the normal prison noises began. I needed a shave, and a toothbrush, and a drink of whiskey. I hollered for the guard.

He arrived, towing Tony Driscoll, the poor man's mouthpiece. Tony had a shaving kit, cigarettes, and no whiskey. He draped his long body over the bunk and lit a cigarette. He mussed his carefully rumpled hair.

"Well, Tony," I said bitterly. "I hope this isn't too early in the morning for you."

"Sorry, Mike," he said. "I wasn't home. I just got word. What's the story?"

I told him the story. He only showed interest once, and that was when I mentioned the redhead and told him to get the FBI on the case.

"That redhead," he said. "She was really all right?"

"She was," I said. "Are we going to discuss her, or are you going to put that massive brain of yours to work and get me out?"

"Get you out? How can I get you out? There's no bail for murder."

"Yes, Tony, but I didn't murder the guy." I looked at him closely. "Or do you think I did?"

He walked to the tiny window. "If you killed a man, even in self-defense, I'm the president of the WCTU."

I relaxed. "Thanks, Counsellor. What'll I do?"

Tony chewed his lip thoughtfully. "I don't exactly know." There was a tap at the door of the cell. The gate opened and Morello shuffled in.

"You've got your lawyer now, Blair. Come down to my office. I'd like a statement."

We sat in Morello's office, with a stenographer, and Morello began reading from a notebook.

"It seems that the bartender thinks Farrow had a gun on you when you came in. He heard you arguing about a girl named Flame—a singer at the Club Torna-do. Then, it says here, you moved to a booth. Your voices were raised, you argued in the booth.

"Then *you* got up and left. Farrow followed you. He called your name. There was a shot outside and the bartender looked out the door and saw Farrow lying on the sidewalk. Then you came back in. What have you got to say?"

"I—"

Tony broke in: "Did you question the bartender, Mo-rello? Personally?"

Morello looked up. "Me? No. These are the facts that the boys on the night shift got. Why?"

Tony shrugged. "I just wanted to know." He walked to the window. "No, Morello, you're on the wrong track. My client wasn't even in the bar. He never saw Farrow."

I gasped. Tony sounded as if he were taking it in the arm. My prints were on the beer glass at the Club Tornado, the bartender had seen me twice. Tony's sad story just wouldn't stick.

Morello laughed. "Honest, Driscoll, sometimes I won-der. The bartender will identify him. Anyway, we're checking the prints on the glass he used. What's your angle?"

"I want a lineup."

"What for? We've got a print, probably. You're wasting our time."

"I want a lineup anyway. The print won't prove anything. My client was in there the night before—maybe you have a glass he used then. How do I know?"

Morello pushed a button and a cop came in. "Chuck, call the bartender at the Club Tornado. Have him get down here right away. Then get seven or eight vagrants out of the cell-block for a police lineup." He looked at Tony bitterly. "Or do you want a couple of dozen, to make it harder?"

Tony said calmly. "Seven or eight will be fine. Well, do you mind if I go back to the cell with my client?"

Morello shook his head and left with the guard. When they closed the cell door, I swung on Tony.

"That bartender can identify me. Besides, they have my prints on the glass."

"Mike, you used to be a cop. Would any of the boys on the night shift be around this time of the morning?"

"No. Why?"

"Then there won't be anybody at the lineup who saw the bartender last night."

"Nobody but me. What are you driving at?"

"Listen. Whatever happens at the lineup, don't be surprised. Even if the bartender doesn't identify you. Understand?"

"He'll identify me. Don't forget, he saw me two days in a row. Besides, what about that glass with my prints on it?"

Tony lit a cigarette.

"Suppose he claims that he didn't wash the glasses. Suppose he says the guy that shot Farrow might have had your glass from the night before?"

I peered at him in the gloom of the cell. An idea filtered into my head.

"You're not going to try to bribe this joker, are you? Hell, Tony, you'll lose your license—they'll disbar you."

He recoiled as if I'd hit him. "Mike! Bribe him? How can you say such a thing? Now just sit tight, and leave it to Uncle Tony."

He pounded on the cell door and was gone...leaving me with my thoughts.

It wasn't fifteen minutes before the turnkey came to get me. He led me to a paneled room with a miniature stage at one end. There were half a dozen drunks and pickpockets lined up, horsing around in front of the footlights. When I walked in, they stopped and leered at me. A big cop was in charge.

"Okay, you guys, quiet down. When the man comes in to see you, keep your eyes straight ahead. No pointing, no fooling around. Understand?"

I stood near the end of the line, trying to see past the footlights. The door opened and Tony Driscoll walked in with Morello. A seedy character followed them, a man I'd never seen before, a man who needed a shave. A very self-conscious man, with shifty eyes, who looked as if he wanted to leave. A thought struck me.

"Okay," growled Morello, turning to Shifty-Eyes. "You see them all. Which one is the man who was in the Club Tornado the night of the murder?"

Shifty-Eyes moved to the foot of the stage and gave us a bleary inspection. Finally he shook his head. "I don't see him here, nohow, Inspector. He ain't any of these."

Morello jerked as if he'd been stabbed in the back. "*What?*"

I tried to look as if I'd known it all the time.

"Look 'em over again," barked Morello.

Shifty-Eyes inspected us again. He wagged his head sadly. "Nope, Inspector. The guy in the bar was kind of skinny. He ain't here."

"All right," said Morello sharply. He turned to Driscoll. "We'll have word on those prints this afternoon. I'm holding your client until we find out."

"Just a minute," said Tony. He looked at Shifty-Eyes. "That glass you showed the police. Had it been washed from the night before?"

The character looked away. "Don't tell my boss, but I didn't have time to wash them glasses. Busy day."

* * *

Morello acted as if he were going to blow a gasket. *"You say that glass hadn't been washed from the night before?"*

Shifty-Eyes shook his head regretfully. "Can I go now?"

Morello grunted. "Yeah. Get out. But stay in town!" He looked at Tony. "You know," he said dangerously, "if I didn't know you better, I *might* think you'd been doing a little cabbage passing on the side."

Tony frowned. "Watch it, Morello. Did you ever hear of slander?"

Morello grated, "I'm keeping Blair anyway. There's something funny about this."

Tony said: "Good, I'm glad to hear that. Blair hasn't got much dough, but when we slap an attachment on your salary for false arrest, we'll both be fat."

Morello reddened. "All right," he yelled suddenly. "Get you and that phony private eye out of here. But see he stays in town, or so help me, I'll—"

Tony nodded toward the door and we left. Shifty-Eyes followed us out. As we rounded the corner toward the desk, he tapped Tony on the shoulder. His voice was hoarse. "Say, buddy, you think that job was worth another fin?"

Tony reached into his and slipped him a bill. "Okay. Now stay out of sight. In about ten minutes, every cop in town'll be looking for you."

The little guy scurried away.

"Tony," I said quietly. "How the hell did you get rid of the *real* bartender?"

He started to answer.

"Shut up," I whispered. A man was standing at the desk as we passed. A tall, lanky guy. A guy I'd seen before. The guy I'd seen behind the bar at the Club Tornado. I turned my face away, my heart pounding. The desk sergeant had my valuables—but he could keep them. Then we were out in the street, and climbing into Tony's car.

"How'd I get rid of the *real* one?" said Tony. "That's easy. I just beat him to the punch. I didn't get rid of him."

"You're telling me," I breathed. "You're telling me...."

We went to a little bar called the Friars and sat in a booth near the back. We ordered two boilermakers and lit two cigarettes. My hands were clammy and I still needed a shave.

"Well," said Tony.

"Well," I answered.

A pretty blonde waitress arrived with our drinks and was rewarded by Tony with a pat on the hand.

We lifted our glasses. "I guess," said Tony, "I'm the cagiest, smartest, sharpest character practicing law in this town."

"I'll say you were," I agreed. "What are you going to do for a living when Morello finds out what you pulled?"

"Break rocks at San Quentin," Tony said sadly.

"Greater love hath no man," I said sweetly. "It was such a nice practice, too."

We drank to Tony's practice. We drank to Tony. We ordered another round and drank to the waitress. We drank to Morello, then we drank to me.

"Mike," said Tony. "From here on, you've got to clear yourself. I don't want to be around when Morello discovers that I ran in a ringer on him. I'm leaving town."

"He's already found it out," I said. "The *real* bartender was at the sergeant's desk when we left."

Tony shrugged. "Well, what are *you* going to do?"

I thought it over. "I'm going to Reno. I'm going to find that girl, if she's still alive. Then I'm going to head for Outer Mongolia. I'll come back when Morello drops dead."

"That seems like a very good idea, but why bother with the girl?"

He had something there. Why bother with the girl? Why not head for Mexico, or Canada, right away? Wait until things cooled down, and then come back and try to clear myself? I thought of the red hair and the laugh that had brightened up the grimy kitchen; the taunting lips and the desperate look in her eyes when I'd left. I decided to find the girl.

"First the girl, *then* the Big Skip," I said. "I'll need some money."

"How do you like that?" said Tony reaching for his hip pocket. "I wreck my career for you and now you want me to pay for the privilege. Such a client shouldn't happen to a dog. Will two hundred do you any good?"

"Thanks, Tony," I said. "Thanks a lot."

CHAPTER FOUR

A Gambling Fool

I figured the cops would be watching the Municipal Airport, so I grabbed a cab and went to a little field near Palo Alto. I bargained with a hangar bum who wore a tattered Air Force jacket and owned a battered surplus trainer.

We staggered into the air heading east. It was very rough, especially going over the mountains, rougher than the Aleutians in '41. But we made it, landing with a bounce and a bump and a sigh of relief at a little airport outside Reno. I tottered out, shook hands with the pilot, and called town for a taxi.

Reno was hot, glaring hot after San Francisco. I registered at an air-conditioned hotel under the name "Paul Remsen." I was very proud of the name. I might not be so smart, but I had improved since the night before. I bought a razor and finally got my shave and shower. Then I gulped a beer.

I was in Reno, and the cops were looking for me in San Francisco. What did I do now?

Well, the only way to get a line on the redhead was to find the gambling establishment of one Nino Costa.

Of course, I might call the FBI. But suppose I was wrong? If I was wrong, the FBI wouldn't do the girl any good and I'd land in the same smelly cell in San Francisco. I decided to give myself twelve hours. Then I'd call the

FBI, spill the whole story on the phone, and light out for far-away places and strange-sounding names.

This eased my conscience. If Nino Costa, whoever he was, had the girl, I might be able to get her. If I could convince him that Kid Farrow had told me where the twelve grand was, maybe he'd release her. Of course, when Nino found out I *didn't* know where the money was, I'd probably end up at the bottom of the Truckee River....

I decided to visit Nino. I asked the bartender for the name of Nino's club. Strangely enough, it was "*Nino's*," and only a block away. I slapped four bits on the bar and moved out into the shimmering heat.

Nino Costa ran a nice place. Just as Kid Farrow had said, he had roulette wheels, crap tables, blackjack games. It was clean and cool. A bar stretched across one end of the room, a mirrored bar, gleaming with chromium and nickel. There were a few cowhands, genuine and tourist, leaning on it. There were waitresses, pretty little girls dressed in cowboy boots and Stetson hats and fake guns and not much else. I liked Nino's.

Stepping to the bar, I said, "Where do I find the boss?"

The barkeep was a tall, baby-faced young fellow with carefully groomed hair. In spite of the baby-face, you felt that you didn't want to tangle with him.

"He's not here just now, sir. Do you want to leave a message for him here?"

"Tell him a friend of Kid Farrow was here to see him."

The bartender nodded. "A drink, sir?"

"A shot of bourbon and a bottle of beer."

He poured it and stepped under the bar. In a moment he was back. "Mr. Costa was in, after all. He'll see you in his office."

"That's what I figured," I said. Taking my time, I finished the whiskey and beer. I swung off the leather barstool and stared straight into the eyes of a blackjack dealer behind me. He was absently dealing to an empty table, and he had been watching me.

Short and fat with thick, greasy lips, he had cloudy blue eyes. As I looked, he shifted his glance. Next to him stood a big man, all shoulders and broken nose, carefully not watching me. They looked as if they'd seen me before. I wondered if I'd seen *them*. Maybe in the Club Tornado two nights before? Who could say? Guys in my racket should stay sober.

I walked to the rear, found a door labeled *Manager*, and walked in.

Behind a polished desk sat an immaculate, saintly character with snow-white hair. He smiled and stuck out a hand. His grip was firm and friendly.

"Nino Costa," he said. "You're a friend of Kid Farrow's?"

"I was."

"Was?"

"Kid is dead. Killed, in San Francisco."

"No!" He allowed himself to look surprised. "This *is* a blow. What happened?"

"Somebody shot him. Outside a bar."

Nino Costa clicked his tongue. "That's a tragedy. He was a good boy. He used to come in here often."

"So he told me."

The old boy looked at me sharply. "Is that so? And what did you say your name was again? I didn't quite catch it."

"I didn't. Remsen. Paul Remsen."

"Would you like a drink, Mr. Remsen?" He moved to the wall and pressed a button. A bar swung out from a panel. He turned and smiled. "A man works all his life to own a gadget like this. Just like in the movies. What'll it be?"

"Bourbon, straight." Watch it, I thought. Always watch the boys with the charm. Like a hawk, watch them.

He brought me my drink. I heard the door open and close behind me and knew without turning that it was the lad with the shoulders and the broken nose. It was. He walked silently across the room and sank into a leather chair. He pulled out a detective magazine and began to read it, about as relaxed as a steel spring.

"William," said Costa. "Kid Farrow was killed in San Francisco. Did you know that?"

William looked up. "No," he said. He went back to his magazine.

Costa turned to me. "Kid used to come in here all the time. A good boy. Free with his money when he had it, always paid his debts. A good gambler."

I sipped the bourbon. It was older than I was. Apparently I was getting the full treatment.

"Yes," I said. "He told me he won twelve thousand dollars here a while back."

Costa shrugged. "That might be. That might very well be. A good gambler."

"Twelve thousand dollars is a lot of money," I ventured.

"Yes it is," agreed Costa. "A lot of money."

This was getting us nowhere. I began to wonder if Costa already knew where the money was. Well, I could try a bluff.

"Before he died, Kid told me where the money was."

Costa's expression didn't change. Still not interested. I looked at his hand on the desk. His fist was clenched. His knuckles were white. He was interested.

He walked to the window.

"He must have trusted you, to tell you where he put it. I imagine he put it in a vault?" Yes, he was interested, and it meant Flame hadn't told him where the money was, and it meant that Flame was probably still alive. I wasn't in a very good spot, but for the first time in two days I felt good.

"No," I said. "He didn't put it in a vault. First he gave it to a girl to keep for him. Later he took it back and put it away."

Costa turned. His expression had changed. He wasn't smiling now, and his lips were tense.

"Listen. I've got a story to tell you, about your friend Farrow. About your friend Farrow and that twelve grand he won. You know how he won it?"

"No."

"He slipped in a cold deck on my dealer."

Having known Farrow, it seemed like a good theory. It would explain why Costa was so keen after the money, too. When a legitimate gambler loses twelve grand, he doesn't go chasing around trying to get it back, unless he had a bum shake in the first place.

"That money's mine," continued Costa. "Where did he put it?"

I lit a cigarette. "You know, I *thought* you'd ask that question."

Costa nodded to his trained ape. The ape put down the magazine and strolled over. He stood in front of me, leaning back against the desk.

"The boss asked you a question," he said hoarsely.

"I heard the boss." I glanced at Costa. "Get this monkey out of here. I don't like to be threatened."

Costa offered me a cigarette. He was smooth again.

"All right, Remsen," he said. "If that's your name. What's your angle?"

"Where's Flame?"

"Flame?"

"The girl who used to work for you. The girl Kid gave the money to. The girl your boys snatched. Where is she?"

"Now, wait a minute. I know who you mean, but I never had her snatched. *I* don't know where she is."

I shook my head. "That's too bad, because until you produce her, nobody's going to know where the money is but me."

"I don't know where she is."

"I guess you didn't send your hoods down to San Francisco to get her."

He hesitated. "What do you want?"

"I want you to let the girl go. Then I'll tell you where the money is."

"Tell me where the money is, and *then* I'll let the girl go." He pushed a buzzer on his desk. Behind me, I heard the door open. I watched Costa closely, but I never had a chance. He nodded, I started to rise, there was a crashing blow behind my ear, and my brain exploded in a shower of stardust....

When I came to, I was propped in a corner and someone was pouring water over my head. I opened an eye. Willie was bending over me. He drew back his foot. It flashed and landed in my chest. I felt as if I were going to die.

I rolled on the floor, trying to get my breath. He got in two kicks as I squirmed, and I felt a rib snap. In the distance I heard Costa's voice. "Hold it, Willie. Are you ready to talk, Remsen?"

Remsen...Remsen. That was me. I tried to say no. All I got was a groan. I shook my head. Willie's foot landed on my jaw and the stardust dropped again....

The rest was a nightmare. I remember rolling around the floor, with the taste of blood in my mouth and searing pain racing up my back and down my chest. I remember a kick to the throat that almost strangled me....The last time I woke up, I kept my eyes closed.

"Wait'll he comes to again, boss. He'll talk or buy new teeth."

Half-conscious, I heard Costa answer: "He isn't going to talk, Willie. You're wasting your time....Is he all right?"

I felt Willie's tremendous hand on my aching chest.

"He's still breathin', boss."

"Okay, Willie. Go on out and get the boys. Have them take him to the ranch."

The ranch? I wondered if Flame was at the ranch... Flame . . . Flame . . . go away . . . come again another day....My brain spun crazily. My lungs were on fire, and a drop of blood tickled my cheek. I tried to tie down my thoughts.

Something was bothering me...somebody I'd seen tonight, I'd seen before....One of the hoods who'd been in the fight at the Club Tornado? Maybe.

Thinking hurt my head. Breathing hurt my chest. I didn't believe I'd ever move again.

Very carefully, I opened an eye. Costa was sitting at his desk, watching me. From his drawer he lifted a heavy service automatic, cocked it, and laid it down. He turned and poured himself a drink.

Come on, Mike, I thought. *This is it.* I tensed my muscles. Even thinking of getting across the room hurt. But now was my chance, with Willie gone. I could move faster than an old guy like Costa—or could I?

CHAPTER FIVE

Playing for Coffins

Quietly, painfully, I gathered my legs under me. Costa turned suddenly and I relaxed. I heard him shoot soda into his drink. Then I was up and surging across the room in a flash of pain.

Costa turned, spilling his drink.

Diving for the desk, I tripped, and crashed into it. I got a finger on the gun as I fell. The gun slid off the desk and into the wastebasket. I jammed my hand in after it, grabbed it, and rolled away. From the floor I groaned, "Okay, Costa. Stay where you are!"

He froze.

Painfully I got up.

"Sit down at your desk." I limped to the door. "When Willie and the rest of your boys get here, have them come in. This gun's going to be pointing right at your head, so you'd better play ball. Then you and Willie are going to have your teeth kicked out."

"You won't get away with it."

"Shut up!" There was a knock at the door. "Tell them to come in."

He hesitated. I waved the gun.

"Come in," he said. The door opened and I moved behind it. Willie came in first, followed by three flashy characters and the blackjack dealer. "Hey, boss," said Willie. "Where's—"

"Here I am. Put up your hands."

Slowly, five pairs of hands came up. I limped over

and frisked them. They were carrying enough artillery to pull a job on Fort Knox.

I tossed it in the corner.

"All right, turn around." They turned around.

Suddenly I had it. The blackjack dealer! I'd seen *him* before. But where?

I stared at him. He looked away.

"What's your name?" I asked. "You, short and fat."

"Lippy," he muttered. "Lippy Larson."

"And where have I seen you before?"

"One of Mrs. Astor's tea parties, maybe?"

"Very funny," I said. I had an idea, for a change. Kid had won twelve grand at a blackjack table. A cold deck? Maybe; but very unusual. Very, very unusual, unless—

Unless the blackjack dealer had cooperated. Unless it was an inside job. Suppose it was an inside job. Wouldn't Costa have known it? I turned to Costa.

"This guy Lippy. Was he the dealer Kid Farrow won the twelve grand from?"

Costa nodded. "Yes. Why?"

"Did you ever figure it for a put-up job?"

"No."

"Why not? Do you let your dealers throw that much money away?"

"Farrow slipped a cold deck in on him."

"That's right," Lippy broke in eagerly. "He cold-decked me."

"Nasty break," I said. "How long you been dealing blackjack?"

"Look, buddy," said Lippy, "like I said, it was a cold deck."

Well, it was none of my business if Costa had been taken for a ride. I was interested in Flame. I waved the gun at Costa.

"All right, Costa. Where's the girl?"

"Like I told you, I don't have her."

"Like you also told me, you'd get her if I got the money."

Costa flushed. "That was a bluff. So help me, I don't know where she is."

"I guess you never sent these boys down to San Francisco to get her?"

Costa leaned forward intently. "Yes, I did. When she quit her job here, I figured Farrow might have given her the money, in case we found out about the cold deck and rolled him. I'd heard she went to San Francisco. So I sent these three guys down to San Francisco to get her." He nodded toward the three flashy hoods, went on, "But some drunk at the joint where she worked cut loose at them when they tried to pick her up. So they came back without her."

One of the hoods, a kid about twenty with a pimply face, spoke up:

"Boss, *this* is the guy that broke it up."

Costa stared at me. My brain whirled. If Costa was telling the truth, where was Flame?

"Was Lippy on that caper in San Francisco?" I asked. Costa shook his head. "No."

I looked at Lippy again. I knew I'd seen him, but where? Short and fat—the man in the fog. The man outside the Club Tornado. The man who'd shot Farrow!

"Costa," I asked slowly. "Did Lippy work yesterday?"

"No. He went to Tonopah on business."

"And his buddy Willie? Did he work?"

Costa shook his head. "He had the day off."

"That's what I figured," I said. "That's what I figured." I swung on Lippy. "All right, Larson. Where's the girl?"

Larson turned white. "What girl?"

I stepped over and let him have it across the mouth with the flat of my hand. "You still want to know *what* girl?"

I heard a rumble from Willie and he was on me before I could swing my gun. Instinctively I lashed out with my foot. He dropped, white-faced, and sat stupidly.

"All right," I said to Willie, drawing back my foot again. "Now *I'm* doing the drop-kicking. Where's the singer?"

Willie was yellow. Clear through. He groaned: "At Lippy's. In the cellar."

I looked at Costa. He was standing, his eyes wide. "What—"

"Skip it," I said. "Come on. Everybody. And nobody make a quick move."

I marched them out of the gambling house like Sergeant York. The three hoods I released outside. I got a cab and filled it with Costa, Lippy, Willie, and myself. I let Costa give the directions to Lippy's house, a nice little place in the suburb, not far beyond the city limits.

Lippy unlocked the door sullenly, prodded by the .45.

"The cellar," I said. He hesitated and then led me to a door. I herded the whole outfit to the basement and switched on the light.

The cellar was filled with old newspapers, bottles, garden tools—a normal cellar. But in the corner was a folding cot, and tied to the cot, gagged, wide-eyed, and angry, was Flame.

"Untie her," I snarled. Lippy looked at Willie and Willie looked at Lippy. "Untie her," I repeated. "Both of you."

Reluctantly they moved to the cot. Nervously they released her hands and feet. They jumped back, but not fast enough. Her hands lashed out at their faces. As they stumbled backwards, I saw angry red scratches on their cheeks. Flame whipped off her gag.

"Why, you—" she began. Her voice broke. She weaved unsteadily and then she was in my arms. "Oh, Mike..."

Flame sat close to me in the cab going back. Her face was dirty and her hair was tangled and she was sobbing, but she still looked like a million dollars. We got out at Costa's and I marched the boys back to his office, my hand on the gun in my pocket.

"All right, Costa," I said. "I want you to call the San Francisco Police. Homicide bureau. Get a guy named Morello on the phone."

"Never mind. Get your hands up." The voice came from behind me. I got my hands up. I turned and stared. Morello stepped from behind the door.

"What—Boy, am I glad to see you," I began.

His hands went over me expertly. He slipped the gun out of my pocket. "And I'm glad to see you. Very glad. Didn't you think I'd check *all* of the airports?"

"Here's the man who killed Farrow," I jerked my thumb at Lippy. "And the ape here drove the car for him."

Flame broke in: "Kid was *killed?*" I nodded. She moved to the window and looked out.

"This guy shot him?" asked Morello. "Very interesting. What makes you think that?"

I took a deep breath.

"I was there. This man, Lippy Larson, I saw in the fog the night of the murder. He's a blackjack dealer here. He let Farrow slip a cold deck in on him; let him win twelve grand. They were going to split the score. Farrow gave the money to Flame, in case Costa might have him rolled. Then Farrow lit out for New York and Flame went to San Francisco. She didn't know it was a crooked deal."

Flame turned. "Thanks, Mike."

"She didn't know it was a crooked deal," I repeated. "But when Lippy told Costa about the cold deck—*that* was according to plan, so he wouldn't lose his job—when he told him about the cold deck, Costa guessed that Flame would be holding the money for Farrow. They'd been going together here. Right?"

Costa nodded.

"So he sent three of his boys down to pick up Flame. They didn't get her. For various reasons," I added modestly. "In the meantime, Lippy thought maybe his cut wasn't going to be enough—he'd take the whole works. He went to San Francisco with his buddy Willie. *They* snatched the girl, right out of her apartment.

"She wouldn't tell them where the money was, so they decided to take her back to Reno. They knew she worked at the Club Tornado and they checked to see if Kid Farrow had arrived in town and might be waiting for her there. They were lucky.

"He was there, with me. Lippy left the girl in the car with Willie, and waited outside the club. When Farrow followed me out, Lippy stepped past me and let him have it. I remember where I saw him now—it was in the fog that night. Then they got away with the girl."

Morello turned to Flame.

"Did these men kidnap you?"

She nodded.

Morello glared at me. "You know, Blair, I've got a good mind to run you in for obstructing justice. If you knew this girl was kidnapped, why didn't you call the FBI?"

I hung my head. "I forgot."

"You forgot! Did you forget what the *real* bartender in the Club Tornado looked like? That was a slick deal, too."

I stepped forward and grabbed his arm. "Morello, don't hold that against Driscoll. Don't get him disbarred."

Morello seemed to be fighting a smile. Finally he said, "You think I'd let that story get out? I'd be pounding a beat. You can tell your lawyer to come back to town—if he'll keep his mouth shut." He jerked his head at Lippy and Willie. "All right, you guys, you're coming with me. I'm having the Reno police arrest you for kidnapping—and murder."

Costa broke in, turning to Morello, his eyes blazing. "Mister," he said, "before you take Lippy, let me have him alone for ten minutes...just ten minutes. Let my boys talk to him. You'll save the state money."

Morello laughed. "No soap, Costa. After this, pick your help better. Blair, be at the station tomorrow. And you too, sister." The door closed behind them.

I turned to Flame. "This guy Farrow. Did he mean a lot to you?"

Her eyes filled with tears. "I went through hell to keep his money for him. Now I find out it wasn't his. I guess I knew he was no good. I just wouldn't admit it."

Costa was smiling. "Yes," he said smoothly. "That money. What do you think ought to be done with it?"

"It goes back to you," Flame said quickly. "It's yours."

Costa shrugged. "Suppose we split it? After all, you kept it for me."

Flame opened her mouth and I cut in sharply. "That sounds good," I said. "Where's the money?"

Flame smiled. "I should tell you to turn around, I guess." She raised her skirt on the prettiest gam in the world and dragged a slim pack of bills out of her stocking. "A very unusual place for a girl to keep her money," she said.

I looked at Costa. Costa looked at me. We shook our heads.

"I'll be damned," I said.

For Auld
Lang Crime

◆

*When the Blimp's lethal
legmen toasted the tin-
horn Casanova into hell,
tearful Lynne coaxed pri-
vate eye Blair—into crashing the fatal festivities.*

CHAPTER ONE

Sucker Trap

I listened to the voice. *No*, I
thought. *No*. In the dim light I stared at the familiar
bottles, the same old labels.

I tested my eyesight on the brand names. I clutched
the bar. Same sticky, lacquered bar. Glasses sweating.
Pools of water by every drink. A watch-your-coat-cuff
bar. I was still sober. I swung around.

Leaning on the piano in the blue glare of the cheap
spotlight, she was singing in the throaty, offhand way
she had, the way that made you cry inside for every
woman who had ever lost a man.

It was a song she'd sung years ago, sometimes for
me alone; a song that in a different place and a different
time had become almost a symbol of the girl who sang

it.. Her hair was blonde now instead of burnished copper, and it was worn bobbed to match her sleek, shimmering dress.

But it was Lynne.

Shakily I lit a cigarette and groped behind me for my drink. *Easy, boy,* I told myself. *Easy. Don't get burned again.* Her eyes, sweeping the lounge languidly, rested on mine, and for a second I thought her voice quivered. Then she shifted her gaze quickly. I tore my eyes away from her and turned to the barkeep.

"New singer, Joe?"

"Yeah, Mr. Blair." He frowned as he wiped the glasses. "Christine...Christine something."

I almost smiled. Christine, hell. Lynne. Lynne Woodstock. A name I'd hoped I'd never remember, but a name that still thrilled me. Lynne....

Now she was through and the applause was as loud as ever before. She hadn't lost her touch with an audience. I slid off the barstool, cut across the lounge, and caught her outside the manager's office.

"Hello," I said. "Hello...Christine."

She turned and stared at me blankly.

"Hello. I don't think—"

I shook my head. "Come on, honey, none of that stuff." I jerked my chin toward an empty table. "Sit down, Lynne."

She hesitated. "Not Lynne—Christine," she said absently. "And I'm not supposed to sit with the customers."

"Sit down."

She moved over and sat at the table. "I—"

I ordered her a drink. "Still scotch and water, I presume?"

She nodded. I looked at her curiously.

"What's the idea of the act? You didn't expect to fool *me*, did you? After all...."

"After all," she said sadly. "No, Mike, I didn't really expect to fool you."

"Why'd you try?"

She shook her head miserably. "I don't know. I don't know."

I tried to look cheerful. "Well, what's the difference? This is a hell of a gloomy way to meet after— How long? Five years?"

She nodded. "Five years."

My mind went back. Another bar, another time. Lynne and I together. Lynne on her way to the big time...Lynne with burnished hair and a smile in her eyes. Singing in a little place down south, near Los Angeles. A little bar with a gambling room in the back and Lynne the star of the show in front. Happy days, then. Until one night....

"Have you heard from Rip?" I asked, casual like.

She looked up quickly. "No."

"His time," I remarked, "ought to be about up."

She shrugged.

I swished the drink in my glass. "Still in love with him?"

Her voice was dead. "Don't be silly."

"Silly? I don't know. *Some* girls have waited five years. But," I said bitterly, "you always were kind of fickle."

Her eyes flared. "Since you're so damned curious, Rip is out now. And I did wait."

My heart sank, but I gave it the old British try. I put my hand on hers and smiled. "Say, that's swell. I'm really glad."

She looked up, distracted. "Please, Mike, don't mention that he's out of jail. And don't tell anyone my name."

Well, I could understand that. A guy who's been in the cage for five years has to start all over. So does his girl. I decided to change the subject.

"Have you heard from Juanita, or anybody else from the Club Silver?"

She shook her head.

I said, "The Blimp is running a new place now. Up here."

She nodded. "I know," she said in a tired voice. "I know it."

My heart chilled. "Say, Rip isn't in *town*, is he?"

She looked up sharply. "Why?"

I shook my head. "Skip it."

Her hand grew white on her glass. "Why did you ask that?"

I shrugged. "I don't know. There was a rumor...."

"That Rip was framed?"

"That's right."

"It isn't true. It isn't true at all."

I looked at her curiously. "That's a funny thing for you to say."

She sighed: "Oh, I don't care if he *was* framed. He did his time. Why can't he let it go at that?"

"Did *he* hear that he was framed?"

She nodded miserably. "In prison."

"Well, I don't believe it. There were too many witnesses. Of course, they *were* all crumbs. Even Juanita might have crossed him for enough dough. Does Rip think the Blimp framed him?"

"Yes."

"He isn't up here to get the Blimp, is he?"

"I don't know what he wants to do. I was waiting for him when he got out last week. He told me he'd heard he'd been framed. Said he was leaving L.A., that he had a job to do. I begged him to stay there. He wouldn't stay and he wouldn't take me with him. I was sure he was coming up here to get the Blimp so I came up too, alone."

"Is that why you changed your name? Is that why you're a blonde?"

"Yes," she said tensely. "If I could only find him! If I could only get him to listen."

It sounded bad. A guy can get awful mad after five years in that big iron box. Especially if he thinks he's been framed. "And you haven't been able to find him?"

She shook her head. "Oh, Mike, what'll I do?"

I thought for a while. Finally I decided to let her have it.

"Listen, Lynne, the guy isn't worth it. He's a cheap tinhorn gambler. He's a bum. If he was framed, it couldn't have happened to a nicer guy. If he knocks off the Blimp, there'll be one less phony in the world. When the cops get *him*, there'll be two less. This isn't because he took you away from me, Lynne. This isn't jealousy. Forget him and go back to Los Angeles. Let him fry in his own grease."

She lowered her eyes. "No, Mike. No, I've got to stop him." Her gray, serious eyes met mine. "Mike, you've got to help me."

Great. Swell. The crummiest character on the face of the earth steals your girl and you're supposed to take care of him like a kid brother.

Not me.

"You're talking to the wrong guy, honey. The hell with him. That guy was made for the gas chamber. How about another drink?"

The gray eyes filled with tears. "Mike, please."

"No, Lynne. I'm a private investigator. My racket is finding people. But if I found that guy, I'd probably kill him on sight and *I'd* be up for murder."

She started to speak and changed her mind. She stood up. "I have to sing now. And thanks for the drink."

She walked across the lounge with the easy careless stride I remembered. She had always walked as if she were swinging down a country lane in the springtime, square shoulders set, eyes straight ahead. I felt a pang of regret. She stood by the piano, smiling stiffly at the house.

"I have an encore," she said. Then she sang it again, the song she'd always sung for me. I toyed with my drink as chills raced up and down my spine. She sang to the past and she sang to me, and as she sang she swayed, and the vibrant voice reached deep into my memory.

I paid for my drink and left.

I hit every bar on the waterfront and consumed half a year's whiskey production, but wherever I went the song went with me. The song and a vision of Lynne, alone in the harsh blue spotlight. And finally, of course, I reeled back into the lounge where she sang, and by the time she helped me up the steps to my apartment I'd promised to find Rip if it took twenty years.

Clipped by a Cutie

I woke up with an army of little men in my head; two armies, fighting over my brain. I had a quick shot of whiskey, contemplated the day ahead, and shuddered.

People who think the private eye racket is a breeze should try to find a person who wants to stay hidden in the city. You try to put yourself in his place, and figure what you'd do if you were he—but you're not he, you're you, so you usually have to do it the hard way.

You walk until your legs are ready to fall off, and you ask questions until your tongue is ready to fall out, and you watch the passing parade until your eyeballs feel as if someone had sandpapered them. And sometimes it takes a day and sometimes it takes a week and sometimes it takes a year, and if you are doing it for free it's worse because you can't put the refreshments you need on your expense account.

So you try to figure the angles. There was one angle in this case. If Rip Torrance was looking for the Blimp, the Blimp's new gambling house might be a good place to pick up a few angles on Rip.

Another shot of whiskey got me shaved, and the next shot got me dressed. I grabbed a cab and went to the Club Golden. The Blimp had come up in the world since the Club Silver in Los Angeles.

It was 11:30 in the morning when I walked up the stairs to the Blimp's new sucker trap, but the bar was ready for business.

You can tell a lot about a place by the bar. This bar was clean, uncomfortable, and efficient—designed to pour as much mediocre liquor into as many mediocre people as possible in the shortest time. Designed to get them drunk, away from the bar, and into the backroom where the easy money lay.

The bar reminded me of the Blimp's other bar in the Club Silver five years ago. The bartender was at the far end, his back turned, already setting up old-fashioned glasses for the afternoon rush. His back was turned, but it was a back you never forgot.

"Tiny," I yelled. "Tiny, you old poisoner, come down here and give me one on the house."

Tiny turned like a startled elephant. His pudgy cheeks bulged and his fat eyes closed to slits. He looked as if he were going to cry, or laugh, or something. It was Tiny's long-lost-friend look. He waddled toward me, his puffy hand outstretched.

"Mike," he bellowed. "You old alcoholic. Where've you been for the last five years?"

"Up here in heaven."

"How come I haven't seen you?"

"I've been living clean. That's how come, you old reprobate."

Tiny laughed. For Tiny it was almost a giggle, but my ears rang and the glasses danced on the bar.

"What'll you have, Mike? I thought you were dead. Thought some husband of some daffy blonde had caught up with you."

"For that crack, I'll have a shot of the best scotch in the house and a beer chaser."

Tiny poured my drink and one for himself. He raised his glass. "To old times."

We clinked glasses.

"Speaking of old times," I said, "did the Blimp bring his whole rotten crew with him, or are you the only slave he imported?"

Tiny laughed again, and the windows rattled. "Well, let's see. He brought Moxie—"

"Natch. And Moxie brought his gun."

"Yeah, Moxie's here. And Kiddie LePlant, and a couple of the dealers, and Leon—remember, he was the headwaiter at the Club Silver—and you know that little girl who peddled cigarettes? The one that went for Rip Torrance?"

"Juanita?"

Tiny nodded. "Juanita. She's up here too. The rest of the gang stayed down south with the guy that bought the Club Silver."

"So Juanita's still working for the Blimp," I said slowly. "That's funny. When they jugged Rip, I thought she'd quit."

Tiny looked at me curiously. "Why should she quit?"

I shrugged. "I don't know. She was in love with him, and the way the Blimp testified in court, I didn't think she'd want to work for him anymore."

Tiny began to polish a glass absentedly. He said, "Well, *she* testified against Rip too."

"That's right, she did. Well, I guess she had to. They had the goods on him."

"Yeah," said Tiny. "It's a funny thing, though...." He paused.

I waited. "What's a funny thing?"

Tiny's eyes veiled themselves. "Skip it. How about another drink?"

He poured me another shot and we sat in silence for a while. My mind went back through the years.... A hot, stuffy courtroom, with a schoolhouse smell. Lynne sitting beside me, listening to the testimony mounting like a tidal wave against the man she loved. The young District Attorney, confident and smug, riding the crest of victory. Questioning the Blimp, "And now, Mr. Manz, tell us what transpired in your nightclub on that evening." And the Blimp's voice, suave, smooth, floating across the room, "Rip—that's Mr. Torrance—had been drinking all night. Snowy Carroll was all hopped up with dope. He's been gambling heavily. Snowy wanted a ride back to town, but no one was leaving. He said he'd walk. About ten minutes after he left, Rip Torrance decided to drive home. We tried to talk him out of it—he was all tanked up.

"He left anyway, and about a half hour later came

back. He staggered through the door to the back room and said he'd just hit Snowy Carroll and killed him. We thought he was kidding, but I sent Moxie down the road to see. He found Snowy dead."

And testifying after the Blimp, Moxie; and after Moxie, Kiddie LePlant, and then to clinch the case, Juanita. So Rip had pulled five years; not more, because Snowy was a dope fiend on a jag; not less, because the sovereign state of California doesn't like its drunks killing its hopheads.

And now the grapevine said it had all been a frame-up. Well, maybe.

I glanced at Tiny. "With good behavior, Rip ought to be out by now."

Tiny thought for a while. He nodded, "I guess so. Well, that's no great break for society."

Anyway, Tiny hadn't seen him. "Where's the Blimp?"

Tiny jerked a thumb like a sausage back toward the rear of the dark bar.

"Back there thinking of some way to get us to work for nothing. Why don't you drop in and see him?"

"I will."

The Blimp hadn't changed. A little less hair, maybe, but the same white flaccid face, the same slim gambler's hands, and, when he stood up, the same narrow shoulders, wide hips and little feet. A build like a flour sack tied at both ends.

"Michael! I haven't seen you in years. Didn't even know you were in town. Sit down. How about a drink?"

All right, he could give me a drink—he'd taken enough money from me in the old days. "Sure, Blimp. Thanks."

He reached into his desk drawer. His private stock, no less. He settled back in his swivel chair. I looked around.

"This is quite a place you have here, Blimp. What made you sell out down south?"

The Blimp hesitated. "Well, you remember that kid

Torrance...Rip Torrance? There was so much in the paper about that case, on account of the gambling angle, that it got pretty hot. I decided I'd do better up here."

I nodded casually. "Oh, yeah. I wonder if Rip's out yet?"

The Blimp looked at me sharply. Suddenly he said, "Are you still in the private eye game?"

"Sure," I said. "It takes all kinds to make a world."

The Blimp drummed his fingers on his desk. He lit a cigarette and leaned back in his chair. He cleared his throat, said finally, "How'd you like to do a job for me?"

It doesn't pay to let them think you're starving to death. "Well, I don't know. I'm pretty busy now. What sort of a job is it?"

"Profitable."

"They're all profitable, or I don't take them. It's somebody you want tailed?"

"Found."

"Who?"

The Blimp took a deep drag from his cigarette and snuffed it out.

"Rip Torrance."

I had to play dumb. I had to have time to think. "Rip? It ought to be easy to find him. Unless he's out of jail by now."

"He's out, all right. And I want him found."

"Why?"

He didn't answer the question. "What do you charge?"

"It depends. You're in the chips. For you, thirty bucks a day. *If* I take the case. Why do you want him found?"

"For thirty bucks a day you'd have to know why?"

"I always have to know why I'm on a job. Otherwise, no soap."

"I think he's out to get me."

Buddy, I thought, *you're not the only one who thinks so.* "Why should he be trying to get you?"

"He was blacked out the night he killed Snowy

Carroll. Doesn't remember anything. He doesn't think he killed him. He thinks I had him framed."

"That's ridiculous," I said. "Or is it?"

"Of course."

I did some fast thinking. This was a problem in ethics. Also a problem in business. Trying to track down Rip Torrance for free wasn't doing my pocketbook any good. Thirty bucks a day was a different matter. Two birds with one stone. There was one thing, though.

"And if I find him, what happens? Do the cops find him later in a ditch somewhere?"

"Not at all," the Blimp said smoothly, "I'll give him enough money to get started somewhere else. I didn't frame him, but I don't want him getting in my hair out here."

I trusted the Blimp about as far as I could throw his bartender. On the other hand, what he said made sense. As long as Lynne and the Blimp were both interested in the same thing, there seemed to be no reason why I couldn't work for both of them at the same time. I stood up.

"Okay. But if I find him, and he's knocked off afterwards, I'm spilling the whole story to the cops."

"Don't worry."

"And that'll be five days pay in advance."

The Blimp scribbled on a piece of paper. "Give this to Tiny in the bar. And good luck."

"I'll do my best."

Tiny was talking to a girl at the end of the bar. I walked over and handed him the Blimp's note. Without a word he walked to the cash register, rang up "No Sale," and brought me back three crisp new fifties. The girl watched with interest.

"Mr. Blair," she said, "Mike Blair?"

I squinted at her in the dim light of the lounge. Shimmering, raven hair, hazel eyes; slim, with a build that you see once in a lifetime.

"Juanita," I said. "Juanita Lorez, Mexico's gift to

the tobacco industry. The cigarette girl with the mink coats. How've you been?"

"For the last few minutes, thirsty."

I bought her a drink. We talked for a while about old times, and once I asked her if she'd heard from Rip. She raised her eyebrows.

"Rip? Is he out?"

"I didn't say he was out. I asked if you'd heard from him."

"Me? Why should I hear from him? You ought to ask your old girlfriend, Lynne."

"That's right. You lost a man—a kind of a man anyway—and I lost a girl."

"Yes," she said thoughtfully. "Yes." She moved closer and looked up at me with the soft, amber eyes. "I always thought we two should get together after what happened."

The lush amber eyes had a cash-register brain behind them. I decided that it was time to leave....

CHAPTER THREE

Tanked-Up Hero

Downtown, the cocktail lounge was crowded with businessmen buying their secretaries a drink before they had to go home to face the ball and chain. Lynne's song floated above the babble of voices and the tinkle of glasses.

She found my eyes among all the eyes that watched her, and she smiled at me, and the old feeling for her was back. When she was through, she walked to my table and seated herself.

"Hi, Mike. How's the head?"

"Okay, considering. Nothing that another drink won't cure." I signaled a waiter. I moved closer to the table. "I've been looking for your boyfriend all day."

She frowned a little. "Any luck?"

"No. Maybe he's not in town."

"He's in town, all right," she said thoughtfully. "Mike, you don't have to look for him any longer."

"What the hell," I said. "Did he turn up?"

"No." She paused. "I changed my mind, that's all."

A tiny golden ray of hope flashed through me. "Decided to give him up?"

She lit a cigarette. "No, I'm not giving him up. He phoned me this afternoon."

"He did? From where?"

"From the Hotel Traynor. He's been staying there all the time."

"Well, I wish you'd make up your mind. You owe me thirty cents for shoe leather. I can't get rich this way."

She smiled. "Thanks anyway, Mike. Everything's going to work out all right."

Well, that was a matter of opinion. "What did he say?"

Her eyes shone happily. "He said someone was staking him to a trip back East. Somebody's setting him up in a nightclub."

I'll bet, I thought. Anybody who'd trust Rip Torrance with more than a buck at a time wouldn't have had the brains to earn a dime in the first place.

"Did he mention the guy's name? Or is it Santa Claus?"

She looked hurt. "No, he didn't say. He said it would take one more day for the deal to go through and that he was lying low until it did."

"How did he know you were here?"

"He saw my picture outside." She tinkled the ice in her glass thoughtfully and smiled up at me. "Don't worry, Mike. We'll make out."

I wasn't worrying, but I was wondering. Rip had something up his sleeve, and it sounded like an ace. Well, it wasn't any of my business.

But what was I supposed to do now? I could tell the Blimp where Rip was, of course, and keep my advance. But I might have a tough time convincing him that Rip and Lynne were actually leaving town.

And if I couldn't convince him, there was a good

chance that Rip would leave in a casket; in my estima-
tion not a bad idea, but a little rough on the girl with
the faint, happy smile. Besides, I told myself, acting as a
finger-man for the Blimp wasn't a very good job for a
private eye. Unethical. A guy could lose his license.

"Okay, Lynne—Christine, I mean," I said bitterly.
"Then you're going back East with him?"

She nodded, dreamy-eyed. *The hell with it*, I thought.
I paid the check and got up. "Good luck. And you'll need
it."

It was like old times in the Blimp's office—a gathering of
the clan. Moxie Scarborough, a blank-faced little guy
who looked like a bank clerk and thought with a .32
automatic, cleaning his fingernails in a corner, smiling
at me, his eyes the color and hardness of slate.

Kiddie LePlant, a rugged, flashy lad, with heavy
eyes and a slack mouth, staring at me dully. The actors
in the Blimp's road company hadn't changed.

The Blimp looked up and nodded coolly. "Sit down,
Mike. What's the good word?"

"That job I was doing for you—"

For a moment he looked puzzled. "Oh, yeah," he
said. "That. Have any luck?"

I shook my head and pulled out my wallet. "I
decided to quit. Here's your advance."

In the old days, people who worked for the Blimp
didn't quit—they waited to be fired. I braced myself for
the explosion. Instead of blowing his top, he shrugged.

"All right," he said absently. "Never mind. Keep the
money."

I laid it on his desk. "Just to have things straight," I
said. "Okay?"

He nodded. "Well, drop in again, Mike."

And that was that. As I left, I almost asked him
why he'd lost interest in the whereabouts of Rip Torrance.
Later I wished I had.

I walked into the bar. It was crowded now, crowded
with well-heeled citizens on their way to the gambling
room in back, and poorer citizens on their way out.

Juanita sat at the far end, sipping a tall, fruity drink. I slid onto the stool next to hers.

"Aren't you working tonight, Beautiful?"

She shrugged. "Maybe, maybe not."

"The cigarette industry will never recover."

"The liquor industry would appreciate it if you bought me a drink."

Always the lady, Juanita. I signalled to Tiny. "Get Juanita another of these floating gardens, and make mine a boilermaker."

Tiny whipped them up, and left the whiskey on the bar. Juanita and I touched glasses. *I might be*, I reflected, *temporarily unemployed, but there were compensations.* "And what do you do if you don't work, Gorgeous? Besides caging drinks, I mean?"

"Sometimes I let old friends buy me a dinner."

"You know," I said slowly. "I don't know why you bother peddling cigarettes. It doesn't seem to cost you anything to live."

She laughed. "I won't be peddling cigarettes anymore after tomorrow. I'm quitting."

"Seriously?"

She nodded. "I'm going East."

Everybody seemed to be going East. A regular gold rush, in reverse.

"You might," I remarked, "see one of your old boyfriends back there."

She raised her eyebrows. "Who?"

"Rip Torrance."

She looked away quickly. Finally she said: "Not that I give a damn, but what makes you think he's going East?"

I glanced up sharply. "I didn't say he was *going* East. How did you know he wasn't there already?"

She lit a cigarette and looked at me squarely. "He was in jail in Los Angeles the last I heard. I didn't even know he was out."

"I thought *all* you girls were counting the days," I said sarcastically. "He's out, all right. In fact he's in town. But tomorrow he's going East."

She sipped her drink. "How did you find out?"

"He called his girlfriend and told her to be ready to leave," I said bitterly.

Her voice was flat. "His girlfriend? Who's that?"

"Lynne Woodstock. Who else?" It slipped out before I remembered my promise. Well, what the hell...Lynne was leaving tomorrow.

She stared at me. "Is *she* in town?"

I nodded. "Different name, different hair. But the same girl, and still in love with her poolroom Casanova."

"Where did you see *her?*"

I'd talked enough.

"What's the difference? How about another drink and then that dinner you're trying to ace me out of."

She looked at her watch. "I just remembered. I have a date. I'm late." She smiled absently and touched my arm. "I'll take a rain check."

And then she was gone. I stared at the bottle moodily. I was beginning to feel like the villain in a deodorant advertisement—nobody wanted to play with me. I was also beginning to feel the drinks. I crooked a finger at Tiny.

"Tiny, ignore these apes and have a drink with your old buddy."

Tiny poured himself a small one under the bar and grunted. "Working too hard tonight. Don't know why they drink here, the kind of rotgut we serve. Well, here's to us. Where's Juanita?"

"I mentioned Rip's name to her and she froze. Said she had a date and left."

"I heard he was in town. Maybe she went to see him."

"He's in town, yeah. But I didn't tell her where he was." I had another shot of whiskey. My head was singing. "No," I said. "All you have to do is mention that guy's name to a girl. She gets to thinking about him, and from then on you're out in the cold."

Tiny nodded ponderously, scowling down a patron who wanted a drink. "Yeah, I remember the night he ran over Snowy Carroll. Couldn't tell who took it worse, Lynne or Juanita. Dames carrying on all over the place."

I remember the night too. Strictly a rat race. Typical of Blimp's parties; free liquor, beautiful women, and drunks knee-deep at the bar. Lynne singing, dim in the blue haze, and me trying to forget that she was singing to Rip Torrance and not Mike Blair. A very rugged night. And ending, as the rotogravure boys would say, in tragedy....

"Yeah," I said. "I remember too."

Carefully I poured another drink. My mind slipped back again to the night five years ago. Rip Torrance ignoring Lynne and heading for the crap tables in back. Lynne, after her song, sitting with me at the bar and glancing occasionally, impatiently, at the door to the gambling room.

Half an hour, an hour maybe, and then the door opening. Rip, firm in the grip of Kiddie LePlant and Moxie Scarborough. Rip, his eyes bleary and his legs rubbery, being steered toward the door. Lynne, her face taut, moving to help them, and Blimp, coming up quickly and drawing her aside. Saying, "He's in trouble. He went out the back way. Said he wanted to drive home. We tried to get him to wait until he sobered up, but he wouldn't. I sent Moxie after him in my car, to see that he got home all right...."

Lynne, her face white, "He didn't...."

And the Blimp nodding. "Snowy Carroll, walking down the highway. Snowy was dead when Moxie got there; Rip must have been doing fifty. We'll have to take him to the cops...."

Tiny served a customer and came back. I helped myself to another shot from the bottle in front of me.

"It's a funny thing," I remarked. "Rip was never worth a damn, and he never will be, but that was the first time I ever saw him sop up more liquor than he could hold. He was out on his feet that night, never knew what happened."

Tiny shrugged. "You can never tell. Sometimes a

guy can drink all night, sometimes it only takes a couple. As a matter of fact...."

He moved away and jammed a glass on a mixer. I had another shot and my head cleared. There was something funny about that night five years before. Tiny came back, punched the cash register, and leaned on the bar.

"As a matter of fact, what?" I asked.

"As a matter of fact, I only served Rip two drinks that night. And they must have hit him late, because he was okay when he left the bar."

He was okay when he left the bar...and now they said he had been framed.

"Look, Tiny," I said, moving closer to him. "Confidentially, what would happen if I suddenly got rough at the bar? Too rough to handle? Would they call Kiddie to throw me out?"

Tiny glanced around cautiously and shook his head. "No. That'd cause a scene. Bad for business."

I nodded. "I'd get a Mickey, wouldn't I?"

Tiny's blue eyes met mine. "That's right."

"And if, say, instead of getting rough, I won twenty or thirty grand in the back room. What would happen then?"

Tiny rubbed his chin. "Well, I hate to admit it, but you'd probably get the same treatment. Outside, they'd roll you. You know how the Blimp feels about dough, anybody's dough."

"Yeah. I know the Blimp. Frankly, I'd hate to win too much dough around here. Snowy Carroll won a lot of money that night. It wasn't on him when the cops got to his body. Everybody thought that Moxie had lifted it. There just wasn't any proof. Right?"

"That was the general impression. But so what? That was a long time ago. Why worry about it?"

I lit a cigarette. "I'm not worrying about it. It just seems kind of funny, that's all."

Tiny's blue eyes were serious. "You think the Blimp had Snowy killed?"

I shrugged. "They say Rip was framed. It could be."

Tiny tossed his head angrily. "It's one thing to slip a guy a Mickey and roll him—it's something else to run him over and rob him. The Blimp can't go around murdering everybody that wins money from him."

"Thirty grand isn't exactly peanuts. And don't forget—Snowy didn't drink. With Snowy it was purely dope. How can you slip a guy a Mickey if he doesn't drink?"

Tiny shook his head doubtfully. "You can't."

"You can't. So you have to use another way, or let the money go."

"You think they slipped Rip a Mickey so they could use his car for the murder, and then hang it on him. Is that what you think?"

"Why not?"

"Why should they pick Rip? The place was lousy with drunks that night. Rip was a good customer."

"Too good a customer. Remember the night the Blimp caught him trying to bribe a dealer in the blackjack game? That would be enough, right there."

Tiny served a blonde a tall, frosted drink, and came back to wipe off the bar. He said quietly, "Well, like I said, that was a long time ago, and nobody cares now. I'm about through with this dump anyway. I'm gonna buy me a nice, clean chicken farm somewhere and retire."

"Chicken farm," I said absently. "Tiny, if I looked like I needed a Mickey, who'd slip it in my drink? Not you."

"You're damn right not me. I let 'em handle their own troubles—I just work here. No, if you'd just won thirty grand, say, pretty soon your little buddy Juanita would skip up with her little cigarette box, and when she left you'd be drinking whiskey with a sleep chaser."

So Juanita was the knockout artist. That made sense, even in Rip's case. Five years ago she'd been dropped like a hot potato for Lynne—and girls don't like that. Besides, anything you did for the Blimp was like money in the bank. And Juanita had dollar signs floating in her hazel eyes. Yes, it made sense all right. But there was something else.

Why was Rip leaving town? Why had he come in the first place unless it was to get the Blimp? Maybe his story to Lynne was true. Maybe somebody was setting him up in business. But who?

Well, the Blimp had said that if I found Rip he'd buy him off, get him out of town. Maybe the Blimp had found him without my help. Or maybe Rip had contacted the Blimp, and blackmailed him. The trouble was, you didn't blackmail the Blimp unless you had the goods on him, and as far as I knew, there was nothing but rumor in the case of the late Snowy Carroll.

On second thought, you'd have to be pretty desperate to blackmail the Blimp, even if you had the goods on him. You'd be just as likely to end up in the bay as in the chips. Well, it was none of my business.

I helped myself to another slug out of the bottle and looked over a redhead at the far end of the bar. Very nice. But I just couldn't manage to keep my mind on her.

On the surface, it looked as if Rip expected a payoff tonight or tomorrow. If he expected the Blimp to cough up any dough, he'd be liable to get a surprise—the Blimp was freer with slugs than cash. And the boys were gathering in the Blimp's office.

I decided that I'd hate to be in Rip's shoes, if he was really trying to get anything out of the Blimp. Anyway, I was glad that I hadn't found him for the Blimp. Whatever happened, my conscience was clear.

Just to clear my conscience a little more, I poured myself another drink. I smiled at the redhead. She smiled back. I toyed with the idea of moving down the bar.

But somehow I kept remembering Lynne's happy, glowing smile when she'd told me that she and Rip were leaving town. And a nagging little voice told me that Rip wasn't leaving anywhere if somebody didn't warn him.

I groaned and stood up. "So long, Tiny, old pal," I said thickly. "See you sometime."

Tiny looked at the bottle. "You're not leaving the joint while this whiskey bottle's alive?"

I nodded and steadied myself on the bar. "Yeah," I muttered. "Gotta see a dog about a man."

CHAPTER FOUR

Leaving—in a Casket

I was feeling very proud of myself as I staggered to the desk of the Hotel Traynor. The desk clerk, a shoddy old rum-pot with a drooping moustache and bleary eyes, inspected me coldly.

"Look," I said. "A guy lent me some dough. Flashy character, blond hair, about thirty. Forgot his name, but he said he lived here. Know who I mean?"

"Maybe. All except his lending you some dough. There's a man named Thorne in 411 sounds like the one you mean. Thorne's probably not his name—none of our guests give their right names. Now, if you got this guy to lend you some money, tell me how you did it.

"He's a week behind in his rent, and I think his luggage is full of bricks. Say," he said, sniffing. "You ain't got that bottle with you, have you, Mac? A guy gets thirsty sittin' here all day."

I waved my hand carelessly and started for the elevator.

"Never mind the elevator," the old guy yelled after me. "That's for guests. You use the stairs."

Nice place. I staggered up the stairs.

I knocked on the door to 411. There was no answer. I tried the handle and the door opened. The lights were off, but intermittently a flashing neon sign outside lit the room. I could see a dark shape on the bed.

"Rip," I shouted. "Rip, you rotten no-good tinhorn gambler, wake up. It's drinking time."

No answer.

I tried falsetto. "Rip," I squeaked. "You big hand-some thing, wake up and give us girls a break. We've missed you and we want to see that nice prison tan you've got."

Still no answer. I stumbled to the bed and poked at the shape.

It was limp and warm and I had a drunken desire to roll it off the mattress. But something stopped me. I lurched back to the door and flicked on the light.

The shape on the bed was Rip Torrance. His eyes were open, as if he were searching for a hole in the ceiling, and his mouth was open, as if he were about to deliver some profound commentary on the state of the nation. Buried neatly in his chest was a slim, wicked letter opener.

I was too late. He was very, very dead.

There is something about finding a body that sobers you up. Much quicker then black coffee or tomato juice. There is also something about finding a body that makes you want to get the hell out. I almost did. Instead, I decided to look around.

I went into the bathroom and looked around. I pushed open the bathroom window and looked around. I went back into the bedroom and stuck my head under the bed and looked around. Strangely enough, there was no one there. Okay.

Now, I told myself, like any law-abiding citizen, you call the cops. I reached for the phone and paused.

Or do you call the cops? Suppose the victim stole your girl five years ago. Suppose you've been hired by one of the roughest gangsters in the state to track him down. Do you still call the cops? I hesitated.

Of course you call them. They can't do anything to an innocent man. I reached again for the phone.

"Hold it," said a voice from the door—a voice loaded with authority. "Get your hands up and don't move."

I got my hands up and I didn't move. At all. The floor behind me creaked, and a hand went over me. Very professionally, too.

"Okay, boss," said the voice. "He don't have no rod."

"Turn around, Blair," said another voice. A familiar voice—the Blimp's. I turned around. The Blimp, Moxie, and Kiddie LePlant lounged by the door, all smiling.

"Well," I said pleasantly, trying to keep my voice from cracking. "I've heard of returning to the scene of the crime, but I never saw it happen before. You guys getting sentimental about your work?"

The Blimp laughed. "You're pretty smooth, Buster. I hope you keep it up when the cops get here."

"I will," I said. "If they get here."

"They'll get here, all right. We're calling them." He nodded to the phone. Moxie looked at him strangely and picked it up. "Call the cops, Moxie," said the Blimp.

"Well, hey, boss," blurted Kiddie LePlant. "You sure you want the cops here?"

"I said call the cops, Moxie."

Moxie shrugged and asked the room clerk for the police. He covered the mouthpiece. "What'll I tell 'em, boss?"

"Tell them to get here quick, there's been a murder and we have the murderer."

Moxie shrugged and got the police department. "Listen flatfoot," he growled. "See if you can get this straight. There's been a murder at the Traynor Hotel, room 411. Better write the number down before you forget it." He hung up.

"You," I said to the Blimp, "got a lot of guts. So *I'm* the murderer. You think the cops will go for that, when I tell them you hired me to find Rip Torrance? What'd you want to find him for? A fourth at bridge?"

The Blimp laughed.

"Never mind why I wanted to find him. He's dead, and we caught you with the body."

"How are you going to explain your being here to the cops? A social call?"

"Oh, no," said the Blimp seriously. "No, you got drunk at my place and threatened to kill Torrance. We tried to head you off, but we got here too late. I have witnesses to that."

Kiddie LePlant looked at his boss in admiration. Moxie shook his head and chuckled mirthlessly. I chilled. This movie I had seen before.

"Wait a minute," I said. "You're not pulling that Snowy Carroll deal again—Listen, that won't work with me. That poor sucker"— I nodded toward the bed—"that poor sucker was blacked out when you pulled the frame on him. *I'm* not—I *know* what I've been doing!"

"I," said the Blimp smoothly, "don't know what you're talking about." He turned to Kiddie LePlant. "Do you, Kiddie?"

Kiddie shook his head slowly, his mouth slack. "Hell, no, boss. This guy said he was gonna kill Torrance, and he did. That's all I know."

"Listen," I said, trying to keep calm. "Your boy Tiny can shoot that story as full of holes as a bachelor's socks. He knows I didn't threaten to kill Torrance."

"So he does," said the Blimp thoughtfully. "So he does."

I heard the clumping of heavy feet down the hall and the room began to fill with uniforms. A quick-eyed, nervous little man in plainclothes darted through the crowd. I recognized him from news photos—Foxy Farnsworth, of the homicide detail.

"What goes on here? Well, Blimp Manz. I figured you'd get in trouble sooner or later." He peered at the body on the bed. "And who's Lucky Louis? A friend of yours?"

"An old friend, Foxy," said the Blimp. "Rip Torrance. And I'm not in trouble. This man murdered him." He flicked his thumb at me.

Foxy's alert brown eyes traveled over from head to toe. "This guy?"

"Mike Blair," I said. "Licensed private investigator. And your friend the Blimp is crazy as hell."

"He's not my friend," said Farnsworth. "Nobody's my friend. Suppose we start at the beginning."

"I got up here," I said evenly, "to warn Torrance

about the Blimp. Torrance had evidently been trying to blackmail him, and I figured the Blimp might try to knock him off. I was too late. I started to call the police, and the Blimp and his boys came back."

"Who *did* call the police?" asked Farnsworth.

"I did," said Moxie.

"Hmm." Farnsworth turned to the Blimp. "And what's your story?"

"This man Blair has been drinking at my place all afternoon. He used to know Torrance. Torrance stole his girl, a long while back. This afternoon Blair got drunk and told us he was going to finish him off.

"Only we didn't pay any attention until he started waving that envelope cutter around." He pointed to the thing in Rip's chest. "Then we tried to follow him in the car. When we got here, it was too late."

"That's right," said Moxie. "We found him staggerin' around in here, lookin' for somethin'. I kept a gun on him and called the cops."

"Check for a license on the gun, Pete," said Farnsworth automatically. A policeman took down the number. Farnsworth turned to me. "You got anything else to say?"

"Plenty," I said. "Why don't you ask the room clerk and see who was up here first, me or them?"

"I did, on the way up. Twenty minutes ago one man came up, drunk." He darted over and sniffed at my breath. "That was you. Fifteen minutes ago three more men came up. That was apparently the Blimp and his playmates."

My heart dropped. "Maybe he didn't see them come up the first time."

Farnsworth shrugged. "Maybe not. Well, I'm taking you all in, so it doesn't matter—"

"Wait a minute," said the Blimp. He reached into his coat and pulled out a yellow slip of paper. "A half hour ago I was at my club. I can prove that. I'd been there all day. I can prove that, too!" He looked at his watch.

"It's 7:30 now. At 7:00 I left my club, to try to beat

Blair down here. Coming in, I picked up this. Way out in the sticks."

Farnsworth took the yellow slip and studied it. "Forty miles an hour in a twenty-mile zone. Time: 7:05. Place: Steiner and Jackson Streets. Let's see—Officer's name: Rudy C. Knox. Check on that too, Pete." Farnsworth stared at me speculatively. "Well, Blair, what do you say to that?"

My mind was whirling. "I don't know," I stumbled. "It looks phony as hell to me."

"Just the same," Farnsworth said softly, "just the same, you'll admit that it'd be hard for a guy to pick up a traffic ticket way out there at 7:05, get down here to nab a man, and leave before you got here at 7:10. Wouldn't it?"

I nodded numbly. My head began to ache and my eyeballs grated when I moved them. I needed a drink, fast, or a new brain, or something. My mind was cloudy and creaky. I slumped down in a chair. With a real effort I tried to think.

The cop at the phone looked up. "Knox remembers the pinch. Says he's sure about the time, and he kept them there about five minutes."

Farnsworth shook his head sadly. "Well, I guess that clears you, Blimp. I kind of hoped. . . ." He shrugged. "Oh, well, you and your boys stay in town, Come on, Blair."

"Where?" I asked dully.

"Where do you think, Mac. Down to the station. I'm booking you on suspicion of murder."

Down to the station. The words bounced around my whirling head. Once I was there, the Blimp and his boys would have time to get rid of Tiny and fill in the weak points in their story, if there were any. When they finished with me, I'd be in the same spot as Rip Torrance five years ago.

"Come on, Blair," said Farnsworth. "Get out of the chair. Let's go."

He spoke tolerantly, as if I were drunk. Well, maybe I was, but not drunk enough to want to start on the first leg of a trip to the gas chamber. I closed my eyes, played possum, and tried to think.

I had to get away. I had to get away to do some thinking, to get hold of Tiny, maybe. I had to get away.

But how do you get away from a room full of cops on the fourth floor of a hotel? You don't. Drunk or sober, you go quietly. Drunk or sober.

Well, sometimes a drunk can get away with murder. And they thought I was drunk. Suddenly I had it. One chance in a million, and I doubted whether I had the guts to go through with it, but it was a chance. If I had enough ham in me to make it work, it was a chance.

I opened my bloodshot eyes wide. I took a deep breath and let go with the most blood curdling yell I could muster. It was a beautiful yell. It even scared me, and the effect on Farnsworth, the Blimp, Moxie, and the cops was out of this world.

Farnsworth leaped backwards, grabbing at his coat. I screamed again, enjoying it now, and suddenly dashed for the open window. I swung one foot over the edge and yelled again, louder.

One of the cops lunged for me and I swung the other foot onto the sill.

"Don't touch me," I shouted.

"He's nuts, Foxy," muttered the cop "Nuts. He'll jump."

"Don't touch him," said Farnsworth quietly. He jerked his head at the phone and one of the boys picked it up and began to talk, cupping his hand over the mouthpiece.

"Turkeys," I yelled. "Little turkeys with top hats." I waved my arm. "All over the floor. Keep 'em away from me. Keep 'em away from me!"

"He's got the DT's," whispered Farnsworth. "Leave him alone until the rescue squad gets here." And then, to me, "We won't let the turkeys get you, Blair. Now come out of the window, and we'll have a drink. Okay?"

"No," I shouted. "Keep 'em away. Keep 'em away or I'll jump!"

The Blimp stared at me from a safe distance across the room, his mouth open. Sweat started out on Farnsworth's brow. "Now, take it easy, Blair. You don't want to jump. Nothing's going to hurt you. Just take it easy."

I put my head out the window and looked down. The street below was crowded with movie-goers and the nightclub set. I gave them one of my better yells and almost caused a riot. White faces flashed in the light of the street lamps and a forest of arms pointed upward.

I looked back in the room just in time. One of the cops was three feet away and edging toward me slowly. I jerked myself farther out on the ledge and for a sickening moment almost lost my balance. Below me I heard a woman's shrill scream.

"Stay away," I told the cop. "Stay away, turkey. I'll jump."

In the distance I heard a siren wailing. The rescue squad. I glanced out the window again. I was playing to a full house. The street was mobbed—tense, craning bodies packed together, fascinated, waiting for the leap. Directly below, a respectful clearing for my plummeting body. Windows creaked open across the street and someone shouted to a neighbor. A regular sell-out. Just what I needed.

I turned back to the room. Farnsworth and the men in uniform watched me cautiously, guns out.

"Take it easy," said Farnsworth again. "Nobody's going to hurt you."

"Turkey!" I yelled and sneaked a glance out the window. There was a bustle in the crowd below, and a movement as a well-drilled unit of men in blue shouldered through the mob. Quickly and efficiently they set up a life net. From the fourth floor it looked like a postage stamp.

I hesitated. If I could make the net without breaking my neck, I'd be able to get into the crowd in the excitement, and no one could shoot into the bystanders. *If* I could hit the net....

The phone rang behind me and I turned. Farnsworth picked it up, watching me carefully. He nodded and hung up.

"Okay, boys," he said quietly. "They're all set." Slowly the cops edged toward me. My heart beat wildly—it was now or never. I crossed my fingers, shot a quick glance at the net below, and jumped.

I felt the wind in my hair and heard a faint sigh go up from the crowd. White-hot needles played along my skin. I tried to relax for the impact and began to wonder if I'd ever hit.

Something that felt like the Superchief whacked my back. For a desperate second I thought I'd missed the net. Then I was in the air again, with the neon lights gyrating around me. I tensed myself. When I hit again, it was on the sidewalk, sprawling into the gutter, my neck wrenched.

But I was alive, and I could move. I scrambled to my feet, looking around wildly, trying to get my bearings. Ten feet away, lunging at me, was a policeman, his gun half drawn. I dove into the crowd. For a fighting, squirming half-minute I battled the press of frightened bodies, and then I was free, and sprinting up an alley, with the roar of the crowd behind me....

I skidded around the corner of an alley, praying for a cab. Everything on wheels was crawling up and down the street—everything but a taxi. A few blank-eyed derelicts were lined up outside a burlesque theater. They stared at me incuriously.

I looked around wildly, heard a shout from the alley, and muscled in at the head of the line. I was buying a ticket at the window as I heard the feet pounding by. I stepped inside, handed my ticket to a hard-eyed usher, and slipped into a dark seat in the back.

On the stage a tall redhead with a painted smile was giving her all for her art, but I kept thinking of another show—the Gas Chamber Follies—starring Mike Blair.

I stood it for half an hour and then I crawled over the knees of ten or twelve old guys and left by a fire exit. A squad car cruised by as I stepped outside. I waited in the shadows, my heart racing, until it turned at the end of the block, and then followed it as far as the drugstore on the corner. I squeezed into a phone booth and called the Club Golden.

CHAPTER FIVE

Too Fat to Fry

Tiny was downtown in twenty minutes, still in his white uniform, driving a ridiculous miniature auto that fit him like a straitjacket. Somehow I crammed myself in beside him.

"Let's get out of here, where I can talk. Did you tell the Blimp you were leaving?"

He shook his head, pulling away from the curb. "Nope, I just left. Always wanted to leave those customers with their tongues hanging out. What's the story?"

I briefed him on the latest adventures of Mike Blair. When I came to the suicide act, he almost burst a blood vessel. "No," he kept saying. "No. It's impossible. And they tried to frame you?"

I nodded. "Said I'd threatened to kill Torrance before I left the club."

"That's a damn lie," said Tiny. "I can clear you on that."

"That's why I phoned you," I said. "The Blimp knows you can shoot that part of his story full of holes, and I figured he might try to put you away."

Tiny swerved the impish car between a delivery van and a bus. "Where to now? The police?"

I thought it over. I still couldn't prove that the Blimp had killed Rip Torrance, but that wasn't my job—that was one for Foxy Farnsworth. At least, with Tiny's help I could prove that I hadn't left the Club Golden with murder in my mind.

"If you tell the cops," I warned, "you'll lose your job."

"I was quitting anyway. And it isn't my job I'd worry about."

I knew what he meant. Tiny's frame could hold a lot

of lead, and he'd make a wonderful target. Now we were in the deserted warehouse district, driving aimlessly.

"I don't know, Tiny," I said slowly. "Maybe—" I felt his hand on my knee and glanced over. His eyes were intent, staring into the rearview mirror.

"Wait a minute."

My blood chilled. "What's the matter?"

"That pair of lights. It's been following us." Suddenly he swung off into a side stret. I craned my neck. Behind us, powerful headlights swept around the corner. I tried to get a look.

"Cops?" whispered Tiny.

"I hope so," I said. "I really hope so."

The threatening headlights moved closer, and I knew suddenly that they belonged to no squad car.

"It's the Blimp's car," I muttered. "Try to get back to the main drag."

Tiny shot around the next corner like a private in a jeep, but the headlights crept closer. Suddenly they swung out to the left and drew alongside. A horn spoke once, with authority. I caught a glimpse of Moxie's bored, ferret face, and Tiny was nudged over to the curb.

"They must have followed me when I left the club," said Tiny. "Oh, brother."

In the feeble yellow glow of Tiny's headlights two men walked back to the car, two men with blue-black badges of authority held in their right hands. Moxie Scarborough opened my door and beckoned me with his head.

"Come on, Blair," he growled. "You're going with Kiddie. I'm going with Tiny, and we're going to have a picnic all by ourselves in the country. We'll follow you."

"Why don't you kill us here and save the gas?" I asked bitterly.

"No gas shortage now," said Moxie pleasantly. He jabbed me in the ribs with the gun. "Now get goin'!"

I looked at Tiny. In the dim light his eyes were bleak and hopeless. "Well, Tiny, old pal," I began. "I guess this is it."

"Come on," said Moxie impatiently. "You boys can

kiss each other good-bye later. You're going to spend a long time together. Let's go."

Reluctantly I climbed into the other car with Kiddie LePlant, my heart cold and clammy. He glanced in the rearview mirror, shifted his gun to his left hand so he could cover me as he drove, and pulled out into the darkened street.

You read a lot about that last long mile; the thirteen steps to the gallows; that final breathtaking second in a plummeting airplane. And I used to get a strange feeling ploughing through the Pacific on a carrier, waiting for dawn and flight quarters.

But nothing I ever read about or experienced before compares with a long automobile ride with a man you know is going to kill you. You want to argue with him—"Now, look, LePlant, we've known each other a long time." But you know it won't do any good to argue with him; he's just earning his pay.

You want to threaten him—"Listen, LePlant, you won't get away with this"—but you *know* he'll get away with it, because he's smart and he's got away with it before, and you know *he* knows it.

You want to plead with him, "I got a wife and six kids," but if you did, you know he'd express regret and knock you off anyway.

So you sit there, stiff and silent, and try to keep from showing how quaking, jelly-scared you are, and your thoughts bump against the padded cell of your brain and you promise that if you ever get out of this one you'll sell women brushes for the rest of your life.

We drove west, past the park and the zoo, and then we were cruising down the coast, with the glare of the city behind us and the black Pacific thundering on the rocks below. We came to a deserted roadside park and Kiddie swung off the road. He parked at the edge of the cliff and clicked off the lights.

I didn't feel much like joking, but at least I could try. "Why, Kiddie! I didn't know you cared."

"Very funny, wise guy. This'll be a pleasure. Get out."

I stepped outside as Tiny's midget car crunched over the gravel and stopped, facing the cliff. Moxie climbed out and motioned to me to take his seat. I began to get the idea. For a sickening moment I toyed with the thought of making a run for it, and then decided that I'd be a portable lead mine before I'd get five feet. Meekly, I squeezed into the car. Moxie closed the door.

Tiny leaned forward over the wheel. "Moxie," he said, his voice tired and low, "I got friends. You know that. And I swear, you'll never get away with this. They'll get you if it takes twenty years."

Moxie shrugged. "I don't think anybody'll ever know what happened to either one of you. Just in case your car doesn't clear the rocks, though, you can take this along."

In the darkness I saw him take something out of his overcoat. It was a whiskey bottle. He uncapped it and shoved it through the window, dousing the upholstery. He sloshed some of the stinging liquid into my face and tossed the bottle behind the seat.

"If you drink, don't drive," he said. Suddenly he stepped back from the car, braced himself, and swung with the gun. I caught the flash of blue metal in the light from the dash. I half ducked, too late, and a searing, roaring sheet of flame exploded in my brain....

I fought my way up from the dark, liquid blackness. A great weight was pressing on me. I groaned and opened my eyes.

Tiny was slumped over me, jamming me in the seat. Weakly I tried to push him away, and almost passed out from the effort. Behind me I heard an engine race. Suddenly I remembered where I was. I grabbed for the door. I was too late. There was a heavy bump and Tiny's car gathered speed, pushed from behind.

I clutched at the wheel but Tiny's mammoth body pinioned me. There was a squeal of brakes and a rumble of locked tires on gravel behind us, and then we were crashing through the rickety fence and over the cliff, soaring through the air. I saw the breakers exploding below.

For a long moment the tiny car seemed to hang nose-low in the air, and then it flipped over. The black rocks, the white foam, and the dark water flashed in front of the windshield, and then there was a deafening roar. My head banged against the dashboard and Tiny stirred and fell away from me.

Then we were plummeting to the depths, with salt-water pouring into the car through the open window. I yanked at the door handle. It was jammed.

This was it, I figured. At last Mrs. Blair's little boy has had it. The water in the car was up to my eyes now but I could see that Tiny was awake and struggling feebly, trapped behind the steering wheel. His eyeballs rolled toward me wildly. I twisted toward him, braced my shoulders against my own door, and jammed my feet into his side. As the last inch of air-space closed over my head, I took a deep, final breath and kicked out hard with both my feet, straining convulsively.

For an angry moment I cursed every potato that my fat friend had eaten. I kicked out once more, felt something give, and suddenly Tiny was gone. I pulled myself under the wheel, my lungs bursting, and followed him.

I shot toward the surface blindly, salt in my mouth and eyes, blood pounding in my head, clawing my way to air. My eardrums sang under the pressure and I felt as if Davy Jones were trying to squeeze out my brains with a monkey wrench.

Suddenly my head broke clear and I gulped fresh, cool air. I floundered in the surge and ebb of the tide, trying to keep away from the wicked black rocks towering above me. Automatically I kicked off my shoes.

A dozen feet away I heard a groan. In the starlight I could see a round shape bobbing with the waves. I fought my way over and grabbed at Tiny's meaty head.

"Okay, Tiny?"

I heard a hoarse gurgle that might have meant anything.

"Turn on your back," I sputtered. He heard me and relaxed. He was buoyant as all fat men are buoyant, and once on his back was more help than otherwise. I faced the shore, treading water, and sized up the situation.

There were cliffs rising from the water all along the coast, with nasty rocks jutting out of the water in plumes of spray. About fifty yards up the cliff, though, was a dark, flat object lying along the water. It looked as if it might be a pier.

I was wrong about the pier. It was a rock, covered with shells and barnacles and slippery as a pickpocket at a county fair. But we made it, me feeling like a tug pushing an ocean liner, and Tiny gradually coming to the point where he could help a little.

I clambered onto the rock, losing half my skin and clothes in the process, and heaved Tiny up behind me. We collapsed on our backs, gulping air and feeling as if we'd just swum the English Channel. Finally Tiny gasped, "Thanks, Mike."

"Think nothing of it. You make a good life raft. Besides, you can do the same for me sometime."

Tiny looked up at the towering cliffs. "I know what you mean. Let's get started on it now. If you think we can crawl up there at night."

I pointed at the water. "I hate to press you, but we have to. Unless you want another swim. The tide's coming in, and in another hour a seal wouldn't be able to hang on this rock. Let's go."

The climb up the cliff was rough too. I went first, following a fault in the rock, and Tiny puffed along after me, clinging to the face of the cliff with his fingertips. I heaved myself over the edge, helped Tiny, and stood up.

We were on the coast highway, and it was a long walk back to town. I looked at my watch. It was stopped at 1:20. About 2 o'clock now, I figured, and no use even trying to hitchhike.

"Let's get started," I said to Tiny. He groaned and crawled to his feet.

"Brother," he said, "I'll bet I've lost twenty pounds in the last hour."

I thought of the trouble I'd had getting him out of his car and said: "Off you it looks good. Let's hit the road."

We walked for half an hour, and I did a lot of thinking, mainly about the ticket that the Blimp had picked up. You can't hang a murder on a man that's being pinched for speeding when the murder happens. Well, if it wasn't the Blimp, who was it? Nobody else had any particular reason to knock off Rip Torrance.

Or did somebody else have a reason? I had a sudden flash of inspiration.

Suddenly we were caught in the glare of headlights. For a chilling moment I thought of Moxie and Kiddie LePlant. Then I realized that their first move after they sent Tiny's car hurtling from the cliff would be to get as far away as possible. Optimistically I turned and stuck out a thumb. The car slowed to a stop, a big state police seal on its side.

"You guys lost?" asked a pleasant voice. "Hitchhiking is against the law, you know. A flashlight shone in our faces. "Say, Joe," said the voice. "Did you know people were swimming off cliffs?"

"We weren't swimming, Officer," I told him. "We were pushed. And I want to turn myself in to Foxy Farnsworth."

"It's Blair, Joe," I heard the driver mutter. "Guy that jumped out the window downtown. Cover him."

The door opened and Joe got out, trim in his khaki uniform. "Okay, Blair," he said, easing me in the backseat. "We're in a position to make your dream come true. Foxy Farnsworth is just the guy you're going to see. You too, fat-stuff—up front...."

Foxy looked up when we entered the office. He half rose from his chair and then collapsed weakly. He mopped his brow.

"Nice goin', boys," he said. "Nice goin'. Where'd you find him?"

"On the coast highway. He gave himself up."

"Gave himself up? That's not so good." Farnsworth

glanced at me sharply. "What made you change your mind?"

Tiny cleared his throat. "It's a frame-up, Chief. I'm the barkeep at the Club Golden. Blair was with me all afternoon, and he never threatened to kill anybody."

"That's your story," said Farnsworth. "What about these guys that tried to knock you off?"

"They shoved us off a cliff in Tiny's car," I volunteered.

"Maybe," said Farnsworth. "Maybe. And I guess you figure they killed Torrance. How about the traffic ticket?"

I shook my head. "They didn't kill Torrance. But they killed a guy named Snowy Carroll five years ago."

Farnsworth pushed a button and spoke into an intercom. "Get the Blimp, Moxie Scarborough, and Kiddie LePlant."

"And while you're at it," I said, "see if he can't pick up the cigarette girl. Juanita Lorez."

Farnsworth looked at me quizzically. He shrugged. "Get a girl called Lorez, while you're out there. He leaned back in his swivel chair. "All right, Blair. They'll be here in half an hour. But me, I still think you killed Torrance."

I shook my head. "I didn't."

Foxy raised his eyebrows. "There's a girl in the outer office that thinks you didn't, too."

My heart surged. "Christine?"

"Christine...Lynne...whatever you want to call her. She's all broken up about her boyfriend, but she swears you couldn't have murdered her boyfriend, Torrance."

I began to feel better already. "That's a woman's intuition. Can I see her?"

Farnsworth shrugged. He called into the intercom, "Show Miss Woodstock in."

Lynne came in, her eyes tired and her hair rumpled. She walked over and kissed me.

"I know you didn't do it, Mike."

"Thanks, Lynne," I said. "I'm sorry he's dead."

And strangely enough, I was.

* * *

There was a long wait until the Blimp, Moxie, and Kiddie LePlant strolled in. The Blimp faltered when he saw us, Kiddie LePlant blanched, and Moxie looked at us coolly.

Juanita Lorez came in, jerking her arm away from a policeman.

"What's the idea?" she hissed.

Farnsworth nodded at me. "His idea, not mine. Okay, Blair, start talking."

"Well," I said, "This starts five years ago. A guy named Snowy Carroll won some money at the Blimp's place, and they had to get it back. He was a dope fiend—didn't drink—so they couldn't slip him a Mickey, which is their standard operating procedure. They had to kill him.

"Ran him over in Rip Torrance's car, slipped Rip a Mickey, and even convinced Rip himself he'd killed him. Juanita was the Mickey artist. Right so far, Tiny?"

"That's right. Rip only had two drinks—he couldn't have been drunk. He was doped."

The Blimp's lips tightened. He stared at Tiny with cold, beady eyes. Tiny glared back.

"Now," I continued, "Rip heard in prison that he was framed. When he got out, he decided to come up here and blackmail the Blimp. He shook Lynne in Los Angeles, and put up here at the Traynor Hotel. He needed a contact man for the Blimp—he was afraid to see him in person.

"So he looked up his old girlfriend, Juanita, and told her where he was, and what to tell the Blimp. I guess he promised her she'd go with him when he left town—"

"That's a lie," whispered Juanita. "I didn't know he was in town."

"But apparently," I went on, "he still loved Lynne. Because when he found out Lynne was in town, he called her and told her to get ready to go back East. He told her to be ready a day earlier than he'd told Juanita."

"That's a lie," said Juanita, her voice rising.

I shook my head. "All I did was mention to Juanita

tonight that Rip had called Lynne. Suddenly she remembered that she had a date, and had to leave. A half hour later, Rip was dead. Incidentally, she could have saved herself the trouble—apparently the Blimp had had her tailed and knew where Rip was. But the Blimp got a traffic ticket, and I took a cab, so Juanita got there first."

"All right," screamed Juanita. "All right! I killed him, I killed him, I killed him!" She lunged for Lynne. One of the state cops caught her. "I killed him," she yelled, "but *you'll* never get him. Never, never, never."

It was dawn when Lynne and I stood on the station steps. Lynne was quiet now, her eyes clear and dry. I needed a shave, a drink, and about forty-eight hours sleep; outside of that, I was feeling pretty good.

"How about coming up to my place for a drink, Lynne? Or is it Christine?"

She slipped her arm into mine and squeezed it firmly. Her clear gray eyes looked up into mine.

"Lynne, Mike," she said. "From now on, it's Lynne."

Afterword

◆

by Robert Weinberg

While most mystery fans know that the detective pulps from 1920 through the early 1950's were the birthplace of a new type of crime story—the "hard-boiled" private eye adventure—very few people realize that these pulps provided another equally important service to the mystery field. They offered a marketplace for detective short stories. Without these pulps, many excellent tales would never have seen print. While the slick magazines of the time published some detective fiction, they offered a limited market for the best-selling writers in the mystery field. Rex Stout and Erle Stanley Gardner filled most of their requirements. Authors including John D. MacDonald and Cornell Woolrich needed the pulps as a springboard to greater accomplishments.

Detective pulps were so popular that many of them were published twice a month. *Detective Fiction Weekly* was a 144-page pulp that appeared every week throughout the 1930's—an unbroken run of well over five hundred issues filled with fast-paced pulp mystery fiction. During the late 1930's, there were several dozen mys-

tery pulp magazines being published, printing everything from short short stories to complete novels and
long serials. The market for mystery fiction was immense.

Even in the late 1940's and early 1950's, when the
pulps were in a steep decline, there were more than a
dozen mystery magazines. With 128 to 160 pages to fill
each month, the editors of those magazines were hard-
pressed to find enough detective and private eyes adventures to satisfy their readers. Fans were able to pick and
choose among numerous titles all featuring mystery stories by the top names in the mystery field.

With such a wide-open market, the mystery short
story flourished. Beginning authors found a ready market for their stories. Pay was often low, but the top
magazines paid as well as many of the slick magazines.
And once an author established himself as a steady
contributor of good fiction, the pulps took all he could
write and demanded more. Erle Stanley Gardner made
over $20,000 one year writing for the detective pulps—
before Perry Mason. *Shadow* author Walter Gibson lived
in a New York City penthouse apartment during the
1930's, financed by his work for the pulps.

John D. MacDonald and Louis L'Amour both started
out as pulp authors. Each contributed many dozens of
stories to the pulps of the 1940's. Recent reprint collections
from both authors vividly demonstrated that even at the
beginning of their careers, they could write exciting, mem-
orable stories. The pulps provided them with a starting
place for their careers. And did so for many other authors.

Hank Searls is another author who saw his earliest
fiction published by the pulp magazines. Known throughout the world today as the author of *Overboard, Jaws II,
Jaws—the Revenge* and other best-sellers, Searls's first
novel did not appear until 1959. Long before that, his
Mike Blair series headlined the pages of *Dime Detective*.

Born in San Francisco on August 10, 1922, Searls
attended UCLA at Berkeley in 1940. He joined the U.S.
Navy in 1941 and received his B.S. from the Naval Academy
in 1944. From 1941 through 1954 he served in the Navy,
rising to the rank of lieutenant commander. After leaving

the Navy, Searls worked as a writer for Hughes Aircraft, Douglas Aircraft, and Warner Brothers before becoming a full-time freelance writer in 1959.

Searls married Berna Ann Cooper in 1959, and is the father of a daughter and two sons. Most of his novels have dealt with the flying field (*The Big X, The Crowded Sky*) or the sea, as in his recent best-sellers. Only a few collectors of the pulps ever realized that his earliest stories were hard-boiled mysteries.

"Murder Is a Tough Rap" was the title of Searls's first submission to Popular Publications, the publisher of both *Dime Detective* and *Black Mask* magazines. It was bought and paid for on March 9, 1949. The title was changed to "Shiv for Your Supper" and appeared in *F.B.I. Detective Stories* in June of the same year. It was the first story featuring hard-boiled detective Mike Blair in a tough world of small-time crooks and sudden murder.

This first sale was soon followed by "Murderers Prefer Blondes" which was bought by Popular on May 27, 1949, and appeared in *All-Story Detective* for August of that year under the title "Kickback for a Killer."

Searls's first two stories appeared in Popular's second string of detective pulps. The success of Mike Blair's first two adventures provided the necessary leap into the publisher's lead titles. "A Dish of Homicide" (originally titled "Suitable for Framing") was published in *Dime Detective* for November 1949. Mike Blair and his creator had made it to the top of the line in the detective pulp field.

Eventually, Searls left the pulp field for the better-paying market of the slick fiction magazines. The detective pulps had provided him with a first step in his long climb to the best-seller lists. Now, with this first appearance ever of the Mike Blair stories in book form, Searls's fans can sample the early writings of this major author.